"I don't know why you decided to offer me this job, but I hope it means you believe that you and I can…get along."

"Get along?" he repeated.

"Cricket," she said, twisting her hands nervously, "I know that you know what I'm talking about. But I'll say it anyway to avoid any possible chance of miscommunication. There's been weirdness between us for a lot of years now. And I admit it's my fault."

A tightness grabbed hold of his heart. Her fault? How could she possibly believe that? "Hazel—"

"I've made things difficult at times. I know that. It took me forever to get over you, and there were times when I'd be angry and hurt because I thought you were lying to yourself, and to me, about only seeing me as Tag's little sister."

He shifted toward her but then stopped because what purpose would that serve? Admitting his feelings now would only complicate this situation more. He couldn't be with her. Not in the way he wanted.

Dear Reader,

Sometimes in life, against all odds, against all advice and against what we think is our own better judgment, love happens. True love. The kind that won't listen to reason. It's brilliant, and breathtaking, and perfect. But sometimes it's also wildly inconvenient.

Hazel James has been in love with her older brother's best friend, Cricket Blackburn, for as long as she can remember. Cricket has been trying *not* to be in love with Hazel for far longer than he wants to admit. A long-ago kiss cemented feelings for them both, ruining romance for Hazel and torturing Cricket with the memory. What followed were years of coping—avoidance, excuses, rationalizing, a few misunderstandings and even some "list making" on Hazel's part. But now, with an extra-special Christmas brewing in Rankins, these familiar and comforting "rules" no longer apply. It's time for Hazel and Cricket to face the past—and their feelings.

Like one of my favorite songs of all time declares, *You can't hurry love*. And I believe that's true. Hazel and Cricket prove that you definitely can't stop it, either.

Thanks for reading, and I hope you enjoy *The Secret Santa Project*!

Carol

HEARTWARMING

The Secret Santa Project

Carol Ross

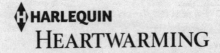

HARLEQUIN
HEARTWARMING

HARLEQUIN®
HEARTWARMING™

ISBN-13: 978-1-335-42635-2

The Secret Santa Project

Recycling programs
for this product may
not exist in your area.

Harlequin Enterprises ULC
22 Adelaide St. West, 40th Floor
Toronto, Ontario M5H 4E3, Canada
www.Harlequin.com

Printed in U.S.A.

Carol Ross lives in the Pacific Northwest with her husband and two dogs. She is a graduate of Washington State University. When not writing, or thinking about writing, she enjoys reading, running, hiking, skiing, traveling and making plans for the next adventure to subject her sometimes reluctant but always fun-loving family to. Carol can be contacted at carolrossauthor.com and via Facebook at Facebook.com/carolrossauthor, Twitter, @_carolross, and Instagram, @carolross__.

Books by Carol Ross

Harlequin Heartwarming

Return of the Blackwell Brothers

The Rancher's Twins

Seasons of Alaska

Mountains Apart
A Case for Forgiveness
If Not for a Bee
A Family Like Hannah's
Bachelor Remedy
In the Doctor's Arms
Catching Mr. Right

Second Chance for the Single Dad

Visit the Author Profile page
at Harlequin.com for more titles.

To all my readers who have asked when Hazel would be getting her own story, here you go, and thank you. Thank you, also, to those of you who've suggested that Cricket get his own story, too. But most of all, thank you to Jean, who told me several times that "Hazel *and* Cricket need *their* own story." You were so right.

CHAPTER ONE

On a good day, texting was only slightly more tolerable than a visit to the dentist. So composing this particular message was more like a root canal without the Novocain. Cricket analyzed what he had so far.

Hey, can you give me a call when you have a minute? I'd like to chat.

No, that didn't sound right. They weren't besties meeting for lunch. Deleted *chat*. Added *talk*. Rearranged.

Any chance you could give me a call? I'd like to talk to you about something important.

Hmm. *Talk* might imply that he wanted to have a *conversation*. Like a heart-to-heart with sentences that included *I feel* or *what I'm hearing you say is*... Never a good thing, and definitely not the goal here. Especially with the way his last encounter with Hazel had gone.

Even now, the memory of what had happened in Florida made his stomach churn with the hot acid of regret. That didn't mean Cricket wanted to talk about it, though.

For reasons known only to his deceased mother, Lynette, Cricket had been dubbed Jiminy Malcolm Blackburn at birth. According to his father, Frank, she'd barely lived long enough to fill in the name on his birth certificate. He also maintained that they'd previously agreed on David Malcolm, but she'd changed it at the last second, and who was he to argue with a woman who'd just suffered through untold agony giving birth to his child? If Frank's tale could even be believed. Cricket's older brother, Lee, had been too young to remember any of these details.

Regardless, growing up with a famous cartoon insect as his namesake could have set the stage for a rough childhood. And likely would have if his surname hadn't already ensured as much. *Blackburn* was a true badge of dishonor in the small town of Rankins, Alaska, where he'd grown up.

Years of staying out of trouble had managed to fade the stigma somewhat, but with a criminal con man for a father and a thief for a brother, it was always there. Lurking like a shark beneath the surface, waiting for the next **opportunity to strike. And frequently, a story** about yet another scam or theft or arrest would arise and unleash the gossip monster all over again. Cricket often imagined he could feel the less charitable townsfolk watching, waiting, wondering how far the apple had truly fallen from the tree.

A lifetime of weathering this fallout had made Cricket extremely cautious. He trusted very few people. It was a tricky balance trying to keep a low profile while fostering a positive reputation in a community this size. He'd learned at a very young age that words, once spoken, could never be taken back. Texting, in his opinion, was even worse than talking; phrases were misconstrued, statements spun. Every mistake or misstep indelibly recorded.

Bringing him back to his current dilemma. Hazel. He'd phoned her twice now, and she hadn't answered or returned his calls. That probably told him all he needed to know. Likely she was still upset with him, which was fair. Although this was business, he reminded himself as he deleted the entire message and started over.

Call me. We need to talk.

That sounded like the precursor to a breakup. He ground out a frustrated sigh. This was ridiculous. He shouldn't be agonizing over a simple text to a woman he'd known her entire life. If it were any one of her three sisters, he wouldn't even hesitate. The Jameses were like family to him. But that was the problem, wasn't it? Hazel didn't *feel* like family. And hadn't for a very long time.

Ten years since "the incident" that still filled him with regret and from which he knew he'd never completely recover. He'd tried to move on. Over the years, he'd dated plenty of women, hoping someone would take her place. One unsuccessful attempt had followed another until, ultimately, he'd accepted his fate.

What had happened in Florida a few months ago only proved how little progress he'd made with Hazel. They'd argued. Yes, he'd started it, but he'd also apologized. Then, foolishly, he'd taken her in his arms, and before he knew it, a simple hug had turned…intense. He'd almost kissed her. Again. As if he needed the memory of another kiss, and the long-ago promise he'd broken, to keep him up at night. This time, at least, he'd resisted. Was he proud of how he'd walked away and left things? No. And undoubtedly, that was the source of her anger. Was she *that* upset, though? Enough not to return his calls?

Finally, he settled on a simple Call me. I need to talk to you.

With a final grumble, he hit Send, set the phone aside and turned his attention back to the computer monitor, where he didn't see things getting better anytime soon. Not without help. Ideally, Hazel's help.

The familiar *stomp, stomp, stomp* of boots shedding snow sounded on the front mat outside the entrance of the newly appointed office of Our Alaska Tours. He looked up to see Tag James come through the door, here to fetch him for their outing to Glacier City. Today was the first donation pickup on behalf of Operation Happy Christmas, a charity Tag's mom, Margaret, had started and in which Cricket had played an integral part.

"Hey, buddy, you ready?" Tag asked.

"Yep. Rebekah said we could pick up the load anytime after three."

"Sounds good." Tag walked forward and leaned on the reception counter, behind which no one yet worked. Our Alaska Tours wasn't officially open for business. They were slated to launch this spring, but unfortunately, they were behind schedule—the reason he needed to talk to Hazel.

Tag was Hazel's oldest brother, and his oldest friend. His first friend, his *best* friend since first grade. He'd been the one to give him the nickname Cricket because Tag went by a nickname, too, and thought being called Cricket would be "supercool." Beyond that, though, Tag had never cared about any of Cricket's names, first or last, or what they implied. His pedigree, his poverty, none of that mattered to Tag. Or to the rest of the James family, for that matter.

That same often-hungry, without-prospects poverty might have prevented Cricket from participating in the everyday activities typical of a small-town Alaska childhood if it hadn't been for Tag. His friend had handled this obstacle the same way he did almost everything in life: with generosity, discretion, casual efficiency—and extreme loyalty.

When it came time for a game of basketball, snow-machine ride, hike, fishing trip or whatever the boys had set their sights on, and Cricket didn't have proper-fitting sneakers or a warm-enough coat or the right gear, Tag would give him something from his own closet. Or borrow something from his cousin Bering, or one of his sisters, and loan *that* to him. And when Cricket had been skirting the edge of the foster system, it had been Tag's parents who'd taken him in.

Bering, who was also a close friend and

Cricket's business partner in the newly formed tour business, entered the office only seconds behind Tag.

Crossing his arms over his massive chest, he nodded toward the monitor and asked, "What do you think of Hazel's suggestions?"

Cricket considered the two men standing before him and wondered, as he often did, where he'd be if it weren't for the James family. No place good, that was for sure, if he were to base the probabilities on his own family's history. Instead, with hard work and the encouragement of Tag and his parents, Margaret and Ben, he'd become an airplane pilot. And then a helicopter pilot and finally a business owner.

Tag's sister Hannah was his partner in JB Heli-Ski, a backcountry adventure ski company for which Cricket also piloted. After Tag, she was his closest friend. The rest of the year, Cricket flew clients into the backcountry for Bering's other business, a guide and outfitter service, and for Tag's air transport company, Copper Crossing, which flew just about anything anywhere it needed to go.

This new partnership between him and Bering, while taking him in a different direction, felt like a natural evolution. The formation of Our Alaska Tours was also one more tie binding him to the James family. And one more reason to keep his distance from Hazel, the James woman who could unravel it all.

Keeping a literal distance usually wasn't too difficult. Her life as a travel writer and blogger meant that typically, thousands of miles separated them. Ironically, it was her expertise in that field now forcing this point of contact.

And this latest bout of Hazel anxiety must, as always, remain his secret and was not the aim of Bering's question, which he now addressed with a wryly delivered, "Ghost tours? I didn't even know we had ghosts in Alaska."

Tag laughed.

A smiling Bering said, "Emily says these tours are very popular everywhere right now." Emily was Bering's wife and director of Rankins's tourism bureau. She'd been filling them in on popular tourist draws. "And you have to admit, it's interesting. You guys know Kerry Cottons, right? He says Gold Bend's history is spooky that way. Maybe we could tack on a day to the coastal tour—for the mining history, not the ghosts." Kerry was a fellow pilot who lived near the historic old mining town a short boat ride away from Juneau.

"We know him," Cricket said. "Great guy. Honestly, Hazel's entire proposal is full of interesting ideas." Mostly. Some of them seemed a little out-there, but Bering had asked her for any and all suggestions, and she'd delivered.

"I agree. What do you think about her recommendation to hire someone?"

"Why don't you just hire *her*?" Tag joked. "I'd love for my sister to quit wandering around the world all alone and come home for good."

"We'd all love that," Bering concurred.

Would we? Cricket silently pondered. He could barely handle being in the same room with her without giving himself away. How would he manage to live in the same town? Then again, Tag had a point, too; at least they'd know she was safe.

He had to admit that Bering's idea to seek her advice about their tours had been a good one. He could see now that they should have done it months ago. Technically, they'd planned to in Florida, but then there'd been the argument followed by a crisis involving her brother Seth, and the opportunity had been lost.

Nevertheless, the clock was now ticking to get their tours finalized in advance of the travel season. Cricket felt responsible for the delay. Partly, anyway. There'd been plenty of other obstacles they could never have foreseen. All of them heightening his anxiety as money and time had been invested, commitments and promises made. He needed to fix this, get them back on track.

Expression turning thoughtful, Bering asked Tag, "Do you think that's possible? That she'd want a job?"

"No." Tag sighed. "It'll never happen. Traveling is her life. I don't think we'll ever get her back here for good."

Cricket tried to decide if Tag's declaration caused him more disappointment or relief. He said, "I texted her, asking if she had time to discuss some of this stuff." Or, at least, that was what he planned to ask her when she called him back.

"Great," Bering said. "Maybe we can set up a video call."

Cricket agreed. Until then, they had a load of Christmas donations to fetch.

Pushing to his feet, he looked at Tag and said, "Let's hit the road."

"SO... NO FACEBOOK, Twitter, Snapchat, LinkedIn, Instagram, TikTok, Marco Polo, or any social media or photo-sharing platform out there that we may or may not have heard of."

Hazel James nodded along while her private guide, Kai Montauk, outlined the rules for touring Montauk Caves, the limestone caverns named for his grandfather.

Piercing dark brown eyes snagged hers and held on tight as he added, "No photos whatsoever." Like she was a naughty middle schooler trying to sneak her phone into class.

"I understand," she politely responded, while desperately wanting to joke, *Principal Montauk, sir.*

"I'll also reiterate that your Instagram *story* cannot include photos or *video* of the caves, or of me, or you, or Buster, or anything or anyone else that you see once we step through that gate."

Even with the borderline hostility, he was a nice-looking guy. Midtwenties, she estimated, with a chiseled jawline, strong chin and black shoulder-length hair tucked behind his ears. She suspected a set of dimples would slash his cheeks if she could ever bring him to a smile.

He was pointing toward the trail, where a security fence stretched as far as she could see in both directions, an endless parade of shiny black metal spears protruding menacingly from the ground and intersecting at a tall gate. The way he'd drawn out the word *video* was enough for her to infer that some genius of the self-proclaimed variety had likely capitalized on the distinction between a still and moving picture by posting a "video" on their social media "story."

"Got it," she stated a bit more firmly. "I won't be taking or posting any photos or videos."

Kai's squinty-eyed skepticism was a match to his dubious tone. "I thought my brother said you were a travel blogger."

Ah. Of course. This was the reason for his borderline hostility. Understandable. Franco had told her about how, several months ago, after seeing a post from a popular "social media influencer" about the "#secretcaves," a group of teens had broken in. They'd carved their initials next to sacred Native hieroglyphs and destroyed some precious and irreplaceable stalactites and helictites.

As if that weren't bad enough, they'd rappelled down to the bottom of the largest shaft, where one of the kids had broken his ankle. Then they'd taken photos and posted them all over Instagram, accusing the Montauk family of "allowing" unsafe conditions, and #deadlycaves had trended. A lawsuit was filed. More graffiti and vandalism followed, prompting the family to close the property to the public and adopt these extreme security measures.

Such desperate actions were becoming more common as travel increased across the globe. All it took were a few rude or destructive individuals to ruin it for everyone. The number of locations where you were no longer permitted to take photos or video was rapidly growing, too. Sites where it had never been allowed were cracking down. Even as a professional traveler who took great pains to advocate for "travel respect" and responsibility, Hazel understood and felt torn about her role in it all.

"What else did Franco tell you about me?"

"Not much," he said. "I haven't spoken to my brother in days. With the time difference and our busy schedules, we keep missing each other. He emailed, asking me to show you around, and here we are."

Not overly thrilled about it either, she couldn't help but note. Suppressing a sigh, she conjured a smile. "I am a travel writer and blogger. But today, I am just Hazel, a friend of Franco's and a fellow cave enthusiast, taking him up on an invitation to visit his family's caves. No agenda. No assignment. A free day just for me. Believe it or not, I like to keep certain experiences to myself." Lately, she'd been feeling that inclination more and more. Maybe she needed a break.

A few months ago, an unfair and devastating social media attack had been unleashed on her brother Seth's girlfriend, Victoria. They'd been in Florida competing for the same professional spokesperson job when Victoria had become the victim of a vicious smear campaign. The incident had nearly derailed Victoria's career and her relationship with Seth.

Hazel had played a small part in rectifying the injustice, but the episode had left her disheartened and disappointed and launched an unprecedented bout of soul-searching. Or it had contributed, anyway. The questioning, the disquiet, ran deeper than that.

So much deeper.

All the way down to the black hole of her life called Cricket Blackburn, with whom she'd had a different, *more personal* altercation with while in Florida. Even now, the memory made her face flush hotly with mortification. They'd been arguing, and then they weren't. Apologies were exchanged and then a hug coalesced into a moment, and she was sure that he returned her attraction. But she was wrong, and the memory of what he'd said next and the vision of him walking away was almost physically painful.

"So, you just want to *look* at our caves?"

The question pulled her back into the moment. Where she belonged. Where she *wanted* to be. After all, that was what her life was all about—living in the moment. For the last ten years, she'd devoted herself to doing just that. Because when she lived in the moment, she did not waste time daydreaming about an impossible future or agonizing about the past. It was just that, lately, she'd been finding the execution of this philosophy more and more problematic. Was she having some sort of early-onset midlife crisis? An early-life crisis—was that a thing?

"No," she answered. "I want to experience your caves, to hear them, to smell them and, yes, to see them. You are welcome to hold on to my phone if that makes you more comfortable." Digging into her daypack, she then removed her cell only to see two missed calls from... No, it couldn't be. She squinted at the screen. *Cricket.* Before she could stop it, her insides erupted in this fluttery happy dance. The same sensation used to fill her with hope and anticipation and leave her reeling with dreamy-eyed fantasies. Now it made her feel foolish and immature. And maybe a little angry.

Ugh. She needed to get over this. What she needed was to get over him, once and for all. If she could only figure out how to do that.

There was a text, too, which gave her pause. Until she read, Call me. I need to talk to you.

That's it? "You've got to be kidding me," she muttered, irritation pulsing through her. She knew he hated texting, but he could do better than that. How about a *please* or maybe even an *I'm sorry*? "Too little, too late," she concluded.

He'd made it perfectly clear that he didn't want to discuss what had happened or make any effort to resolve *anything*, so why should she talk to him now? She looked back down at the phone and quickly counted. Eight words. That was what he could spare for her?

Looking up, she noted Kai's curious expression. His features had softened, dimples twitching as if toying with a smile.

"You okay?" he asked. "Did you get some bad news?"

"Yeah, no, I'm fine."

"If you need to make a call or send a text, I understand. The reception here is not great, but if you head back toward the parking area, you'll probably have better luck."

"Nope. Do *not* need to do that."

Pausing for a moment, he shuffled his weight and then heaved out a sigh. "Sorry if I sounded like kind of a jerk before. I'm just frustrated. Ever since the vandalism and the lawsuit."

"Don't sweat it." Hazel added a sincere smile. "I understand. Franco told me what happened."

"Thanks," he said simply, sincerely. They walked to the gate, where the trail led toward the stunning red rock canyon beyond. He lifted a little door to reveal a keypad and deftly tapped a sequence of buttons. The lock opened with a crisp click. He pushed the gate forward and waved her through.

On the other side, she waited while he secured the gate behind them. Something occurred to her then. "Can I ask you a question?"

"Sure."

"Who is Buster?"

He turned to face her, and she felt validated as those dimples officially made their first appearance. They were every bit as cute as she'd anticipated.

"You'll see."

"You promise?"

"You're not going to take photos, are you?" he asked, but she could tell he was teasing.

"No," she joked. "Just some video."

He laughed. "In his email, Franco said you were cool and funny."

"Well, Franco would know—he is also cool and funny."

That induced another grin, and Hazel decided Kai might not be as unpleasant as she'd first feared.

"He also said you were here in Utah working. Can I ask what brought you here, if not our caves?"

"I…" She started to explain, to tell him about the resort story, but that was when she realized she still held her phone in her hand. Like a lightning bolt, another idea occurred to her, a freelance article she could also write. She loved it when that happened.

"You know what? I am going to send one quick text…" She typed out a message for Iris and Seth, letting her triplet siblings know she'd be out of touch for a couple of days. She could easily work on both stories at the same time.

She then made a show of powering the phone off and shoving it to the bottom of her pack. The very bottom. *Ha. Take that, Cricket Blackburn! Now I won't go all dreamy-eyed when I see that your stupid face has called. Maybe you'll even get a taste of how I feel when you won't talk to me.*

"My current assignment is about resorts." Then she said the other story concept out loud, reinforcing the idea and liking it even more: "I'm also working on an article about how to enjoy traveling without being connected."

CHAPTER TWO

CRICKET'S PHONE BEGAN vibrating while he was still in the parking lot. *Hazel*, he thought, scrambling to remove it from his pocket. Despite the current tension between them, he found himself looking forward to hearing her voice. Suddenly, he needed to know that she was okay. That *they* were okay.

Not Hazel. Disappointed, he frowned at the unknown number.

"Hello?" he answered anyway, because unfamiliar callers were a regular part of his life. His cell number was listed as a contact for JB Heli-Ski.

"Mr. Blackburn?"

"Yes, this is Cricket. How can I help you?"

"I'm hoping I can help you. This is Ernie Harris from Otter Creek Correctional Facility."

"Oh, yes, hello. Thank you for returning my call."

"No problem. Your message said that you are having difficulty accessing an inmate's commissary account?"

"That's correct. My brother, Lee Thomas Blackburn." Cricket rattled off his ID number.

"Okay, got it. Not sure what happened, but I'll look into it and call you back."

"Great. I appreciate that. Thank you so much, Ernie. With that account frozen, you've probably got yourself an unhappy inmate, and for that, I apologize."

"Yeah, well," Ernie quipped, "I can guarantee he ain't the only one of those around here."

Cricket chuckled. "I imagine. I'll be down to see him soon. Thanks, Ernie."

"No problem. You have a good day."

"You, too." He ended the call.

"How is Lee?" Tag asked him.

"Same." Cricket lifted one shoulder in a shrug. "Something goofy with his account. Haven't been able to put any money in there."

Tag nodded, and when Cricket didn't elaborate, he let it go. One of the things he appreciated about his friend was how he didn't pry. Not without a good reason anyway, and rarely about Cricket's family, which consisted only of his wayward dad and brother.

Frank, his father, was two years into a three-to-five-year sentence in Michigan for arson and insurance fraud. Lee was currently in the third month of a six-to-twelve-month stint for second-degree burglary. Frank was a career criminal, hard-core. Lee's lawbreaking had never escalated to anywhere near the level of their father's, and despite his occasional foray into lawlessness, his brother was a likable and charming guy.

Cricket had spent a lot of years believing he could help Lee. Show him the light, steer him straight, whatever. He'd given up on that notion a long time ago. The only thing he could do was love his brother and hope that, eventually, his inherently good heart would win the internal battle that plagued him.

Tag said, "I know Operation Happy *Mom* means we need to get these gifts back in a timely manner, and you wouldn't want to disappoint her, but let's stop in Glacier City and grab a burger at Grizzly Quake? I skipped breakfast."

Cricket wholeheartedly agreed. With their busy schedules, and the recent birth of Tag's son, Abe, it had been a while since the friends had enjoyed an afternoon together. Tag had been the one to suggest they both make this first donation run as a creative way of catching up.

The rest of Tag's statement sank in. "Operation Happy Mom?" he repeated with a laugh.

Even though he understood Tag's gibe, Cricket and Margaret had spent a lot of time together lately. He'd been instrumental in helping her launch Operation Happy Christmas. The massive charity undertaking had been in the works for months and had taken countless hours of their time.

With Margaret's connections as a school principal and as an active member of the local Presbyterian church, she and her band of enthusiastic cohorts had identified people across southern Alaska in need of "holiday attention." Her list was long and varied and included kids, families, adults, low-income seniors and veterans. Age didn't matter. The only requirement was need. Everyone, Margaret believed, deserved a happy Christmas.

Cricket had headed up logistics while Margaret rallied the communities and secured donations. A highly capable and committed team of volunteers was in place. Cricket had established a transport chain with Glacier City as the nearest collection point. He'd recruited Tag to help.

Once inside the van, they buckled up. The vehicle was new to both of them, having been donated to the charity by a used-car dealership. He wished his brother, Lee, a skilled mechanic, wasn't in jail so he could check out its condition for them.

"I cannot wait to tell her you said that!" Cricket said gleefully.

"Yeah, go ahead, rat me out," Tag joked. "Like you need another reason to be her favorite."

"OH, CRIKEY!" HAZEL cried and tapped on her headlamp.

"You okay?" Kai asked, shuffling around in the cramped space so the beam from his light illuminated her. They were in a narrow tunnel on their way to a large vertical cavern where they'd descend into yet another chamber.

"Sorry," she said. "My headlamp is on the fritz. I've been meaning to buy a new one. I've got an old spare at the bottom of my pack, but…" Reaching around to a side pocket, she removed a flashlight. "This should do for now, though, right?"

"Yep. Not much farther." Kai turned back around and headed forward. "We'll regroup before we rappel down to the main cavern." Then he picked up right where they'd left the conversation before Hazel's equipment malfunction. "So, you're telling me that you are getting paid to stay at a bunch of different resorts and try all these cool activities, and then write about your favorite ones?"

Hazel had been explaining about the assignment that had officially brought her to Utah. "Yep, '10 Must-Try Resort Experiences,'" she answered. "The title pretty much says it all."

"What sorts of things have you done so far in the name of research?"

"Let's see… Highlights in the last week would have to be goat yoga, the hot-air-balloon ride with a champagne brunch, stargazing and a sculpting lesson that was a ton of fun. Tomorrow kicks off with a guided meditation session. Then I have a paddleboard excursion, kitten therapy in the afternoon and—"

"Wait, did you say *kitten therapy*?"

"I sure did."

"What is—"

"No clue. But if it involves kittens, I'm in. Ask me tomorrow. But it will have to be after my archery session because, as you can see, I am tightly booked until then. Tomorrow night at Darcie Bluff Resort is the debut of their holiday tasting menu. Looking extra forward to that."

"Are you kidding me? You are doing the holiday tasting at Darcie Bluff? That is a dream of mine. There's like a yearlong waiting list. How did you get a reservation?"

"My editor, Rory, the owner of *Travel Inside & Out*, who I am writing the resort piece for, booked this vacation for himself and his wife a year ago. Then his wife got pregnant and is now due any day. Brilliant man that he is, he turned it into a story, and he asked me if I wanted to write it."

"I want to be a travel writer," Kai said in a comical tone of exaggerated envy.

Hazel laughed and replied, "It is a pretty awesome gig."

She meant those words. Totally and completely. Almost completely. Because it was also a ton of hard work. She didn't mention that part, though, or the incredible number of hours she'd logged to reach this point. People rarely believed it. They assumed a career that involved traveling the world had to be the easiest, best job in the world. Just hop on a plane and jet about the globe. But professional travel was so much more than that; it was a way of life.

And establishing herself had taken years. There was the expense of getting started, figuring out *how* to make money, the part-time jobs to supplement her income until she began to earn more than her travel expenses—with never a guarantee that she'd get there. Even with her English degree, there'd been a learning curve to writing short, catchy articles and blog posts with punchy, searchable titles. Not to mention mastering all the accompanying technology and business strategies associated with a successful blog. Effectively navigating social media was a whole other ball game.

Living out of a suitcase could also be a challenge, as was not having a "home" of her own. She couldn't justify the expense. So, at twenty-nine, she still had a room at her parents' house.

But the personal sacrifices were the most difficult. Romantic relationships were more trouble than they were worth. Friendships took special care. Family commitments were tricky. In ten years, she'd been home for Christmas dinner exactly one time. She couldn't begin to count the number of holidays, birthdays, weddings, parties and special occasions she'd missed.

While family and friends were celebrating her parents' thirtieth anniversary, she'd been "returning" to San Juan Capistrano along with the swallows. She'd been running from bulls in Pamplona when her youngest niece was born. Loneliness could hit hard at unexpected moments.

Nor did she mention the dangers. Like when she'd barely survived a tsunami in Indonesia only to discover her hotel, along with all of her belongings save the clothes on her back, had been swept away. And then there was South America.

Not even her family knew about the time she'd nearly been kidnapped for ransom in Colombia. Unless Cricket had told someone—he'd sworn he wouldn't—and she was reasonably certain she would have heard about it by now if he'd broken that promise. No way her brother Tag would stay quiet about that if he knew. If there was one thing Cricket could be counted on for, it was his restraint. Too much restraint, as far as she was concerned.

So lost was she in her thoughts that the shift in the air almost startled her. Untold hours of caving experience told her the space would soon be opening before them.

"Here we are," Kai said a moment later. "I always like to stop here and take a minute just to appreciate the total lack of light."

Hazel clicked off her flashlight and felt herself smiling in the dark. Inky blackness crowded around her, causing her pulse to accelerate. In the course of normal everyday life, such complete and utter darkness was rare. Caves were one of the few places you could experience it. It was exhilarating and slightly spooky, and she loved the sensation. Like other people enjoyed scuba diving or rock climbing, spelunking was her thing.

Surrendering to the dark, she focused on her remaining senses. The chilly, dank press of the air against her skin was such a contrast to the arid world outside. Breathing deeply, she thought she could smell water. Or maybe that was due to the distinctive *drip, drip, drip* echoing loudly around them. There was also a deep whooshing sound mixed with a higher-pitched fizz.

"Cave acoustics are so fascinating," she said softly. "What is that hissing sound?"

"*That* is the Witch's Pot. Down below us, a cold-water stream collides with a hot spring. Hold on…" She heard a click, and then over-head lights dimly illuminated the space. A sturdy-looking metal fence completely en-closed the opening to the shaft. Steam drifted up from below as if from a bubbling cauldron.

"Witch's Pot? How utterly cool!" She quickly located her spare headlamp, slipped it on and peered over the edge.

"Just wait until we get below and you get the full effect. Ready?"

"Ready."

After securing their harnesses, they rap-pelled the one-hundred-three-foot shaft until they landed on solid ground. A few seconds passed while Kai shuffled around and then hit another set of lights.

"Wow…" Hazel breathed out the word while her gaze traveled around the spacious cavern.

The pool, Witch's Pot, was located to one side, where the ceiling sloped gradually down. Gurgling and bubbling, a roiling layer of steam crawled along on the top, where it drifted up in wispy strands.

"Okay," she said. "This is one of *the* coolest cave formations I've *ever* seen. I understand why Franco was so insistent that I visit."

Off to one side, a cluster of stalagmites and stalactites resembled a yawning mouth, complete with jagged, irregular teeth. "That must be Buster."

"That's him."

"Why Buster?" she asked.

"Grandpa thought it looked like a mouth full of busted teeth."

"It does," she agreed. Then she looked up and promptly let out a gasp. Suspended above them, twisting and crisscrossing the space, were a mass of stalactites and helictites. Strands of varying thickness in shades of brown and gold and caramel. All woven loosely together like finely spun threads of glass. But to her, it looked like…

"Candy!" she exclaimed loudly and then laughed. "Sorry, I get excited. But it looks like threads of caramel."

There was relief inside of her, too, and she welcomed the reaction, reminding her of what she most loved about traveling, why she did what she did. There was nothing like seeing something this spectacular for the very first time. She'd explored many of the very best caves the world over, and this was slated to make her list of all-time personal favorites.

"That's funny," Kai said. "Emma thought the same thing."

"Emma?" she repeated, as curious about the person as she was about Kai's wistful tone.

"Oh, sorry, my ex. She always said it reminded her of making hard candy with her grandmother."

"Exactly!" Hazel said. "My first thought was this toffee my mom makes at Christmastime." A sharp pang of longing struck her, and she suddenly yearned to be home for the holidays this year.

Kai said, "So grateful the delinquents couldn't reach high enough to do any damage in here. Or, more likely, the broken ankle put a damper on their *fun* before they could get to it."

"I am thankful for that, too," she said and then gave him a moment in case he wanted to elaborate. When he didn't, she said, "It's wonderful how you've positioned the lights. It helps set the tone."

"That was my grandfather's doing. Years ago, before he died. Franco and I were just kids, but we helped him. This place was his passion. Sacred to our family, our heritage. It would kill him if he were still alive to see what those kids did."

"No doubt." An idea came to her then. "Thank you so much for taking the time to show me all of this."

"No problem."

"I'd like to repay you by—"

"Nope. No way," he interrupted. "Franco would never forgive me if I—"

"Inviting you to Darcie Bluff for the holiday tasting menu with me tomorrow night."

"Dissed you after an invite like that," he said, quickly changing course and making her laugh. "Yes, I believe that would be a perfectly acceptable means of payment."

"HMM." MARGARET JAMES studied the tablet she held in her hand. Even if she weren't already like a mom to him, Margaret would still be one of Cricket's favorite people. He knew without a doubt that she was one of the planet's finest humans.

Tall and slender, she had dark blond hair and pretty, greenish-brown eyes that were warm and expressive. She was fit for her age from an active lifestyle that included a regular regimen of swimming, walking and strength training, so it was no surprise that she had the energy of a person half her age. She also possessed the sharp mind and exceptional memory you'd expect in a school principal and mother of six.

"The inventory list is not matching up with what we have here. Let's count again."

Cricket acquiesced, and then they exchanged numbers, which were the same. Looking down at the table again, she said, "We're missing two boxes. One of toys and one of winter coats. Are you boys sure you didn't miss anything?"

"Pretty sure, Mom," Tag said. "Rebekah even invited us inside for a few minutes to show us the storage area in case we ever need to load the van ourselves."

In this case, the storage area was a large, unused classroom in St. Steven's Episcopal Church in Glacier City. Other donation drop points would bring their items to St. Steven's to be stored until they could be picked up and brought to the Faraway Inn. Its largest conference room had been volunteered for use as the central hub. Once there, everything would be sorted again, wrapped and readied for final distribution a few days before Christmas.

"Tag's right," Cricket said. "There was nothing else in there."

"Huh. Well, this is our first pick up. I suppose we can't expect everything to go perfect from the get-go. I'll call Rebekah."

"I almost forgot my good news," Cricket said. "I got a good line on some Squixits out of Edmonton. Hoping to hear back tomorrow."

"Some whatty-whos?" Tag asked.

"The Squixit," Margaret informed him. "It's the hot new toy this holiday season. Cricket has been trying to get his hands on some."

"Cricket needs to get a life," Tag quipped.

Margaret flashed him a playful scowl. "I'll have you know that Cricket and I are up on all the holiday trends. Last week, he scored fifty of those fancy heated lap blankets. They'll be gifted to some of our senior citizens. They've been sold out everywhere. Honestly, I don't know what I'd do without him."

When she turned around to talk to another volunteer, Tag rolled his eyes, pointed at Cricket and mouthed the word *favorite*.

"Okay," Margaret said, facing them again. "That's it for tonight. We've got dinner waiting for us at home. Dad made lasagna—two huge pans. Iris brought Caesar salad and garlic bread. See you guys at the house."

Cricket and Tag went back out to the parking lot, where Tag had left his pickup when he'd exchanged it earlier for the van. Cricket climbed inside and took a minute to check his phone. One call from an unknown number, no voice mail.

Seven texts. Four from Hannah. Hannah lamenting the lack of snow in the weather forecast. Hannah asking when he could drop by the resort in the next day or so to talk strategy. Hannah, "so excited about our tickets"—what that meant he did not know. Her last one was a snowboarding joke, which made him smile even under the circumstances.

There was a group message from Aidan to all their poker buddies, wondering about the next gathering's time and place. And then an answer from Bering.

The final message was from his friend Clark Mayfield, clueing him in on the ticket excitement Hannah referenced. As lead singer for the band Rushing Tide, he'd sent tickets for him, Hannah and her husband, Tate, to a Christmas benefit concert in Anchorage, where their band was performing later this month.

Still nothing from Hazel.

He pulled up her contact and tapped the call button. Straight to voice mail once again. He tried to talk himself out of the bad feeling brewing inside of him. Even if she was still angry with him, not responding at all seemed out of character for her. A short, snarky reply was more her thing.

Despite his concern and in an effort not to cause undue alarm, he marshaled a casual tone and asked Tag, "Have you heard from Hazel lately? Is she going to make it home for Christmas this year?"

"Funny you mention her because Ally just asked me that very question this morning. And the answer is, I wish. But I don't know. It would be nice to have everyone together this year. With all the new additions, Mom wants some family pictures. I texted Hazel this morning but haven't heard back. Probably off in the boonies somewhere, right?"

"Probably," Cricket agreed and quickly changed the subject. No point in worrying Tag before he had more information. "Strange about those missing boxes..."

They discussed possible explanations until they pulled up in front of Margaret and Ben's house. Once inside, Hannah was the first person he saw.

"Hey, you. Get my messages?"

"I did."

"Cool about the concert, huh?"

They spent a few minutes chatting before he found a reason to ask her about Hazel, too.

"I called her this afternoon, and it went straight to voice mail. Left a message, haven't heard back." She shook her head, but her tone was full of fondness when she said, "Typical Hazel, right?"

"For sure," Cricket agreed. Her son, Lucas, approached Hannah with a question, and Cricket used that opportunity to slip away and search for the most promising source for up-to-date Hazel information.

"Found the boxes!" Margaret called out as he passed by the dining room. "They're still at the church," she explained. "They got put in the kindergarten classroom."

Cricket gave her a thumbs-up and continued into the kitchen, where he found Iris holding her daughter, Lily, on her hip with one hand. With the other, she was deftly scooping ice from a bucket into glasses and then filling them from a pitcher with what looked like lemonade. Amazing what parents of young children could accomplish one-handed.

Logical and thoughtful to the point of extreme caution, Iris would also be the person most likely to share his concern about Hazel. He needed to be careful about alarming her unnecessarily.

Cricket and Tag had been in grade school when the triplets, Hazel, Seth and Iris, were born. Back then, Cricket had spent more time at the James home than his own. And, like the honorary big brother he was, he'd watched the trio grow up, happily attending sporting events, concerts, plays and Iris's science fairs right alongside everyone else. He and Tag had even coached a young Seth and Hazel's soccer team.

All of this combined to make his eventual attraction to Hazel both shocking and unwanted. Almost…inappropriate. But all too real. And yet, no matter what he did, he couldn't seem to shake his feelings. For a decade, he'd kept the depth of his affections a secret from everyone— including Iris, who, incredibly, seemed to know everything about everyone.

Ten years of avoiding, fighting against and trying to overcome his Hazel infatuation, all while hiding behind the auspices of this big-brother privilege. A subterfuge that, instead of getting easier, only seemed to grow more difficult with time.

"Hey, you," he said to Iris now, walking across the kitchen to join her. "Hello, Miss Lily," he cooed to the baby, who giggled and kicked her feet like a tiny, determined swimmer. Adorable.

"Hey, yourself," Iris said warmly.

When Iris had finished grad school and moved back home, she'd asked Cricket to give her flying lessons. Under his guidance, she'd earned her pilot's license, and in the process, they'd forged a strong friendship of their own.

"How was the journey?" she asked.

"Good. Van runs like a charm."

"Excellent, especially since Mom or I might have to do a pickup or two, as well."

The baby squealed with delight as Cricket took her and swooped her up into his arms.

"So stinking cute how much she adores you."

He spent a minute making silly chitchat with the baby before asking, "Have you talked to Hazel today, by any chance?"

"Nope," Iris said. "Not since the day before last."

"Are you, uh, certain about the timing?"

"Absolutely positive," Iris returned. "The three of us group text almost every day. Hazel's responses can be intermittent, depending on her current time zone. But I'm sure about this one because, as you know, Seth and Victoria are fishing in Brazil. He sent a photo of an arapaima he caught. They both know how much that fish freaks me out, so I found it odd that she didn't respond with a joke."

Frowning, she went on, "And then, this morning, I had a doctor's appointment. She always texts after my appointments." Frowning gently at her pregnant belly, she gave it a rub and amended, "*Our* appointments? I feel like it should be *our.*"

"That seems completely appropriate to me," he agreed, processing this information. He kissed Lily on the cheek. That meant *no one*, no family member anyway, had heard from Hazel in more than forty-eight hours?

"Why do you ask?" Iris asked, her gaze searching his. "What's going on?"

"Nothing." *I hope.* "I've been waiting to hear back from her myself."

"When did you call her? Because Hannah told me she phoned her today, too." Brow knitting tightly, she crossed her arms, waiting. He decided to explain because he knew better than to try to make an end run around Iris.

Before he could even get through it all, she produced her phone and spent a few minutes navigating around. Her gaze snapped up to latch onto his. "No activity on social media. Although, she's been way less active since the Victoria thing. But still." Tapping on the display, she then lifted the phone to her ear. "Oddness is afoot."

They waited.

"No answer," Iris said, ending the call. She inhaled deeply and then exhaled a sharp, worried sigh. "And it's weird that it went straight to voice mail. Like her phone is dead or she's..."

Iris shifted into her silent and somber mode, and Cricket knew her imagination was off and running. "Cricket, what are you thinking? Should we be worried? Never mind, I'm already worried."

He passed Lily back to Iris and slipped his phone from his back pocket. This time he didn't even have to think about what he wanted to say:

No one has heard from you in more than 48 hours. I have two words for you: South America. If you don't call me back by six pm today (Alaska time) I'm going to assume you need help.

CHAPTER THREE

DARCIE BLUFF SERVED their tasting menu in The Kitchen. Not the resort's commercial cooking area, but a separate, more intimate space designed specifically for this purpose. To make patrons feel like they were dining in the comfort of a friend's home. If your friend was an extremely wealthy gourmet chef who held lavish dinner parties with *other* friends you didn't know.

Hazel thought they pulled it off brilliantly. Every inch radiated tasteful luxury, from the gleaming hardwood floors to the high, decoratively paneled ceiling. Even the silver, red and gold holiday decor shimmered with elegant perfection.

Seating for the meal was at a sleek black granite bar adjacent to The Kitchen, where diners could enjoy the interaction with the chef and his staff for two-plus hours while they prepared ten elaborate and innovative "petite" courses served on artistically presented plates.

The offerings varied with the seasons, availability of fresh ingredients and the chef's whims. Kai was clearly beside himself with excitement, and Hazel was pleased to share the experience, especially with a fellow foodie.

The Kitchen also had a full bar and encouraged their guests to arrive at the holiday party early to sample their creative beverage menu. In the interest of fairly evaluating the experience, she and Kai happily obliged. They were currently standing before the floor-to-ceiling windows that made up one entire wall and provided a stunning view of the pine-dotted landscape with the sweeping canyon below. The sun was just setting, and the constantly changing colors were breathtaking.

Hazel sipped a festively titled Sugar Plum, a delicious plum, cranberry and orange concoction served in a sugar-and-spice-rimmed martini glass and garnished with fresh cranberries. Kai had opted for the Night Before Christmas Lager, which he'd cheerfully declared "merry and bright." The acoustics were so impeccable that the holiday orchestral music's subtle strains seemed to seep from the air around them.

"I read somewhere that tasting menus are the new dinner theater," Kai commented. "Dinner theater has always seemed a little awkward to me, though. I can't shake the feeling that it's kind of rude to eat while someone is performing."

Hazel smiled. Kai was proving to be an excellent companion. Yesterday, when they'd finished touring the caves, he'd invited her to lunch, where he'd continued quizzing her about her adventures. Smart, funny and an avid traveler himself, he seemed up for anything. This morning, he'd even joined her for the guided meditation session.

If he weren't still hung up on his ex, Emma, whom he'd mentioned no less than fifty times, he'd be fun to date. Not that *she* wanted to date him. For her, the Emma mentions were a relief. If he was pining for another, there was little danger of him becoming attached to her. They'd spent two days together, and so far, there hadn't been a single "list" violation.

Over the years, Hazel had come to recognize certain behaviors that indicated a suitor's intentions. The blogger in her had compiled them into a "Romantic Interest List."

"Offenses" included actions like calling or texting more than once a day, the giving of flowers or gifts (the more thoughtful, the more "dangerous"), expressing a desire to meet one's family and closest friends, sharing food, delivery of a favorite food to a place of work.

The list went on, and to avoid romantic com-plications, or eventual hurt feelings, she attempted to stave off undue interest before it escalated into relationship territory.

Kai said, "I need to tell you something. When I said I wanted to be a travel writer, I wasn't completely joking. Well, not the *writer* part but the travel. I majored in tourism and travel management at the University of Nevada."

"What! Kai, why haven't you mentioned that before?"

With a sheepish shrug, he admitted, "Self-conscious. I looked you up, and you're kind of a big deal. I even realized that I'd read some of your stuff before." With an apologetic wince, he added, "Sorry."

"Oh, please." She waved him off. "Why would you remember?"

"Because I'm hoping to work in the industry. I've done consulting work for a few local tour companies, in addition to guiding."

"That's awesome," she said and then pointed out, "Sounds like you're there, already."

He agreed but not with an excess of enthusiasm. "But I'd like to do something different. Live somewhere besides the Southwest. I need to get out of here."

"You *need* to get out of here?" she repeated

in a teasing tone even as the phrase resonated through her like a familiar song.

"Yeah, I, um… That might sound a little dramatic, but you know that ex I've mentioned?"

"Emma."

"Right. Well, she's back in town, and I…" Inhaling a breath, he filled his cheeks with air before puffing out a sigh. "I don't want to be where she is. I don't want to be within five hundred miles of her. Do you think that's cowardly?"

"Ha!" she sputtered. "If it is, then I'm the biggest coward on the planet."

"Really?"

"Trust me. I get it. It was a romance disappointment that originally had me packing my bags."

A bit more complicated than that, but after the fiasco of her breakup with her high school boyfriend, Derrick, and the simultaneous rejection by Cricket, she hadn't wanted to remain in Rankins. But there wasn't anywhere else she'd particularly wanted to be either.

The summer before college, she'd toured a portion of Europe and fallen in love, wished she'd had time to see more. So that was what she did, spent her sophomore year of college studying abroad. And then every break, every summer, almost every weekend until graduation, she'd gone somewhere. Anywhere but home.

On a whim, after a visit to Paris had excessively strained her bank account, she'd begun submitting articles to magazines and sites on topics she wished someone would realistically cover. Like "How to Enjoy Paris Cuisine on a (Real) Budget" and "Useful Tips for a Woman Traveling Alone in Southeast Asia."

Keeping her expectations low, she'd started her blog, *Hazel Blazes Trails*, telling herself it was a way to keep track of her experiences. But it grew steadily as she slowly ventured further and wider, turning her passion into a career.

Had she been running away? Maybe. But she didn't regret it. Only lately had this inexplicable longing started nipping at her heels. The problem was she couldn't identify the exact cause, or even what she wanted, or where she wanted to go anymore. Chalking it up to both Iris and Seth finding their soul mates, and now Iris's pregnancy, she hoped it was just a phase. A simple case of nest envy that would pass.

"That is so cool!" he cried and then immediately realized how that sounded. "No, not cool for you, I mean, but…"

"No, I get it," Hazel said with a snicker. "It's always nice to know you're not the only one who's suffering, right? I recommend traveling for getting over just about anything that ails you. And for discovering who you are, what you like, who you want to be. Learning how to rely on yourself is one of the most powerful tools you can have." For her, that was possibly the best byproduct of her lifestyle. There wasn't much she was afraid of.

"That's what I'm hoping to do. Hey, if you hear of anything interesting, will you let me know?"

"Sure, I will," she answered immediately.

"Thank you." Kai's phone began to emit a quiet buzz. "Shoot, sorry, I forgot to turn this off." An eager grin spread across his face as he checked the display. "It's Franco. Do you mind if I take this?"

"Not at all," she said. "Go! Tell him I said hi."

"Thanks. Be right back." Hurrying toward the French doors that exited onto the veranda, he stepped outside.

Behind her, the sounds of shuffling feet and the murmur of cheerful voices provided a pleasant backdrop. More people were arriving, and the crowd was shifting to accommodate. Softness brushed across the bare skin of her back, maybe a shirtsleeve or jacket, sending a shiver over her. Even then, the sensation wouldn't have caused her a second thought if not for the scent that drifted along with it.

The familiar yet distinctive combination of sandalwood, cinnamon and vanilla seeped into her consciousness. She'd know that fragrance anywhere. Since her teenage days, she'd puzzled over how a man could smell so singularly delicious and unique at the same time.

Closing her eyes, she breathed in the essence of Cricket Blackburn and tried to talk herself out of what she was thinking. No way he was here. And yet, when the hand landed on her elbow with an accompanying light squeeze, her heart told her otherwise.

"Hazel." The deep baritone of his voice was unmistakable.

A multitude of questions bombarded her. What was he doing here? Could this possibly be an extremely wild coincidence? If not, how had he found her? When had he arrived? But she didn't ask any of them; she couldn't settle on one. Because he was here, and she was shocked, and he was staring at her. She could *feel* that, too, without even turning her head to look at him.

"Cricket." She finally forced herself to meet his gaze and discovered green eyes blazing with startling intensity. "What are you doing here?"

He shrugged a casual shoulder, but she could see the tension radiating from his body. "Looking for you."

A little thrill spiked through her, only to be immediately tempered by concern. "Why would you be doing that?"

"Because you wouldn't return my calls. Or my texts. I texted you three times."

"What are you…?"

"You know how much I hate texting."

She huffed an exasperated "Cricket!"

He sighed. "We were worried, Hazel. And I need to talk to you."

Worried? "Is everyone okay? What do you need to talk to me about?"

"Everything is fine with your family. Aside from the fact that no one has heard from you in nearly three days. Do you want to explain that? Because I can't think of a single reason that doesn't involve you being in serious trouble. And believe me, I've given this a lot of thought."

He went on before she could explain, as if needing to prove his assertion, "If you'd lost your phone, you'd buy another. A quick look at cell phone coverage in this area revealed that the chances of you being out of range around here for that long are slim.

"At first, I figured it was just me that you

didn't want to talk to." A narrow-eyed pause followed, possibly an invitation for her to confirm or deny. When she did neither, he went on, "Then I found out I wasn't the only one—Tag, Hannah, your mom. None of whom would have caused me to fly across the country in search of you. Except, I asked Iris, too." He quit then, not needing to point out the obvious result.

It *had* been just him. Or at least it had started that way. Ugh, she *really* did not want to admit that.

"It was for an article," she muttered, not quite meeting his eyes as she dug her phone out of her bag. A partial truth, because it had morphed into that, hadn't it?

"Was it?" His tone held an edge of skepticism, as if he was trying to imagine how this could be so.

"Yes. My phone has been off, but I texted Iris and Seth to let them know I'd be out of touch."

"Well, she didn't get it."

Staring at the screen, Hazel powered her phone on to check because she'd absolutely sent them a message before heading into the caves.

"Why? Why would you turn your phone off?"

"It's not unusual for me to be…unreachable."

Her fingers flew over the screen, ignoring the million texts and social media notifications lighting up the display.

"That's true," he smoothly interrupted as if he knew the defense she was about to employ. "But you always let Iris and Seth know when you'll be out of range for more than a couple of days. And at the very least, your location alone serves as an explanation. Mongolia or Nepal, for example, might lead a person to conclude that perhaps you are out of cell phone range or lacking electricity with which to charge your electronic devices. The *wilds* of Utah," he added with a twinge of sarcasm, "not so much."

Pulling up Seth and Iris's text thread, she saw the message she'd sent. Tried to, she silently amended as she noted the tiny error icon along with the words *Failed to send*.

"Oh, no." Her stomach dipped, and she met his gaze again. He was right. "It didn't go through." And that meant... "Is Iris worried about me?"

"Yes."

She cringed. Why hadn't she waited to make sure the text went through? Kai had even told her the service was bad. The truth was, she'd wanted to turn it off. Because she had been **trying to avoid the very man now standing** before her. And now here he was. Mission accomplished turned mission backfired. What a mess.

It reminded her that her pregnant worrier of a sister was also fretting about her. She fumbled for her phone again. "I need to call—"

"Iris is with me. She knows you're fine."

"Iris is here?" She glanced around but didn't see her. That's when something else occurred to her. Visions danced before her of police units swarming the grounds and SWAT teams busting through the windows. "Is everyone worried?"

"She'll be by in a minute. She's taking care of something. Not everyone. Iris, Tag, Bering and I were the only ones fully aware of your MIA status. We didn't want to alarm anybody else until we knew for sure what was going on. Iris made some calls but failed to find where you stayed last night or the night before. She found out where you had been, but there was still the question of where you were now, and then the even bigger mystery of why you weren't answering your phone.

"It made for a very pleasant journey, what with your sister pointing out how someone could have stolen your identity." His wry tone assured her it had been anything but. "Or, in true Iris fashion, kidnapped you, murdered you and *then* stolen your identity. You can imagine all the variations on this riveting theme, I'm sure."

"I can." Poor Cricket. Her sister's "caution" was legendary.

"Anyway, after we got here, she made more calls and found out that you attended a guided meditation session this morning. At some point, she remembered you'd mentioned being excited about a sort of holiday menu thing, which by the way, was not booked in your name. And here we are."

Staring down at her shoes, she nodded, thinking this through, realizing how difficult tracking her down must have been. Most of the reservations had been left in Rory's name. Bad timing to go "unconnected."

"Hazel, I was…" His voice went lower and softer and lacked its previous hint of censure. When she looked into his eyes, she saw only concern and affection. "I was terrified. After South America, I…" Gaze narrowing, he trailed off as if carefully considering what to say next.

"Like you said, Utah is hardly South America." She was trying to lighten the mood, but it came out sounding almost flippant, and she immediately regretted the words.

His jaw went tight, and he took his time inhaling a deep breath before calmly but soberly stating, "People disappear everywhere, Hazel. Every single day. On that point, Iris is correct."

"I know," she whispered, feeling terrible about what she'd put him through. And Iris. The unnecessary worry she'd caused her family. "That was a stupid, terrible joke. I'm so sorry. I'm sorry about all of it. You know this isn't like me. I wasn't thinking."

His eyes seemed to search hers for sincerity. Nodding as if he found it, his voice held a rasp as he added, "I couldn't stop…" He paused to take a sip of what she assumed by its amber color to be whiskey, his drink of choice. No festive and fruity cocktails for him. An epicure, Cricket was not, and a holiday tasting menu definitely would not be his cup of tea.

"Couldn't stop what?" she urged, taking a small step toward him.

"Worrying," he said, then looked away and clearing his throat. "Thinking about South America and all of Iris's theories. And also wondering if you were still angry enough with me that you'd go to this extreme to avoid me and…and I'm just incredibly relieved that you're safe. What happened, anyway? You never did say why your phone was off. What kind of article requires you to shut off your phone?"

Her face went hot. She didn't want to admit that he was right about that part, that she'd shut it down on a whim, just to avoid him. "I'm working on a story about how to enjoy traveling without being connected."

"People need someone to teach them how to do that?" he joked, and she appreciated him trying to make this easier on her. She wasn't sure she deserved it. Probably, she should fess up.

But before she could muster the courage, he leaned in a little closer. "You look beautiful, by the way."

Her pulse jumped and set her heart racing. Despite her frustration with him, she loved how he could make her feel.

"Thank you," she said, joy boosting her smile and her ego. "You're looking pretty handsome yourself." And he was. He'd worn neatly pressed charcoal-colored slacks and a white button-down shirt with a tie—gray and dark green with a subtle pattern that perfectly complemented his striking green eyes. Unlike most of the guys she'd grown up around, Cricket didn't mind dressing up, and he was oddly good at it.

But then he ruined it. "Very grown-up."

Because *that* she hated. The way he quali-fied his compliments with subtle reminders of his honorary "big brother" status in her life. Something she never heard him do with Shay or Hannah or even Iris.

"Now, let's get out of here. Like I mentioned earlier, I do want to discuss something with you. I'll buy you and Iris dinner. I haven't eaten all day."

"I'm sorry." She felt guilty about that, too, knowing that stress stole his appetite. "I can't. I have a reservation for the tasting here, also for an article. But I can maybe meet you guys after?"

"I was afraid you were going to say that." He gave a playful wince. "I was looking forward to the prime rib they're serving in the dining room, but if you insist on staying, we'll hang around here with you and eat tiny plates of things I can't pronounce. Is it acceptable to order a regular-size entrée on the side?"

She gave him an apologetic look. "Unfortunately, this is an extremely popular event. Very trendy. Seats are booked months in advance. It would be impossible to get a spot now."

"Yeah?" He sounded doubtful and scanned the room as if he couldn't quite believe all these people were here for such an occasion.

"Yes, and besides, I have a date, so I'll be fine." Not that she needed company, anyway. She did this kind of thing all the time. Alone.

"Hey, you," Iris said, approaching them and immediately enfolding Hazel in a hug. "So, so, *sooo* glad you're not in the bottom of an abandoned mine shaft. There are so many of those in this part of the country."

"Iris," she said, squeezing her sister tight. "I am beyond sorry. I sent you a text, but it didn't go through."

Nodding, Iris took a step back but held on to her upper arms. "My imagination went off the rails, worse than normal. Possibly, hormones contributed. Regardless, unfortunate circumstances made for a perfect worry storm. We can talk about those details later. Or not. Thankfully, Cricket is a man of action, right? And a pilot with several planes at his disposal. He flew us to Anchorage, we hopped on a jet, and here we are."

Shifting toward Cricket, she held out two tickets and said, "Good news. It worked. We got seats."

Hazel gaped. "Iris, how in the world did you get those? They're supposed to be impossible."

"Hazel," Iris said, the sparkle in her eyes a perfect match to her self-satisfied smile. "A lot of things are impossible unless you know what to ask."

CHAPTER FOUR

IRIS WENT ON to explain how she'd managed to score the tickets, but Cricket was barely listening. He was too busy fixating on that last thing Hazel had said. Specifically, the date part.

When they seemed to be wrapping up the ticket topic, he said, "So, where'd your date scamper off to? Can't wait to meet him." He'd been trying for lightheartedness but could hear the bitter infusion in his tone.

Hazel gave him a sharp, curious look as he silently acknowledged it for the jealousy it was. He should have known better than to drink on an empty stomach. But he'd worked himself up into quite a state on the way here, imagining the myriad ways she could be in danger.

The relief he'd felt upon arriving and finally locating her had left him shaken. Admittedly, he hadn't thought much past finding her, so when he had, he'd been torn between pulling her into a hug or delivering a lecture. He'd gone with lecture because if he hugged her, he wouldn't want to let go. The backless emerald-colored dress she wore complemented her hazel eyes and hugged her curves without being tight. She'd left her long, light brown hair to curl softly around her shoulders, and when she moved, the golden, sun-kissed tones shimmered in the soft glow of the holiday lights. Yeah, he still wanted to hug her.

But now he was rather peeved, for lack of a better term. Had they really flown this distance because she was so infatuated with a new love interest that she couldn't be bothered to turn on her phone?

Miraculously, Iris seemed to miss his edginess, no doubt due to the greater reveal. Eyes wide, she looked at Hazel and lowered her voice to a whisper. "You have a date? Is that why we haven't heard from you? Has my perpetually single, relationship-abstaining, list-observing sister finally fallen in love?"

Hearing his fear voiced aloud, Cricket felt himself scowl.

"Hazel," a man's voice interrupted, and before she could answer, he joined them. "Sorry, that took a little longer than I thought. Franco is coming home, and I— Oh, sorry…" The guy—*the date*—looked at him, then Iris and back to Hazel. "I didn't mean to interrupt."

"You're not," Hazel assured him. "Not at all. I'd like you to meet some people." Her hand came up to rest briefly on the guy's shoulder. Jealousy squeezed Cricket's lungs like a vise. "Kai Montauk, this is my sister Iris Ramsey. And this is Cricket Blackburn. Cricket is a friend from our hometown."

"Pleasure to meet you both." Kai shook hands with Iris and then Cricket. "You're Alaskans, too, huh? Hazel has been regaling me with tales of Alaska, and I gotta say I am ready to relocate."

Relocate? Cricket felt his entire body tense. How serious were they? It didn't seem possible that she could even have a boyfriend without him knowing. He considered himself an expert in the subtle art of keeping up with Hazel's life. The logic being that he couldn't have her but he could admire her from afar. And occasionally fantasize about a life where they could be together.

It took a monumental degree of effort to compose his face to friendly when it felt as if he'd been punched in the solar plexus.

"Nice to meet you, too," he managed.

Of course, he knew that Hazel dated. He'd just never *seen* her in the act of dating before. Not since Derrick, her high school boyfriend. She made it a point never to get serious with anyone.

"You guys are old friends?" her date asked.

"Yes, Hazel and I have known each other forever. She's like a little sister to me." That was such a lie. No matter how much he wanted it to be true. His attraction to her was so far from brotherly it wasn't even funny. But this was suddenly turning a little uncomfortable because how would Iris explain their presence here?

Kai glanced curiously at Hazel. "So, you didn't mention anyone else was joining us. Is this, like, a surprise visit?" Looking from Cricket to Iris, he added, "What brings you guys to Utah?"

"It's a bit of a surprise, for sure," Iris answered with an amused, theatrical flair, her thoughts not quite caught up with Cricket's yet. "We came here looking for Hazel."

"Looking for Hazel?" Kai's concerned gaze darted around the three of them before settling on Hazel. "Why...? Is everything okay?"

Iris, now realizing how her statement could be construed, started to clarify. "Oh, I—"

"Yes, everything is fine," Hazel said at the same time. "You're sweet, Kai, to be concerned. It's just..."

Cricket could see her trying to decide how to explain without providing too much detail. Embarrassing to confess that you'd been out of touch with your family, and as a result, they'd come searching for you. He felt a wave of sympathy because, presumably, their relationship was new, and she should be able to spin this her way. Or not. Bottom line, it wasn't any of this guy's business unless she wanted it to be.

That's what prompted him to announce, "Iris and I decided to surprise her. She doesn't know this part yet, but I'm here to offer Hazel a job."

Technically, this wasn't that far-fetched. Bering had agreed with Tag that hiring her would be a good idea, while Cricket had secretly agreed with Tag that she would never accept. Making the offer was a win-win. Hazel gets out of her current predicament, and he gets to come to her rescue. After all, he'd contributed to creating it, hadn't he, by traveling all the way here to check on her? Besides, discussing tour options wasn't that far from a job offer. And that he did want to do.

"You… You're what?" Hazel asked, clearly shocked.

A nodding Iris remained silent and went with the flow.

"Remember when I said I had something to talk to you about? Well, Bering and I would like to offer you a job."

"A job? Doing what, specifically?"

Thinking fast, he elaborated, "Designing

and organizing our tours. We need help. After the suggestions you gave us, we can't think of anyone more knowledgeable or capable to get us up to speed. We're behind the eight ball now and want to hire you for a few weeks. What do you think? You could come home for the holidays and help us out at the same time?"

"Uh…" she drawled.

Cricket could have laughed at her reaction. She wasn't an easy person to catch off guard. Even more than that, he was happy to have gotten her out of an uncomfortable situation. Never in a million years would he have dreamed that he'd just talked himself into one that was so much worse.

SPEECHLESS, HAZEL GAPED at Cricket and struggled to absorb what he'd said. It was one thing for Bering to ask her advice. That was flattering, for sure. But it was a whole other level of praise for Bering and Cricket to seek her out like this, offer her a job, pay for her expertise. This kind of compliment from two men she so highly respected was…phenomenal.

Her heart went light. And suddenly she knew. This was it! The solution to the unease that had been gnawing at her. She was homesick and hadn't even realized it. Hadn't recognized the affliction because she'd never experienced it before. Not to this degree, anyway.

A big, hefty dose of home was exactly what she needed. She would spend time in Rankins with her family. Play with her nieces and nephews and young cousins. Be with Iris during her pregnancy. Go skiing with Hannah. Ice fishing with Seth. Make candy with her mom! Excitement bubbled inside of her.

Home. For Christmas.

She wasn't presuming this meant Cricket wanted her home, per se, but the fact that he and Bering were even offering her the position meant he supported the notion. He'd thought this through and was okay with working with her.

Sure, it would only be temporary, but this felt huge. Like maybe spending this time together could be a way for them to move forward, to get past this perpetual uneasiness that plagued them. Certainly, it suggested he was ready to try. And if he was, then she was, too.

That was when something else occurred to her. Maybe this was a way to get over him once and for all. A new future unfurled before her, one where she could come home to Rankins and not worry about how things would be when she saw him. No more wondering and wishing and longing for a romance that would never happen.

"Please say yes," she heard Iris whisper beside her.

Cricket said, "We understand if you're too busy. I know you're usually booked months in advance. You're probably planning on skiing in the Alps or something for Christmas, and—"

"No!" she interrupted. "I mean, you guys are in luck. I have nothing planned that can't easily be changed. This fits into my schedule perfectly. So…" Arms up and out, she cried, "I accept!"

Impulsively, she stepped close and hugged him. Okay, too soon for friendly hugs, she realized when she was unable to stop herself from pressing her face to his chest for a sharp inhale of Cricket-scented deliciousness. Hastily, she pulled away.

Gazing into his brilliant green gaze, she said, "Thank you, Cricket. I won't let you guys down."

SEVERAL COURSES INTO the holiday tasting menu and Cricket had yet to taste anything. The current ration before him consisted of a bite of steak, approximately twelve unidentifiable rice-like grains and several multicolored squiggles of sauce that seemed to serve no purpose beyond decorating the plate. Literally, he could scoop the entire portion up with a spoon and eat it in one, maybe two, bites. What was the point? Because just when he decided whether he liked it, it was all gone. They should call the ordeal a teasing instead of a tasting because his taste buds felt both harassed and cheated.

But palate confusion was not the problem.

Nope. The problem was sitting beside him and, by all appearances, having the time of her life. What had he done? How did you take back a job offer that you didn't mean? He was still stunned she'd accepted.

"Oh, wow." A reverent Kai, head bowed over his plate, loudly interrupted his musing, "This is the petite *petite* filet mignon. I was so hoping they would serve this. I'm just wondering how they do it."

"And I can't help wondering," Cricket commented dryly, "where they found such a tiny breed of cows."

Beside him, Iris belted out a laugh. The four of them were seated at one corner of the long bar, Kai and Hazel next to each other, and then Cricket and Iris along the adjacent edge.

"I love how subtle the coriander is," Kai remarked about the next course, consisting of what appeared to be a single chicken nugget swimming in brown gravy. Politely, he asked, "Are you guys picking up on that at all?"

"I probably would have if I hadn't accidentally swallowed mine whole," he murmured.

"Cricket." Hazel snickered quietly before covering her mouth with a napkin.

"I'm sorry, Cricket?" Kai said, placing a cupped hand to his ear. "I didn't catch that."

"He said yes," Hazel answered for him. "It reminds him of a dish called the hallowed sole. Something he once had at a restaurant in Seattle."

And this was how he spent two and a half hours of his life he'd never get back—seated between his best friend's little sisters. On one side, there was Hazel, the woman he coveted and adored but could not have. Talking and laughing and enjoying the company of her *date*. On his other side, Iris was laughing and smiling and reminding him of everything he had to lose, one of the many relationships he would be risking if he ever acted on his attraction to Hazel.

Making matters worse, Hazel kept glancing his way, smiling, her greenish-brown eyes all glittery and joy-filled. All of this he had to endure while the memory of her hug lingered like warm honey. The softness of her arms holding him, the pressure of her fingers when they'd briefly landed on the back of his neck. The texture and heat of her skin as his hands touched her back. Traces of a coconut-laced tropical breeze when his nose grazed her hair. How she fit against his body... And this daydream, this recollection, these feelings were another part of the bigger problem.

She tossed him another sweet smile, this time holding eye contact as it landed right in the center of his chest. More potent than his fine whiskey, the warmth spread through him, leaving him a little giddy and longing for more. That was when he was struck by the fact that in the process of accidentally hiring her, he'd done this, too. Made her this happy. The sensation was both wonderful and terrifying. Because he could never take this away from her now, which meant he needed to figure out a way to live with what he'd done.

Finally, blessedly, the tasting concluded. Exhaustion settled into him. Stress, a lack of sleep and food, followed by the relief at finding her safe and sound—it was all catching up with him. He needed to sleep. He needed to think. And possibly find a vending machine because he'd let Iris have most of his niblets.

After managing a polite goodbye for Kai and a good-night for Hazel, he escorted an equally exhausted Iris to her room. He tried not to imagine how the happy couple would complete their evening. The effort had his teeth clenching, and he reached up to rub his aching jaw.

A morning workout would be wise, too, he decided. That decision, combined with hunger, prompted him to head back down to the lobby, where he located the fitness center, which he was pleased to discover was well-equipped. The vending machine, however, contained only bottled water, sports drinks and breath mints. He bought a water and headed to his room with hopes of finding a well-stocked minibar. Only a few minutes had passed, so he was surprised when Hazel met up with him outside the elevator.

"Glad I caught you," she said, stepping inside the car with him. "So, what did you think of your first tasting menu?"

"Oh, um, let's see…" He pretended to ponder the question before dredging up a wryly delivered, "Delicious, delightful, a veritable amusement park for the senses that took my taste buds on a roller coaster of a ride. Feel free to use that for your article."

She busted out a laugh. "You are not only incorrigible and cliché, you are also a terrible liar."

He grimaced. "I know. But I think it's too late to change."

"It would be a shame if you did." Still grinning, she removed a small brown paper sack from her bag and handed it to him. "The gift shop was still open. I'm sorry you didn't enjoy the meal."

"Was that a meal, though?" he joked even as a rush of tenderness overtook him. Because no matter what was inside, it meant that she'd been thinking about him and not her date. "I have a theory that they're using leftovers from the restaurant's dining room that they chop into tiny pieces, cover with sauce and reheat. It's a brilliant scheme if you think about it…" The teasing came to a screeching halt as he peeked inside the bag. His gaze snapped up to meet hers. "This is my favorite candy bar."

"Two candy bars, actually." Her tone was casual, but the gesture meant so much more than that to him.

He *always* ate at least two candy bars. One wasn't enough, and if he couldn't have two, then he wouldn't eat any at all. The affection coursing through him was almost painful—and precisely what he feared. It was difficult enough to deal with her occasionally or at a distance. How in the world was he supposed to resist when she was up close and personal like this? And for the entire holiday season?

"Thank you," he said with all the sincerity he felt. "You didn't have to do this."

"I know."

The elevator doors slid open with an accompanying ding. They both stepped out and began a leisurely stroll down the hallway.

Glancing at him, she said, "Listen, Cricket, I'm also aware that a couple of candy bars aren't going to repay you for the job offer. But I'd like to talk to you, if you have a few minutes?"

"Sure," he said, stopping and gesturing at the door to his room. "Do you want to come in?" he asked even as he hoped for a no. Hazel in close quarters would not be wise in his current state of mind.

"Here is fine." Facing him, she inhaled a breath. "I know you must be tired, and this will only take a sec. I don't know why you decided to offer *me* this job, but I hope it means you believe that you and I can…get along."

"Get along?" he repeated.

"Cricket," she said, twisting her hands nervously, "I know that you know what I'm talking about. But I'll say it anyway to avoid any possible chance of miscommunication. There's been weirdness between us for a lot of years now. And I admit it's my fault."

A tightness grabbed hold of his heart. Her

fault? How could she possibly believe that? "Hazel—"

Her hand came up to press lightly against his chest. "No, wait, please, let me finish. I've had feelings for you for…forever. Or as long as I can remember, anyway. Ten years ago, I ruined everything with that stupid kiss. And I'm so sorry. I was young, and you were… awesome. I adored you, obviously. You were such a good friend to me, and for a while, we were so close. But then I mistook your kindness and attention for more than it was. Like I said, I was young and inexperienced, and now, looking back, I can see how I misread the signs. Again, not your fault.

"Over the years, I've made things difficult at times. I know that. It took me forever to get over you, and there were times when I'd be angry and hurt because I thought you were lying to yourself, and to me, about only seeing me as Tag's little sister. In Florida, I tried to push you to be honest because I felt… I thought the reality was different than it is."

She paused, her gaze searching his for a few seconds. Nodding, she inhaled a deep breath and then announced, "You were right about my phone—I was avoiding you. I saw that you called. I read your text, and I turned my phone off because I wanted you to know how I felt—all the times I've asked you to talk to me and you wouldn't. But I see everything differently now. Much more clearly. It's been hard to admit, but by not talking to me—telling me how you felt—you didn't want to hurt me."

Her palm was like a hot brand on his chest. But her words were even more painful. It took all his willpower not to sweep her into his arms, confess all and beg her forgiveness. He even shifted toward her but then stopped because what purpose would that serve? Admitting his feelings now would only complicate this situation more. He couldn't be with her. Not in the way he wanted.

Stepping back, she removed her hand, and he instantly felt the loss. "I hope I'm not reading more into this job thing than I should, but to me, your offer is like saying that you wouldn't mind being around me again. I don't know if we can get back what we had all those years ago, but I'd like to try. I want us to be… okay. Friends, even."

"Friends," he repeated, because he was still trying to process her speech.

"Yeah, and I want you to know that you don't have to worry anymore."

"Worry?"

"Yes. I am over you." She held up both hands, palms out, making her point. "You don't have to be concerned that I'll ask you about your feelings or insist that you talk to me. Or worse, that I'll try to kiss you." She forced out a little laugh, one that seemed designed to make light of her embarrassment and write ten years of agony off to a schoolgirl crush. "I get it now. I understand. And I'm done. I promise. I'll do whatever it takes to make this work—the job and us."

"Hazel." He was a veritable one-word wonder here, wasn't he? But he didn't even know where to start with how wrong she was. Didn't she know that if he could be just friends with her, he would? How all of this "weirdness" was his fault because he couldn't stop wanting her? Didn't she know how much it hurt just to look at her?

"Seriously, Cricket, I want to move on from all of this. I'm just really, really excited to be going home for the holidays this year. I have things to figure out, and I…" Eyes shining brightly, she added, "A happy Christmas is all I want right now."

CHAPTER FIVE

THE COZY CARIBOU exemplified everything Hazel adored about small towns. The downtown restaurant was *the* place to gather in Rankins, to celebrate, mourn, commiserate, gossip or just plain old-fashioned chat about nothing. Fresh, home-cooked deliciousness was their hallmark, along with plenty of hot, strong coffee. Or, if you wanted something stronger, you could detour to the bar that made up the other half of the establishment.

The rustic decor was always homey and inviting, but the Cozy Caribou was extra special at Christmastime. A true holiday haven. Twinkle lights crisscrossed the high, open-beamed ceiling, where sparkly ornaments and glittery snowflakes hung from varying lengths of translucent string. Inside the door, opposite the register, there was a brightly decorated Christmas tree. Long lengths of evergreen garland accented the windows. A classic rendition of "Jingle Bell Rock" played softly in the background.

Making her way through the dining area, Hazel hummed along and let the magic sink into her. She found Iris, already seated in their favorite booth, a steaming teapot on the table before her.

"I cannot believe you are going to be here through Christmas," Iris said, standing and delivering a huge hug. After spending an additional two days in Utah finishing her resort story, Hazel had arrived in Rankins the evening before to start her new job today, which she was going to do—right after breakfast.

Hazel settled across from her while Iris added, "I am ecstatic, which means Mom is going to flip. Have you told her yet?"

"I told her last night. She's already making plans and signing me up for her volunteer thing."

"No one is safe from Operation Happy Christmas," Iris quipped. "The name of the charity is also her mantra."

"I always thought when we got older that she would ease up a bit on the holiday enthusiasm."

"Ha." Iris lifted the pot and poured some liquid into each mug before sliding one across the table. "If anything, not having us all around just gives Mom more opportunity to spread her Christmas cheer farther and wider. Not to mention she has grandkids now. Did she tell you she has a surprise announcement to make at brunch on Sunday?"

"She did."

"I can only imagine what she has in store."

"You know what? I don't even care. I'm just happy to be home this year. I am a willing participant in Operation Happy Christmas, Mom's and my own. Starting now, I'm making that my mantra, too." The time was going to go too fast, and she needed to enjoy every second and… *Eww.* What was that smell?

Tipping her head down, she took a whiff of the cup. "What is this?"

"It's tea." Iris patted her belly. "We are drinking this herbal mix that Ally gave me." Ally was Tag's wife, a paramedic with a vast knowledge of natural healing methods.

"Are we, now?" Hazel repeated before bravely taking a sip and shaking her head. "Nope, *we* are not." She pushed the mug away with an exaggerated shudder. "That is disgusting."

"It's good for the baby," Iris countered but couldn't squelch her chuckle.

"I don't see how that could possibly be true," she joked and flagged down a waitress. To Iris, she said, "In case you hadn't noticed, you and I are no longer in vitro. In other words, your tea is not my tea. But I am here for you in almost every other way, and in order to give you my full support, I am going to need coffee."

"So, do you know where you'll be heading after Christmas?"

"Not sure yet, but don't worry, my schedule is pretty open. And March will stay that way. I'll be back before you have the baby." Iris and her husband, Flynn, had adopted Lily after her mother had died giving birth to her, and Iris, despite her brave face, was terrified of everything her own pregnancy entailed.

"That's the detail I was after," she cheerfully confessed.

"I know."

"Hazel…" Iris's eyes filled with tears. "I didn't want to ask, but could you be with me? Like in the delivery room? Shay offered, which is very sweet of her, but you know what she's like. I'm afraid she'll just boss everyone around and make me more nervous."

"That is a distinct possibility." Shay's type A intensity could be a bit overwhelming. Hazel reached across the table and took her sister's hand. "I would be honored. As long as it's okay with Flynn."

"More than okay with him." She directed a mega-watt smile filled with relief and love and gratitude at her. The waitress arrived with Hazel's coffee, and they ordered.

"So, how are you feeling about your new job? Cricket didn't even tell me they were going to ask you. I think I was as surprised as you were."

"Good," Hazel answered. Carefully unfolding her napkin, she thought about the question. "I haven't seen their plans yet. They left the files for me at their office to take a look at, and then they're meeting me there this afternoon to go over everything."

This job thing had seemed like such a good plan in the moment, but now that the time was here, her stomach had worked itself into quite an intricate knot. She had tons of ideas for their tours, but what did she truly know about business?

But it was the Cricket factor that had her on edge. Hannah had informed her that there still wasn't suitable snowpack in the mountains for JB Heli-Ski to operate. Since Cricket wasn't flying, it was likely she'd be seeing him every day. She'd meant what she said about being over him, but how difficult was it going to be to make the declaration true? What exactly did it take to actively fall out of love with someone? Was there any science on that topic? Maybe she needed to read up on it.

Glancing at her sister, she realized Iris was

eyeing her curiously. "Do you want me to get you a new napkin?"

"What?" Removing her hands from the tabletop, she folded them on her lap and willed herself to remain still.

Eyebrows arching high, Iris cast a deliberate gaze down at the curled, twisty strips of tissue now littering the table. "Yours is shredded. You're all fidgety. I just can't tell if it's a good fidget or a bad fidget."

"I'm a little nervous."

"Is this about what happened with Cricket? Do you want to talk about that?"

Hazel's stomach did a fast, hard flop. Iris knew? How had she found out? Truthfully, it was a miracle she'd been able to keep her feelings a secret from her sister all these years. But then again, she'd had a crush on Cricket for so long, and he'd always just been in their lives, so there was no time she could pinpoint where she'd fallen for him. It felt like it had always just…been.

The "incident" had coincided with her breakup with Derrick, and everyone had thought she was devastated over that. And she'd let them all believe it was true. Even Iris. So maybe it was a bit of guilt about that or the worry she'd just put her through in Utah. Or maybe—a thought that would only occur to her after the fact—she wanted to unburden her heart.

Regardless of the reason, she spilled the beans. "Um…well, I guess you could say it started my senior year during track season when Derrick and I were first having problems. But nothing happened until the following spring when I was home from college. But it's over. Not that there was anything to it, except on my part. Although, Cricket… Never mind. That doesn't matter. The point is, it's taken me a long, *loong* time, obviously, but I'm over him. Or, at least, I'm trying to be."

Hazel hadn't been looking directly at her sister as she poured out the details, so she wasn't sure at precisely what point she'd turned into a wax figurine. Clearly, her assumption had been wrong.

Very, very wrong.

"Iris? Oh, no… You didn't know. I thought you were telling me that you knew about us. Okay, um, please, forget everything I just said."

A few very long seconds passed before she spoke, and Hazel could see her trying to process this bombshell.

"No. I was talking about your phone. Cricket said he thought you might have shut your phone off because you were upset with him, something about an argument you had in Florida. That seemed unlikely to me at the time, but…" With a shake of her head, she steered back to the point. "But, Hazel, the only way I could forget what you just said would require drugs I am not willing to take, repeated sessions of hypnosis or possibly even a lobotomy." Quickly, almost furtively, she glanced left and right and then hissed, "You and *Cricket*? When we were in *high school*?"

"Maybe I should start at the beginning."

"You have no idea how much I wish you would."

The waitress arrived with their orders. And so, over fluffy omelets, crispy hash browns and flaky buttermilk biscuits, she told her sister everything.

"Do you remember how Derrick used to work for Cricket occasionally, helping with airplane maintenance and stuff?" At Iris's nod, she went on, "Okay, well, one day, spring of our senior year, he was supposed to take me home after track practice. We'd had a fight, and Derrick didn't show up. He was a jerk that way, bad temper."

"*That*, I remember," Iris said. "Never understood what you saw in him."

"Me either. That day, I called Cricket looking for Derrick. He wasn't there. No surprise,

Cricket came and got me instead. I was upset. He took me out for a burger, and we talked. You know, differently than we ever had before?"

"Mmm-hmm." Iris nodded patiently and drizzled hot sauce on her potatoes.

"So, um, a few days later, I made those oatmeal cookies that he likes and dropped them by his house—to thank him. After that, I started going to the hangar when I knew Derrick was working, and sometimes when I knew he wasn't."

"Uh-huh."

"I started stopping by his house after practice. I know, I know... I knew what I was doing. I mean, I knew how I felt. I liked him *so much*, Iris. We talked about everything and nothing and laughed constantly, and he's so interesting and made *me* feel interesting, you know? Nothing happened that could even be considered inappropriate, but there were these moments where it felt like we had a connection and... Anyway, that doesn't matter. You and I left for college that summer."

"That's why you went home so often during our freshman year?"

"Yes," she confessed. "I would go and see him... And then, Christmas break, Cricket told me about Derrick—that he'd been cheating on me with Kimberly Fitz."

"That I also remember. What a weasel."

"Totally. Understandably, I was upset. Not nearly as upset as I should have been. It was more anger and humiliation than heartbreak. Cricket was there to comfort me. He hugged me. And then…" Hazel closed her eyes and let the memory wash over her. It was burned into her brain because she'd never felt that way before. Or since. Like it was where she belonged.

Opening her eyes, she heaved out a sigh. Because she needed to find somewhere else to belong, didn't she? "And then I kissed him and ruined everything."

"Did he kiss you back?"

"Yes. In fact, at first, he was…enthusiastic. It was more like…"

"A make-out session?" Iris suggested, slathering jam on a biscuit.

"Yeah."

"And that doesn't tell you that he had feelings?"

"He's a guy. Of course he had *feelings*. They just weren't the same as mine."

"Hmm," Iris said, lowering the biscuit to the edge of her plate. "Except, he was, what, like twenty-nine at the time? He was no naive teenager. We're talking about Cricket here."

Hazel winced.

"I meant that he could always have a girl-friend if he wanted one. He just never does, not long-term, anyway. Sort of like—oh, I don't know—*you*!" Iris said firmly. "What I'm saying is that he knew what he was doing."

"Well, he didn't want me." *Doesn't want me*, she reminded herself. Then she revealed the truly mortifying part of the story. "I told him I loved him. I told him…all sorts of embarrassing things. You should have seen him, Iris. I'll never forget it. He looked sick, like physically ill. He told me it was a mistake. We shouldn't have done it. I was Tag's little sister. He broke a promise. We could never be together. He didn't think of me like that, etcetera." She brought one hand up to her forehead, where the heat of embarrassment burned even after all these years.

Scowling now, Iris leaned forward and asked, "What promise did he break?"

Hazel lifted one shoulder. "I assume he meant some silly promise to Tag about never dating one of his sisters."

"Huh." Iris paused for a few seconds, thinking. "Hazel, listen to me. Cricket would *never* have done that if he didn't feel something for you. If you kissed him and he gently pushed you away and patted your head, then yes, I would tend to agree with what you're saying. But that's not what happened, is it?"

"No. But it doesn't matter. Because that's when everything changed. I was hurt and humiliated. I felt like such a fool. It ruined our friendship, and I started avoiding him. That was the worst part. I missed him so much. I missed our friendship."

"This was when you stopped going home," Iris stated with a deliberate nod like it all made perfect sense.

"Yeah, I spent the next semester in Germany, and then I started traveling. When I did see him, there was this uncomfortable tension between us. Like neither of us knew quite how to act. There would be moments when things seemed better. Good, even. We'd get closer, but then he would withdraw again, push me away. Sometimes we'd argue—mainly when I asked him how he felt about me. Then there were a few times, like in Florida, where things got out of control."

"This is the Florida thing Cricket mentioned? As in this past spring, when you were there for Seth's fishing show?"

"Yes."

"What got out of control?"

"We had an argument."

"About what?"

"It was stupid. And after a while, I don't think either one of us knew. At some point, he'd overheard this guy ask me out for a drink, and he claimed the guy had a shady history with women."

"Well, does he?"

"I don't know! I wasn't interested. But he said it like he was jealous. Or, at least, I wanted it to be jealousy. But I didn't appreciate him acting like that. We started discussing that, which was intense and over-the-top for the situation. So, I asked him why he was so upset."

"What did he say?"

"He said it was because he cared about me. He apologized, I apologized, and the next thing you know, we were hugging and... And I know he wanted to kiss me. Or, at least in the moment, I believed it."

Iris grinned. "And then?"

"He didn't. I asked him how, in what way did he care? I said I needed to know once and for all. I needed to hear him say he wasn't attracted to me so I could move on."

"So what did he say?"

Tears pooled in her eyes. Blinking them away, she pressed on, "He said, 'Do you really think it will help, Hazel, if I say any of the things you think you want to hear? That it will make this easier if I'm honest with you?' Then he turned around and walked away."

"Okay, so you believe that…that cryptic non-answer means that he doesn't have feelings for you?"

"Yes. It meant that he didn't want to hurt me again, by telling me the truth. Chemistry isn't feelings—not the kind I'm after, anyway, and he didn't want to point that out."

"Oh, good grief." Iris placed both hands on her head and gave her hair a quick frustrated tug. "Where are you getting this stuff?"

"What do you mean?"

"Hazel, Cricket does not offer me unsolicited romantic advice or get in my business in any way. Ever. Never has. Now that I think about it, he does sort of hover where you're concerned, doesn't he? He talks about you a lot, too. Comments on where you are and what you're doing. And why did *he* insist on flying to Utah? Tag offered, but he was so insistent, no one questioned it. Not even me."

"I know he cares about me." She rolled her eyes. "Like a little sister. He reminds me of that all the time."

Iris tipped her head back as if analyzing the glittering snowflake suspended above them. Then she met Hazel's gaze again with a deliberate look. "He doesn't do that to me either. He made a point of saying that about you, though, in Utah. He said *Hazel* is like a little sister to me. He wasn't compelled to say that about me, was he? When normally, everyone lumps us together."

This was true. As triplets, they were regularly referred to as exactly that, "the triplets" or "the trips," and Hazel and Iris were often Hazel-and-Iris, like it was one word, or simply "the girls."

"I wonder who he's trying to convince," she added quietly. "He's obviously attracted to you."

"But so what? He's right about that part. What would it solve by admitting it?"

"It's what it would complicate. That's the problem."

"What do you mean?"

"You really don't see this, do you?"

"No." She shook her head. "Relationships are not exactly my area of expertise."

"Yes, you and your list. Maybe you should have spent more time having relationships instead of trying so hard to avoid them," Iris attempted to joke. "And then we'd have more to work with here."

"I tried! Early on, I dated more, thinking—hoping—that it would help me move on. But all I did was compare everyone to Cricket. I've never wanted anyone else. That's how the list came to be. I thought it was better to spare someone from getting too attached and then allow them to suffer even a fraction of the heartbreak that I experienced."

"Oh, sweetie…" Iris said sympathetically. "I get all of that now."

Hazel firmly believed that she did. Iris and Flynn had their own rough history that had started with an unrequited high school crush on Iris's part. Their story may have had a bumpy beginning, but they were making up for it with a beautiful middle.

"I never could understand how you were so heartbroken over Derrick. Now that makes sense because you weren't. But the stuff with Cricket does not compute."

"It doesn't make sense that he wouldn't want to hurt me by telling me the truth?"

"Sort of. If it were that simple, but the truth is…"

"Is what?" Hazel prodded.

"Something else," Iris finished in a firm tone, pushing her plate away. "I need to think about this."

"Well, don't waste too much brain power on it," she bravely joked. "Because the truth doesn't matter anymore."

Iris peered at her carefully. "What do you mean?"

"Finally, I know what I want. I want to be over him, Iris. I told him I was. And no matter what it takes, that's what I'm going to do."

ON THEIR WAY out of the Cozy Caribou, Iris stopped at a nearby table to chat with a nurse she knew from the hospital, so Hazel hugged her goodbye and promised to stop in and visit Lily after work. Zippering her down jacket closed, she then flipped up the hood and stepped out onto the frost-covered sidewalk.

Bering and Cricket had rented office space here in town, and since it was only a block away, she'd parked the pickup she'd borrowed from her dad there this morning and walked to the café. Since months often passed between her visits, it was fun to see how her tiny hometown changed during each absence. Typically, that was very little. She used to find this amusing and slightly unnerving, but now, passing the familiar storefronts felt strangely comforting. The addition of multicolored lights and decorations only added to the warm, fuzzy sensation.

Nearing the end of the block, she could smell the delicious yeasty baked goodness that was the Donut Den. She'd traveled the world and had yet to find an equal to the bakery's huckleberry scones. If she weren't currently still stuffed from breakfast, she'd stop in and grab a few.

Lights were on inside the office, but the door was locked. Bering had left her a key at her parents' house, so she let herself inside and took a look around. The reception area consisted of two comfy-looking chairs, a small sofa and an ottoman. Behind a taller reception counter was the work area with three desks, two on one side of the room facing the other. They'd positioned a larger table in the back, around which four chairs were neatly arranged, presumably for meetings or appointments with clients. Nice.

On the single desk, someone—Bering, she surmised from the look of the blocky, no-nonsense handwriting—had left a note card printed with her name. There was a laptop, a separate monitor and a docking station. Stacks of files and papers sat off to one side, all neatly labeled.

She headed to the very back of the room, where a narrow table held a printer, coffee maker, mugs, condiments and assorted office supplies. A bathroom was off to the right, next to a supply closet. The doorway on the left led to a small kitchen.

Back at her desk, she took a seat in her new cushy office chair. That's when she saw the note, this one penned in Cricket's neater, more traditional style.

Hazel,
Welcome home! We tried to make things comfortable for you, but if you need anything just let us know. We've left all the paperwork you need to get started. There are file folders on the computer desktop. (Bering says he told you about this and gave you passwords.) Bering has a meeting this morning, and I have a flight for Tag, but we'll meet you here around noon to talk things over. Coffee in the silver tin on the back table.
Happy to have you here,
C
PS: Bering says to text him if you have any important questions before then.

Hazel reread that last line. *Happy to have you here.* Cricket wouldn't write those words if he didn't mean them. That was another thing about Cricket that she could count on. He might be a man of few words, but what he said, he meant. She could do this. And hopefully, they would soon be friends again. Confidence restored, she powered on the laptop, clicked around the desktop folders and got to work.

CHAPTER SIX

"So, BEFORE WE get too far into the details here, we should probably talk about priorities." Leaning forward, Hazel placed her forearms on the desk and laced her fingers together. "What tasks do you guys most want me to help you accomplish? Because there is more work to do here than I anticipated. More than I can get done in a few weeks…"

She went on while Cricket and Bering sat across from her at their small conference table. Cricket listened to her assessment and battled his guilt about the speech she'd given him a few nights ago. She thought he wanted her here, assumed that he'd offered her the job because he believed they could be friends.

Friends. That was what she wanted. A feat that should be easier since she was "over him." She'd made a point of telling him so, hadn't she? And he'd witnessed it. He'd seen her on a date—a special brand of torture that he hoped never to live through again. Thankfully, she hadn't seemed reluctant about leaving the guy behind.

He knew he should be relieved by her declaration. Wished he could say the same. Not that he didn't want to be friends—he just wasn't as optimistic that they could get there. At least not how they had been all those years ago. Because what they'd had was so much more than a friendship. Even though it hadn't been physical, they'd shared a type of intimacy that only came with a much closer relationship. He'd never had that with anyone before or since.

And he knew he could never be close with her like that again without wanting more. The best *he* could hope for was to get through this holiday season with a minimum of heartache. So he would pretend for her sake. They'd be fake friends. After all, it was only a few weeks. Then she'd leave again, taking with her that temptation of more.

Bering scratched his chin and nodded. "We sort of knew that. Putting this together has been more time-consuming than we thought. Or maybe it's that we haven't had the time we thought we would. For a while there, Tag was short a pilot, so Cricket was flying every hour he could. I had a very good year with my guide business, which pulled me in for extra duties. Plus, we've had a series of unexpected com-plications. This most recent delay is on me. I don't know if Cricket mentioned it to you, but a problem has come up with the federal concession program."

"He didn't."

Bering's guide business was granted permission for the use of certain federal lands by the government. Occasionally, rules changed or new regulations were implemented. Then there was the occasional objection to the program itself, which he was experiencing right now.

"Unfortunately," Bering said when he finished highlighting his latest quagmire, "I'm heading back to Washington, DC, next week. Hoping it will be resolved before the Christmas break."

Cricket said, "We've considered delaying another year, but we've got commitments and obligations that neither of us relishes breaking. Not to mention money invested."

"I understand," she said. "And I don't think you need to."

"What would you recommend?" Bering asked.

"Instead of trying to get all these tours up and running, I would concentrate on fine-tuning three or four of them. Since you haven't advertised any of the specifics yet, no one will even know that you're scaling back. Call them your signature tours and make those your focus. This will also allow you to work out the kinks. If all goes well, then expand. Sort of like a soft opening."

"That sounds good," Bering agreed. "But we could use your advice on which tours to finalize. That's been part of our problem. We're a bit all over the map right now."

"Good one," Hazel said approvingly, grinning at his pun. She patted the stack of files before her. "I see that. And I have a proposal to make. I'd like to hire someone to help me. Especially since you're going to be gone, Bering. And assuming the snow situation improves, Cricket, you'll get busier, too."

This was true.

"If I hire someone with knowledge and experience and we work together for a solid month, I'm confident we could have your signature tours ready, plus a step-by-step plan to implement the next phase."

"Yes from me," Bering said. "What do you think, Cricket?"

The hiring of another employee appealed to him, too. Especially with Bering back and forth to DC for who knew how long. And until the snowpack in the mountains improved, he'd have no excuse not to be here in the office. Another person would be a distraction, a barrier between himself and Hazel, making this friendship thing easier to obtain.

"Sure," he said, fully meeting her gaze for the first time. "Fantastic. Whoever you want to hire is fine with me."

"Excellent." She looked extremely pleased by their answers, and that pleased Cricket. "I have the perfect person in mind."

Bering's phone rang, and he checked the display. "Speaking of my issues, this is Senator Marsh." He answered the call and moved into the kitchen to talk.

Hazel's gaze collided with Cricket's, smile appreciative, eyes soft and warm. Maybe a few weeks of basking in some friendly Hazel-ness wouldn't be so bad, after all.

"SECRET SANTA?" HANNAH repeated flatly. "Mom, you cannot be serious. You do realize that we are all adults now, right?"

"I am quite serious, Hannah." Hands on hips, Margaret frowned at her "middle" child. Technically, Hannah was number three, after Tag and Shay. But with Hannah's arrival five years after Shay and with the triplets sharing the spot as youngest, the title seemed fitting.

With Sunday brunch mostly concluded, they'd all retired to Ben and Margaret's over-size great room with varying combinations of dessert, coffee or hot chocolate so Margaret could "make an announcement."

"That is precisely the point." In her school-principal voice, she addressed the crowd again. "The Christmas spirit is not exclusive to children. And we adults are going to find ours. The level of Christmas enthusiasm, especially toward the gift exchange, has been a bit lackluster in the last few years. Everyone buying gift cards to get out of having to put any thought into it? Pathetic, if I'm being honest."

Hannah's hand shot up. "Can we opt out?"

"Hannah, really!" Margaret huffed.

"Why do you do this with her?" Cricket whispered to Hannah from his spot beside her on the sofa. And then called loudly, "This sounds like a lot of fun, Margaret. I'm in!"

"I agree!" Hazel exclaimed from where she sat in the rocking chair across the room. "I *love* this plan, Mom."

Tate, who'd been standing near the fireplace, tossed Cricket an encouraging glance and stepped over to his mother-in-law. Draping an arm around her shoulder, he then gave it a gentle squeeze. "Margaret, I am on board, too. Don't worry—I'll make sure your wayward child participates."

Margaret patted Tate's hand. "Thank you, and you, too, Cricket and Hazel, for your enthusiasm. It's nice to see that Christmas is alive and well in certain parts of this family." She slid a disappointed frown in Hannah's direction.

"Whatever." Hannah rolled her eyes and gave her head a little shake. To Cricket, she muttered, "I know what you guys are doing." Louder, she declared, "Fine. I'll play."

Cricket, Tate and Hazel exchanged grins because who could resist a little good-natured goading of the most competitive person in the family, and possibly the entire planet? Tate took a seat on the other side of Hannah.

"No gift cards." Margaret went on to outline the rules. "Unless it's something *extremely* specific to the person. Remember, it's not about money—it's about thoughtfulness, giving while genuinely thinking of others. In other words, the true spirit of Christmas."

She paused to let that sink in. "Get creative, people! And I'd like to see at least one gift or deed delivered per week until Christmas. We'll disclose our identities on Christmas Eve. No revealing who you have before then, either on purpose or by 'accident.'" Here she paused to add air quotes and deliver a warning look to Hannah.

"Stop looking at me like that! I will not

cheat. I am not a cheater. In fact, you know what? I am going to win this whole thing."

"Um, sweetie." Tate placed a hand on her knee. "You do know it's not a competition, right?"

"Maybe not to you!" she countered to a room full of laughter. Cricket didn't doubt that Hannah would find a way to turn this into a contest and declare herself the victor.

"That's the spirit," Margaret said approvingly. "Now, I've written the names of every adult on slips of paper and placed them in this stocking." She held the sock aloft before handing it off to Iris, who was seated on a chair to her left. "We're going to pass it around so everyone can draw a name. If you select your own or your spouse's name, please put it back and draw another. You can also have one redraw if, for some reason, you don't want to buy for that person."

Across the room, Cricket watched Iris pass the stocking to Hazel. She reached inside. Poker-faced, she peeked at the slip before tucking it into her pocket. What would he do if he drew her name? The wisest course of action would be to use his pass. The last thing he needed was the added intimacy of buying her gifts, even if he would be awesome at it.

By his count, he had roughly a 5 percent

chance of drawing her name. Odds were against either of them getting the other. So, when the stocking made it around to him, he confidently reached inside, withdrew a slip of paper, read the name and barely managed to keep his features set to blank.

"You okay with who you got there, big guy?" Hannah asked from beside him.

Heart pounding, he stared at Margaret's beautiful cursive rendering of *Hazel* scrawled across the glossy white paper. *Stick with the plan and put the paper back inside*. That's what he told himself. Twice. But he couldn't seem to move. *Hazel*. The name seemed to shimmer before his eyes. He remained motionless. Thinking.

The truth was that he wanted to do this. He wanted to be her Secret Santa. By her own admission, all she wanted was to have a good Christmas, to sort a few things out. She deserved that much, especially when he feared he might be the cause of some of her angst.

He held the power in his hand to give that to her, or at least to contribute significantly. No one knew her better than he did. He was already cataloging all the little gifts he wanted to buy for her, things to do for her. Possibilities that went back years. He could, he realized, finally do some of them. Including giving her the Christmas gift he'd already bought for her months ago that he feared might be too much. But that would be okay now, he told himself, because it was anonymous. By the time she found out that he was her Secret Santa, she'd be stuffing her backpack to leave again.

Fate had just handed him an incredible opportunity.

"Cricket?" Hannah's voice startled him. "What's the deal? You wanna swap yours?"

No way anyone could pry the slip of paper from his fingers now. "Absolutely not," he said. Leaning toward her, he passed the stocking, lowered his voice, and said, "Hate to break it to you, but I am going to be the winner."

"Oh, it is on!" Hannah cried and made a show of shoving her hand into the stocking and withdrawing a slip of paper.

"Hey, everyone!" Hazel called from the doorway. "Can I have your attention for just a sec?"

A few minutes ago, Cricket had noticed Hazel check her phone and then get up and disappear into the hallway. Now she was back with someone by her side. Angled away from the door, he couldn't see who it was.

A figure stepped farther into the room as she continued speaking. "I'd like you all to meet my friend Kai. He's going to be here through the holidays. Kai, this is my family. We're a pretty outgoing bunch, so I'll let everyone introduce themselves…"

She kept talking, but Cricket quit hearing. Likely due to the whooshing sound in his ears, followed by a pounding against the inside of his skull. Was this why she'd been so eager to take the job? Because she'd already planned on bringing the date home to meet her family?

Stunned, Cricket tried to absorb this news. The drawing concluded, people milled about while he sipped his now-cold coffee and pretended to check his phone. That comment Kai had made about being ready "to relocate" to Alaska replayed in his mind. He'd dismissed it because Hazel hadn't mentioned it, or him, since. She'd never brought a man home to meet her family, and the significance of that was obvious. As was the sharp stabbing pain in his heart. Iris had been right about the reason she'd turned her phone off, and this, this…*date* was further proof that she was moving on.

Bering sat beside him. "Seems like a nice guy, huh?"

"What?" Cricket asked, forcing himself to breathe and to focus on Bering's question.

"Kai. Hazel told me you met him in Utah and that she was sure you'd approve. Apparently, he majored in tourism and travel or some such thing. I didn't even know you could do that. Those qualifications should make for a solid employee, though, that's for sure."

Employee? No, no, no… Short of announcing their engagement, he would have bet this situation couldn't get worse. Hazel had hired *him*? He was going to have to see the date every day?

"Said you guys had dinner together or something?"

No, I do not approve, he wanted to shout. But he'd already given his approval, hadn't he? Both he and Bering had readily granted her the freedom to hire whoever she wanted. And he'd thought watching her have dinner with the guy had been a struggle. Now he had to watch them date *and* work together every day? Was it too late to write up a workplace handbook forbidding office romance? Or at least PDAs? If he had to see them kiss, he might do something…

Something that would earn him his rightful place in Blackburn infamy. Even thinking these thoughts was proof of how messed-up he was.

"You okay, buddy?" Bering asked. "You look…weird."

"Uh, yeah, um… Tired. Need to get some sleep." What he needed was to calm down.

Ben appeared, offering him and Bering dessert.

He managed a "Yes, please" and a "Thank you, Ben" and accepted the piece of pumpkin pie with whipped cream and forced himself to think rationally.

The problem, he now realized, was that all these years that she'd been single and available had allowed him to believe in some deep, unconscious place that she might somehow, someday, be available for him. That was what had kept him so stuck. He'd tried to move on, repeatedly and without success, but had finally accepted his fate of forever bachelorhood.

But maybe the answer was for her to move on. Maybe Hazel having a serious boyfriend was the answer to ending this fixation of his once and for all. Making this Christmas that much more critical. He would be the best Secret Santa anyone ever had. Because this might be his last chance to express how he felt—even if he couldn't speak the words aloud.

"THIS IS AWESOME, HAZEL," Kai said, his gaze bouncing around the Spruce Suite. The rooms were decorated to look like the inside of an upscale log cabin with lots of natural-looking wood, mission-style furniture and bold, cheerful colors. Hazel had to agree with Kai. There was even a nice assortment of decorations, including a small Christmas tree and lights strung around the fireplace hearth. "Are you sure? It's way more than I need."

After brunch, Hazel had given Kai a tour of Rankins, which she'd ended at the Faraway Inn, where he'd be living for the next month. She'd hashed out the employment details with Bering and, knowing there'd be plenty of holiday distractions, had committed both herself and Kai to working for Our Alaska Tours until after the New Year. The suite's three-room setup was like a small apartment, and Hazel was confident he'd be more than comfortable.

"Hey, this is all on Bering and Cricket and Shay." Shay owned and operated the inn and regularly housed guests who were also Bering's clients. "Bering called my sister to make arrangements for you, and this is what they agreed on. I have to admit I'm a little jealous."

"No kidding! And I know I've said this already, but I really appreciate this opportunity."

"Stop." Hazel waved him off. "It was meant to be. You're a good sport agreeing to participate in my family's Secret Santa event, though. Scored huge points with my mom."

"It'll be fun and a great way to get to know everyone. Your mom is going to help me out with my gifts—you know, give me some hints since I don't know everyone."

They discussed the gift exchange, made a plan to meet at the office in the morning and then said their goodbyes. Instead of heading out the back exit, Hazel went down the stairs, where she'd pass through the lobby. Shay's office was located there, and she wanted to stop by and copy her schedule.

She'd drawn Shay's name, and Hazel had every intention of spoiling her big sister, who had a habit of spoiling everyone else except herself. Her first gift would be an unqualified challenge to Hannah's quest for Secret Santa supremacy.

This route took her right past the Faraway Restaurant, located inside the inn, adjacent to the lobby. The eatery took up a good portion of the first floor, and the open layout allowed for an expansive view of the dining area.

Hazel had known it was only a matter of time before she ran into her nemesis, Ashley Eller Frye. The woman worked for her brother Tag at Copper Crossing Air Transport. However, what she would never have imagined was that she'd see her now, tucked in at a corner table. With Cricket.

The sensation was much like falling into a snowbank, shocking, cold and suffocating.

Veering toward one of the thick timbers arranged in the center of the inn's main thoroughfare, Hazel stopped. Peering around the beam, she attempted to evaluate the situation and stay partially hidden. Spy, in other words, she guiltily acknowledged. Did she want to be that person? Yep, she decided, and, owning the indignity, she peeked again.

Just in time to see Ashley giggle. The sound barely carried to her, but her brilliant smile, fluttering hands and signature hair-toss all conjured the tone. Hazel knew it well because it was the sound of her sister Iris's torment when Ashley and her friends used to bully Iris back in school. There was the added complication of Ashley being Derrick's cousin. Derrick had cheated on Hazel, and Ashley had not only been complicit, but she'd also lied about it and made Hazel look like a fool.

As if that wasn't enough, Seth had been infatuated with Ashley. She'd broken his heart and then strung him along for years. Just this spring, during the same trip to Florida where she'd sparred with Cricket, Ashley had made a play to win Seth back, but luckily, he'd already been in love with Victoria. After making a grand gesture that fell flat, Ashley ended up looking a little foolish herself. Presenting Hazel with an opportunity that she'd fantasized about for years, to rub it in Ashley's face that her days of playing mind games with the Jameses were over. And briefly, she'd considered it.

But when she'd gone to confront her, Ashley had explained herself and apologized—for everything—and Hazel had been left with more pity than hatred for the divorced single mother of three who'd endured years with a lying cheater of a husband, Roy Frye. Word had it that Roy was also a sketchy businessman whose antics had finally caught up with him in the form of the law.

Karma had punished Ashley enough. Hazel might be done harboring ill will, but that did not mean they would ever be friends. Or that Ashley and Cricket "the couple" made her anything but sick with jealousy. But just because they were sitting together, heads bowed in a conversation so intense neither of them had even looked away the entire time she'd been spy-watching, didn't mean they were a couple, right?

Cricket stood. Hazel slipped out of sight. She hoped nobody she knew walked by because she was literally hugging the post now while peeping around it and looking downright sneaky. Ashley rose, too, and then hugged him. A full-on body squeeze that went on and on and on... And then, finally, gripping his shoulders, she took a small step backward. One that gave her just enough space to push up onto her toes and plant a kiss on his cheek.

CHAPTER SEVEN

HAZEL EXAMINED THE adorably pudgy, plush brown bear on her desk as giddiness bubbled inside of her. Technically, it was what the bear was wearing that was stirring up all the feels—such a needed boost after witnessing last night's Cricket and Ashley display. After the shock had worn off, she'd spent the entire evening assuring herself that seeing them together was a good thing.

Cricket in a relationship could possibly even help her get over him faster. Sort of like a rapid detox. If only it wasn't Ashley! All the women to choose from on this planet, and he picked her?

"Focus, Hazel," she whispered out loud in an attempt to tamp down her jealousy. Refocusing on the bear, she said, "Thanks, little buddy," and slipped the Janek Luna360 headlamp from his fuzzy noggin. "Just going to borrow this for a few minutes." She tested the straps for size, made a few adjustments and then positioned it on her own head.

Already she felt better, silent thanks to her Secret Santa. They'd drawn names only yesterday. How had they managed this so quickly? How could she or he have even known she needed one? And this particular model was top-of-the-line. Most likely, she wouldn't even have sprung for it herself.

She glanced around the office even though she knew no one else was there. She was early, which made the gift even more intriguing. How had they gotten inside the office to deliver it? It seemed too obvious to assume her Secret Santa was Cricket or Bering, but they must have let someone in.

That was a mystery she didn't need to solve right now. Unable to resist, she got up and walked to the light switches, flipped them all off and turned on the headlamp.

"Oh. Wow."

For the next several minutes, she prowled around the office in the dark, playing with her new toy. She was exiting the storage closet when she heard the office door open.

"Hey!" Iris's voice called loudly, "If you're trying to signal to alien spacecraft, you should probably take that outside."

"Good morning!" she called, pivoting toward the sound. "I got the coolest gift ever."

That was when she realized Iris and Cricket

were both illuminated in the beam. Iris reached out and hit the power switch, turning on the overhead lights.

A grinning Cricket held a box from the Donut Den in his hands. "Find what you need in there?" He dipped his head toward the closet, where she still stood in front of the open door.

She laughed, shut the door and switched off the lamp. Pointing at her head, she remarked, "Is this beautiful or what? One-hundred-fifty-meter range, ring focus, six hours on the brightest beam."

"Wow," Iris remarked. "Your Secret Santa is killing it already."

"I know! Impressive, right? How could they already have gotten me something? I mean, something this *amazing*? Who knew that I even wanted one? It almost has to be Kai."

"Why would it have to be Kai?" Iris asked. "My money is on Hannah. We all know she is not going to spare any expense to win this thing—whatever that means."

"Kai and I were caving in Utah—you know, where we met at his family's caverns? My headlamp literally conked out midcave, and I mentioned that I needed a new one. How sweet is that?"

"Pretty sweet," she agreed. "But if it is Kai,

he's not very good at this game, is he? *'Cuz* you're not supposed to give yourself away on the first day."

Cricket, who'd been oddly quiet, now laughed. "I have to agree."

"Besides," Iris added, "you mentioned you needed one on your blog a while back."

"Did I?"

"Yep. Months ago, in that piece you wrote when you were caving in New Zealand. You made this funny remark speculating about how ancient peoples probably invented the first headlamps using glow worms."

"Huh." She did remember that now, but it had been a while ago.

Iris strolled around the reception desk and settled in one of the spare chairs in front of Hazel's desk.

A few days ago, Bering had brought in a small folding table and set it up behind the reception desk for extra storage space and paperwork to be reviewed—and snacks. Cricket moved around the reception area and placed the Donut Den box there.

"Hey, all!" Kai said, charging through the door. "Is this a gorgeous morning or what?" He looked at Hazel and gushed, *"Whaaat?* Nice headlamp! DuoBeam?"

"Janek," she said.

"Luna?"

"Yep. The 360."

"*Sweet!* That is top-of-the-line right there."

"That'll be nice for El Capitan this summer," Cricket commented.

"What? No!" Kai chirped dubiously and then let out a chuckle. "Why would she need a headlamp for El Capitan?" And then to Hazel, "I didn't know you were a rock climber, too."

"The cave, not the rock," Cricket returned blandly.

"He's talking about El Capitan, the cave system here in southeast Alaska," Hazel said and then detailed how ancient fossils had been discovered there.

Iris chimed in, "Hazel has been asked to help explore portions where they think fossil bones might be. Isn't it like a two-week project?"

She replied, "It is."

Kai said, "Wow. That's supercool. Can't believe I haven't heard of it."

"Me either," Cricket said flatly. "Especially in light of your family's property. Donut?" he asked, looking toward her and Iris.

"Don't mind if I do," Kai said.

"Sure," Hazel answered.

"Yes, please," Iris said. "Buttermilk glazed for me."

Cricket used the enclosed tissue paper to hand Iris her request.

"Hey, Hazel," Kai said, peering at the options. "You want a chocolate with sprinkles, a cream puff, a glazed…" He kept rattling off flavors while Cricket returned to the box, plucked out a scone, walked over to her desk and placed it in front of her.

"Thank you," she said, giving Cricket a grateful smile because, of course, he knew what she wanted. "Um, thanks, Kai, but these huckleberry scones are my all-time favorite."

Cricket winked and headed to his desk.

Iris, she realized, was watching the entire interplay with an inscrutable expression. Quirking a brow at Hazel, she leaned in and whispered, "I realize we're not doing the list anymore, but that is a blatant violation right there. Delivering your favorite food to work."

THE NEXT AFTERNOON, Cricket gathered his patience while Bering, Hazel and *Date*—also known as Kai—assembled for their first "staff meeting." Very uncharitable, he told himself, this attitude of his. Probably he needed to start thinking of the guy by his name.

Kai removed a cup from the cardboard coffee carrier he'd brought from the Cozy Caribou and held it out for Hazel. "Cream, no sugar, right?"

"No, black," she replied, lifting another cup from the container. "That's Bering's."

Was this guy for real? First, the scones, and now he didn't even know how she liked her coffee? How was it possible to date Hazel and not know these basic details about her?

"Got it." He handed it off to Bering and then passed the remaining cup to Cricket.

"One quick thing before we get started," Hazel said, glancing between Cricket and Bering. "It probably won't surprise you two that Shay called this morning wondering if we wanted to contribute to the Festival of Trees auction. I know we're not technically up and running yet, but it would be a great way to introduce Our Alaska Tours to the community."

The Festival of Trees was an annual fundraising benefit for the hospital. Held at the Faraway Inn, elaborately decorated Christmas trees were donated by area businesses and then auctioned off for exorbitant sums. Competition among community members was fierce and fun, with generous patrons going to extremes to outbid each other.

This year, the committee had added a silent auction and a raffle. An elegant dinner was always served, and the evening had become one of the most highly anticipated social events of the season.

"Definitely," Bering answered and then glanced at Cricket.

He nodded. "Agree."

"Perfect, I'll give her a firm yes and get started on it. What about donating a tour for the raffle?" They discussed it briefly, settled on their contribution and then Hazel looked at Kai.

"Kai, you want to take the first order of business?"

"Sure!" Kai wheeled his office chair closer to hers. Too close, in Cricket's opinion. Brow scrunching in concentration, he studied the monitor screen on Hazel's desk. Cricket had no clue why the guy couldn't use his own computer. As much as he hovered around Hazel's desk, he wondered why they'd even bothered getting him one of his own.

"Okay, so, what we need to do ASAP is arrange lodging for each tour. Once we have suitable accommodations, we can fine tune the sightseeing details. Have you guys stayed at any of the following places? Blue Spruce Hotel, Northern Nook Lodge, Four Sisters Resort?" Glancing up, he looked from Bering to Cricket and back again, and Cricket hoped he wasn't going to read off the name of every hotel in the entire state. What was the point of this?

"You know what…?" Hazel said, frowning thoughtfully at Kai.

Kai held up one finger. "Hold on a sec…" He tapped the keyboard, and the printer began to hum and then shoot out pages. He pointed at Hazel. "Go!"

"Nothing," she said brightly. "You read my mind." She popped out of her chair and headed for the copy machine. "Kai is printing the list for you guys to take a look at."

Cricket barely managed not to roll his eyes. This was what he'd endured for the last two days. The two of them, working side by side in perfect harmony, cracking "travel" jokes and finishing each other's sentences. Today, he'd taken a break for a couple of hours when he'd gone to Snowy Sky Ski Resort to meet with Hannah on JB Heli-Ski business. Had he purposely lingered to avoid coming back into the office? Yes. He'd had no choice but to return when Kai had texted about the staff meeting. He hoped these weren't going to become a daily occurrence.

Handing copies to him and Bering, Hazel said, "As you can see, we've already eliminated some of these options based on location, size, amenities and other issues."

Kai said, "We're assuming you've visited

some of them. So, we'll see if we can eliminate more or elevate others based on your experiences."

Bering scanned the list and scratched his cheek with one thumb. "Let's see…" He pointed. "Emily and I have stayed at this Bear Paws Guesthouse. Caters to kids. It's got a nice indoor pool. Toasty warm. Big slide." He indicated another hotel farther down the list. "And this one, too, JB's Travel Inn, but never again. Pool is tiny and cold."

"This is what your life has become?" Cricket wryly observed. "Basing your hotel choices on the condition of the pool."

"No!" Bering exclaimed with exaggerated defensiveness. "Not at all. The breakfast is important, too."

Cricket gave his head a sorry shake. "Hopeless."

"Totally." Bering chuckled with a kind of dreamy look on his face. "That's what happens when you have kids. It used to be about whether they had a nice restaurant or a spa for Em but not anymore. Now it's all about the pool and if the continental breakfast has a waffle maker. You'll find out eventually. Maybe."

Not at the rate he was going. A family of his own, kids specifically, had never been a high priority for him. Hazel, he knew, felt the same.

He'd always respected how she wasn't 100 percent certain about motherhood herself. She'd told him once that it was a decision that required thorough analysis and total commitment—from both partners. Precisely how he felt about parenthood, too. He wondered if she and Kai had had that conversation yet. The thought of Hazel having children with anyone else was... He couldn't think about that right now. He was already concerned about the current uptick in his blood pressure.

"I've heard the Ptarmigan Inn is nice," Bering said.

Kai nodded zealously, like a bobblehead doll on a bumpy back road. "That's near the top of our list. Reviews are good. Slight concern about its remote location. You have to get there by boat, although people might enjoy that aspect. Especially if we incorporate it into the experience."

"There are a lot of places we would have to access by boat, or possibly even plane," Cricket said, trying not to allow his growing impatience to creep into his tone but knowing he was failing. "Alaska is like that."

Kai gave a hearty, "Sure, I get that."

Something occurred to him as he studied the list. "I don't see Grey's on here. I always stay at Grey's when I'm anywhere near Denali."

Grey's Lodge was a high-end resort and spa with a Michelin-rated steak house.

"*Gorgeous* pool," Bering reported. "Two pools, technically. And the most incredible porterhouse steak I've ever eaten."

Cricket agreed about the steak. "One of many, many reasons that I like it. The views are phenomenal, too, and the—"

"Grey's is out of our price range," Kai interrupted with an exaggerated cringe. "Unfortunately," he quickly added when Cricket frowned.

Hazel backed him up. "Kai is right. We've already ruled out the high-end destination-type resorts."

Perky Kai went on, "But places with a similar type of Alaskan flair would be the ultimate goal. Even somewhat rustic would be good. Rustic-*looking*, anyway. We still need decent amenities."

"And," Hazel chimed in, "we have to be able to provide breakfast if the hotel doesn't."

Resentment churned inside of Cricket as he wondered if they'd practiced this snappy back-and-forth routine.

"Like Grey's does?" he retorted, feeling, and possibly sounding, unreasonably perturbed.

Hazel shook her head. "That degree of luxury is not necessary."

"But I thought we were catering to the luxury traveler?"

"We are, sort of…" Kai reassured him with a tad too much patience as if Cricket were a willful elementary student.

He countered in a similarly exaggerated tone, "If people want to go camping, *Da*—uh—*Kai*, they can sign up for one of Bering's excursions."

"I would love to," Kai conceded pleasantly. Another gesture, Cricket surmised, designed to placate him. But only managed to annoy him more. "I plan to."

When Cricket scowled, Kai hastily said, "I totally understand your point. But an Our Alaska tour isn't going to come with much downtime, is it? Tour members aren't paying to stay in the room. They're paying for an *experience*. I guarantee that people will be much more interested in what's going on outdoors than indoors. Grey's could be a vacation all on its own."

"Which is why it's so appealing," Cricket reasoned unreasonably.

"The cost would be—"

"But shouldn't every aspect of the tour be a part of the *experience*?" Cricket interrupted. "Including the lodging?" He could hear his tone crossing the line into argumentative, and he knew he needed to dial it back.

"Yes, to a point," Hazel interjected, and Cricket couldn't help but think she was coming to Kai's rescue. "Maybe we should talk about that now—your brand. Kai and I have already discussed this at length, and to us, an Our Alaska tour should be an authentic yet accessible Alaskan experience.

"Like a safe and comfortable adventure. Your goal is to show the outdoors to people who might have the desire but not the ability to get out there and live in it like we do. A taste of the rugged versus the actual roughing it they'd get with an excursion through Bering's guide service. Electricity, hot water, good food. *Comfort*. A soft bed, sure, but maybe one with rough-hewn logs overhead and the sound of an owl hooting outside. Think gourmet coffee on the deck while a bear or a moose grazes off in the distance. Close enough to photograph but too far away to touch."

Pausing to chuckle, she then added, "I keep thinking about the type of tour Iris would like. She's our gold standard here."

Unlike the rest of her family, Iris saw no point in camping out or otherwise "eschewing a decent bed and a proper meal."

"I see what you mean," Bering agreed with a chuckle. "So, how do we choose?"

"We'd like to see some of these places, talk to the owners or managers, get a feel for them and discuss group rates, discounts, meal options, etcetera. Plus, there's nothing like a personal experience, especially from multiple points of view."

"Makes sense. When and where?"

"As soon as possible. We'd like to start in Juneau. The Coastal Gold Tour, as we've tentatively named it, is going to be the most specialized of your signature tours. There aren't as many lodging options there, so we need to nail those down. If we add a day in Gold Bend as you've suggested, we need to make sure that's feasible. So, the sooner, the better."

Bering grimaced. "My flight to DC is set for Thursday. Once again, I'm afraid I'm not going to be much help until I get this federal concession problem squared away."

"We understand, Bering," she conceded. "But, Cricket, you can come with us, right?"

Cricket could not think of a single thing he'd like to do less. Caught off guard and flat-out flummoxed, he answered the only way he could with Bering, Hazel and Kai staring at him expectantly and no excuse readily available. "Uh, sure, as long as it doesn't snow three feet in the mountains." *Please*, he begged the universe, *let it snow.*

"We'll go ASAP." Hazel nodded. "I'll make arrangements."

"Hey, you're flying to Juneau on Thursday, anyway, aren't you?" an unhelpful Bering reminded him.

He was, with Ashley. But he would not disclose the details of that mission with Kai, or Hazel, or anyone else for that matter. It was Ashley's private business. And he'd never cancel on her now; they'd been planning this for weeks.

He'd just have to figure out a way for them to peel off for a few hours. Copper Crossing had a flight scheduled out of Juneau that day. If they timed it right, Ashley could see to her task and then catch that flight back to Rankins. He couldn't see how to explain all of this that didn't involve a lot more explaining than he cared to do. Plus, he needed to run this by Ashley first. She might not want anyone along, and Cricket would respect that if that was what she chose.

"Yes," he answered. "I can fly us. Probably be easier if you guys are comfortable with me being your pilot?" And so much faster. The less time he had to endure this third-wheel torment, the better. "Let me check on a couple of things first, and I'll let you know tonight."

Thinking the situation through had him hopeful this two-birds-with-one-stone excursion could work. There was no love lost between Hazel and Ashley, but at this point, having another person along would be helpful. He almost laughed out loud because he'd thought that about having another employee around, too, hadn't he? And look where that had gotten him. This general mood of grumpy impatience was definitely not what he'd had in mind for Hazel's ideal holiday.

To Kai, Hazel asked, "You okay with flying in small planes? Cricket is *the* best pilot in the entire world. Not even exaggerating." Pointing a finger between Bering and Cricket, she added in a teasing tone, "If either of you tells Tag I said that—you will regret it."

"You bet!" Kai said with over-the-top eagerness. "Sounds like an adventure."

Cricket wondered how anyone could be that enthusiastic all the time.

"Perfect. Thanks, Cricket," Hazel said, gracing him with a brilliant smile, the one that made her eyes sparkle, and even managed to mitigate his irritation slightly.

POKER NIGHT ROTATED from house to house, but in an informal, haphazard manner. Often, like this evening, it ended up being most convenient for Cricket to host. He was the only single guy left in their group, the core of which consisted of Bering along with his brother-in-law, Aidan, brothers Tag and Seth, and their brothers-in-law, Jonah, Tate and Flynn, married to Shay, Hannah and Iris, respectively. Hannah was a semiregular attendee, too, and, when she played, could generally be counted on to take all their money. Except for Cricket's, which drove her nuts.

Cricket enjoyed being the anchor. And he was a good host, if he did say so himself. His roomy three-bedroom house had an open floor plan, including a spacious dining room with a large round table, perfect for card playing. He made a mean pizza, excellent lasagna, a delicious, hearty stew and the best loaded quesadillas. He rotated the four dishes while the guys supplied beer, soda and snacks. Both Emily, Bering's wife, and Janie, Aidan's wife, enjoyed baking and usually sent along a dessert or two.

"Three of a kind," Cricket said, revealing his trio of kings. Tonight, he really needed this time with his friends.

How could Hazel believe Mr. Clueless was her Secret Santa? He hadn't even known about her upcoming stint at El Capitan. Frankly, he didn't seem to know much about her at all. At least not the good stuff, the important little details that a boyfriend should know.

"Full house," Tag said, flipping over a jack and a nine to match the jack and two nines already showing.

"Oh, man!" Tate groaned, tossing his pair of queens onto the pile. "You are so lucky tonight."

"Ah, the thrill of victory is so very sweet," Tag boasted, sliding the massive pile of chips from the center of the table toward him, where it joined the small fortune he'd already amassed. "You losers should try it sometime."

Tag looked at Cricket. "I thought maybe you had me there. You and your poker face. Good thing I know you better than anyone else, and I'm a better cardplayer."

Cricket chuckled. He couldn't resist returning with a gibe of his own. "Yeah, well, another one of your sisters thinks I'm a better pilot than you are, so it's nice that you can play poker. Everyone needs to be halfway good at something."

"No way. Which one?" he demanded indignantly.

"It's totally true!" Bering supplied and then laughed, hard. "Hazel said it—I heard her. I was hoping you'd mention it, Cricket, so I won't be in trouble for telling him. It's too good to keep to myself."

"That's just great!" Tag plopped his beer bottle down on the tabletop. "First, one of my little sisters asks you to teach her how to fly, and now another one is just dissing me out-right?"

"Don't forget about the sister who asked him to go into business with her," Bering gleefully reminded Tag about Hannah.

Silently, Cricket acknowledged that there were reasons for all three of these occurrences. Hannah had asked him because Tag already had his own business, Iris hadn't wanted any-one to know she was taking flying lessons be-cause she wanted it to be a surprise and Hazel had been complimenting him to convince Kai to fly with him. But none of that was relevant when ribbing a boastful Tag was the point.

"Don't sweat it, buddy," Jonah chimed in with mock severity. "Shay thinks her big brother is the best *p-p-p*..." He drew out an exaggerated *p* sound before finishing with, "*Person* in the whole world."

That earned another round of laughter.

"Hey," Tag said, fighting a grin. "What-ever makes you guys feel better about me tak-ing all your money is fine by me." With a sly, knowing glance at Cricket, he added, "When it comes to women and cards, you do have a tell, by the way."

"You wish," Cricket said. "Hannah's been looking for one for years. If she can't find one, no one will."

"My sisters," Tag said flatly and then let out a little snort. "Ungrateful backstabbers. Best pilot? Ha. I'm sure she was simply being kind. However, I will give you credit for helping me look out for them for all these years, even when they thought they didn't need it."

Cricket felt a hitch in his chest. Tag was speaking in jest, but Cricket knew he meant it. That trust meant everything. He was secure in his belief that Cricket would do anything for those sisters. It went without saying that that included keeping his hands off them. He'd broken that trust once—not to mention another outright promise—and the guilt was nearly unbearable. It was a mistake that he'd vowed never to repeat, and one he'd tried to make up for ever since.

"That means the world to me," he deadpanned. "Sort of like winning the silver medal in a race of two."

"Four sisters," Tate said with a shake of his head. "I can't even imagine what that would be like, trying to keep all the fools away."

Tag set his features to mock-serious. "Tate,

you know me. I'm an easygoing guy, but you have no idea how that brings out the worst in me."

"I do!" Jonah joked, raising his hand. "I have an idea."

"Ha, I did my best to get rid of you," Tag responded. "Lucky for Shay—you don't scare easy."

Years ago, when Jonah had first come back to town and set his sights on reconnecting with Shay, Tag had been a less than enthusiastic supporter. To be fair, Shay and Jonah had had a history riddled with heartbreak and disappointment.

"So, you're saying I'm still a loser?"

"I will concede that you're less *loser-ish* than anyone else she ever dated," Tag conceded. They all laughed.

"Good thing only one of them is still single," Tate pointed out.

"Maybe not for long, though, huh?" Aidan observed, munching a piece of pizza. Leave it to the scientist, Cricket thought wryly, to point out this detail. "What's the deal with this Kai character anyway? Are he and Hazel a couple? Should we have invited him tonight?"

Bering gathered the cards, shrugged a shoulder and looked at Cricket. "He seems like a good guy. Great employee, too. So far."

So much for that distraction he'd been hoping for tonight. Couldn't even make it two hours without a reminder. How would he ever manage, he wondered, being friends with the guy who captured Hazel's heart? Was it wrong to hope that it wouldn't be Kai? Sure, he was a nice guy, but Cricket could plainly see that he wasn't right for her. Then again, no one would ever be good enough for Hazel, so what did it matter? A familiar sensation of hopelessness stole over him because he wasn't good enough either, was he?

"Bering, are you going to deal or what?" Tag heaved out a sigh. "Because I do not want to spend the evening gossiping about my sisters or discussing Hazel's love life. I'd rather lose all my money."

"Amen," Cricket wholeheartedly agreed.

CHAPTER EIGHT

THE DOORBELL CHIMED while Hazel was in the kitchen, putting the finishing touches of sour cream and salsa on the breakfast burritos she'd made. With eggs, chorizo sausage and plenty of cheese, they were one of her dad's favorites. The oatmeal cookies piled on the platter were for Cricket, although she was still undecided about whether to go through with delivering them.

Fidgety and unsettled, she'd gotten up way too early trying to decide where the line was between friend and former fantasy love interest. Needing to do something, she'd started cooking—another activity she enjoyed but didn't have the opportunity to do much of with her nomadic lifestyle.

Wiping her hands on a towel, she jogged toward the front door. "I got it!" she called loudly from the foyer because she knew her parents were still upstairs.

She opened the door in time to watch the delivery truck disappearing down the driveway.

A large package bearing her name rested on the mat. Hmm. Funny, the little stir of excitement she felt. Bending over, she picked it up and discovered it was surprisingly light for its size. She carried it into the great room, set it on the floor and immediately began wrestling it open. Marveling at the strength of modern-day packing tape, she quickly became aware that she should have gone in search of scissors or a box cutter. *Can't stop now, already committed.*

After sufficiently shredding the tape enough to pull open the flaps, she dug inside. Peeling away several tissue-paper layers revealed the treasure inside—a pillow. A fluffy, thick, gorgeous, full-size pillow!

Feeling like a...well, like a little kid at Christmas, she belted out a jolly laugh. She would have sworn the headlamp was impossible to beat, but this did it. The thought that *anyone* knew her this well was both incredibly endearing and a bit shocking. She unpacked the delicious puffball and hugged it to her chest.

One of the things she liked the least about traveling was the pillows. You never knew what you were going to get—anything from a thin, flimsy piece of foam to an overstuffed sack of gravel. Worst were the lumpy ones filled with chunks of an unidentifiable substance that crunched like a bag of chips at your slightest movement.

She always packed a small travel cushion with her, but it wasn't anywhere close to the same as a real pillow. Her schedule meant keeping inconsistent, often odd hours that precluded sleeping late, or well. Getting enough sleep was a rare indulgence but oh so treasured. Whenever she came home, taking a literal catnap was one of her very favorite activities.

How had her Santa known about her secret pillow yearning? She was positive she'd never blogged about the topic. Maybe she'd mentioned it in a social media post? Offhand, like complaining about a particularly bad one? She couldn't recall, though, so if she had, it'd been years ago.

There was more in the box, a pillowcase in buttery-soft flannel featuring adorable cartoon cats wearing Santa hats and all tangled in Christmas lights.

She found a card that read:

Since you're home for the holidays, you might as well enjoy all the comforts. Wishing you sweet dreams and plenty of catnaps. Love from your Secret Santa.

Tears welled in her eyes. Not the crying kind but like good old-fashioned happy tears. So many Christmases she'd spent alone, which was okay. That was her choice, but now that she was home, it felt so good to be here—and to be known. And loved. Like someone understood that as the only remaining single James child, she'd been feeling lonely and a bit left out.

Glancing at her mom's gigantic antique grandfather clock in the corner, she calculated the hours until bedtime. Too long. Did she have time for a nap?

In a case of utterly weird and perfect timing, her mom's cat Mica breezed in from the hall, strolled across the floor and parked himself at her feet. Gazing up at her with a slow, lazy blink, he let out a soft meow that could easily be interpreted as an invitation. A cat after her own heart, he was always up for a snooze.

An unexpected sting of tears burned behind her eyes. The sad kind now because another challenge of life forever on the go was no pets. She'd missed the cats, too, she realized while she'd been away. What was wrong with her?

Swiping at an errant tear on her cheek, she crouched to scratch Mica's cheeks. "I appreciate your enthusiasm. Maybe we can—"

The sound of the back door opening caught

her attention, and then Shay's voice called, "Hello?"

She stood. "Hey, Shay. In here!"

Mica wandered over to inspect the now-empty box, no doubt considering it for a potential napping spot.

"Hi, you," her sister said, striding quickly into the living room. She was smartly dressed in a blue-green cashmere sweater and gray wool slacks tucked into stylish but sturdy boots. With her dark brown hair neatly twisted on top of her head, her sister looked every inch the driven, successful, no-nonsense hotel owner that she was. But her gold-brown eyes reflected pure contentment, and Hazel knew that was due to her husband, Jonah, and their sweet baby, Maggie, the daughter they'd believed they could never have and whom they'd named after her grandmother Margaret.

Shay was extremely dedicated to her little family, which included her father-in-law, Caleb. Without a doubt, her loyalty and devotion to those she loved was one of her best traits, but as her Secret Santa, Hazel intended to show Shay that she deserved a little attention, too. She hoped Shay would mention the gift she'd had delivered yesterday.

"Good morning!" Hazel said brightly.

"I'm glad I caught you before you left for work."

"I'm glad you caught me, too. Breakfast burritos in the kitchen if you're hungry. Did you get my message about the Festival of Trees contributions?"

"Yes! Thank you! That's why I wanted to talk to you. Bering dropped a tree off for you guys at the inn. Emily ordered spares through the tourism bureau for any late participants who might need them."

"Of course she did."

"I know, right? The woman is a marvel. All you need to do is get your ornaments and schedule your decorating time."

The trees were creatively themed, usually in relation to the business or organization donating them. The decorations were typically unique, often handcrafted or special-ordered, resulting in trees that were veritable works of art in their own right. The finished products were kept top secret until the "authorized viewing days" before the auction, when they were set up in the Faraway Inn to generate interest and excitement—and sell last-minute tickets. Thus, the necessity of scheduling a decorating appointment.

"Sounds good. Kai and I already ordered the ornaments online. Tiny suitcases, backpacks, little maps and globes. It'll be supercute." She wasn't much of a "crafter" herself, but Kai had volunteered for the job, assuring her he had an artistic side. Since he was already on-site anyway, she'd given him free rein. "Kai will be in touch."

"Will you be back by Saturday for baking day?" Seth and Victoria would be arriving Friday, so Margaret had invited everyone over on Saturday for holiday baking and cookie decorating.

"Wouldn't miss it! Coming home Friday."

"Excellent." Shay's gaze turned curious as if just noticing the bounty still clutched to her chest. "What's with the pillow? Are you okay? Or is that part of a Santa costume?"

"Oh, you must be referring to *this*," Hazel said, making a show of pointing at the pillow. She gave it an affectionate pat. "This is not just a pillow. This happens to be the best gift ever in all the history of Secret Santa gift-giving."

"A pillow?" Shay repeated skeptically. "A pillow is the best gift ever?"

"One hundred percent."

"I hate to disappoint you, little sister, but yesterday, I got the best gift ever."

"Oh?" Hazel asked, her spirits lifting even further.

"My Secret Santa got me a pedicure. And I

don't mean a future pedicure, as in a gift card to add to my stack of unused gift cards. I adore pedicures, but do you think I ever get them? No. I'm always going to, and then I get busy, or I decide to spend my free time with Maggie instead…" She exhaled with a shrug that suggested she couldn't help herself.

"My point here is that my toes stay neglected. See, my Secret Santa knows this about me and delivered a pedicure to the inn. I couldn't say no. Anita came right into my office and set up a portable foot bath. I'm not even joking—I almost cried. Hands down, one of the best gifts I've ever gotten. Ever."

"That is pretty awesome," she agreed casually. *Yesss! Nailed it!* she wanted to shout as she basked in Shay's pure delight.

Their mom was onto something big here.

"Don't tell her I said this, but I think Mom might be a Christmas genius."

"Ha!" Margaret chirped brightly, strolling into the room. "I heard that."

Shay groaned good-naturedly.

"Mornin', Mom," Hazel crooned. "Breakfast burritos in the kitchen."

"Oh, good. You can take one to Cricket."

"Cricket? Why?" Her stomach executed a nervous flip. Had her mom seen the cookies? Did she somehow know their significance?

"His power is out. Dad has his generator, and I was hoping you could drop it off on your way to work?"

So, WITH A plate of oatmeal cookies and an insulated lunch box on the seat beside her, Hazel drove her father's spare pickup to Cricket's house. She wasn't home often enough to justify a vehicle of her own, but she adored this one. Old, but like most everything her father owned, it was clean, perfectly maintained and smelled faintly of fish. She suspected he hung on to it just for her to use.

A lack of snow this winter, and none the past week, meant the road surface was nice and clear. With every second that passed, her heart seemed to grow. As if the closer she got, the more it, too, remembered how much she used to love visiting him here.

She hadn't been to Cricket's place in ages, but the memories returned fast and fresh when she turned onto his driveway. Maybe because, throughout the years, she'd recalled those idyllic moments more often than was probably healthy.

She'd always adored the bungalow-style home with its wide and welcoming front porch lined with tall rectangular windows. The exterior was a combination of natural cedar-plank siding and shingles, all trimmed in white. He took extreme care and an equal amount of pride in maintaining every square inch.

The interior was spacious but comfortable. Homey. Her favorite features were the kitchen, where they'd often cooked together, the partially covered deck on the back of the house and the sunroom. *The sunroom.* Where she'd kissed him. Probably not a good idea to revisit that specific locale. Or to linger around the house for very long.

Yes, she decided, best to make this a quick visit. Ease into these memories like dipping a toe into a hot bath. Give him the cookies and get out. Smart to have a plan.

She pulled around back in time to see Cricket exit through the garage's side door. She drove onto the concrete pad and parked. Now that she was here, her confidence wavered. Was she dredging up too many memories? Would this be painfully awkward? What would they talk about?

"You can do this," she muttered softly. "Friends," she reminded herself. "Friends would not be nervous right now. Stick to the plan."

"Hey!" he said when she climbed out, a smile lighting his gorgeous face. "I was expecting your dad, so imagine my delight at seeing you instead."

Okay, then. This was good. Relief flowed through her. Of course, Cricket wouldn't let this be weird. Considering the depth of her teenage infatuation and the look on his face, it now seemed completely reasonable how she'd once confused his kindness and compliments, those watchful eyes and electric smile for more.

"I'm glad you think so. And maybe I can even add to that delight." Reaching into the vehicle, she retrieved the bounty she'd brought him. "Breakfast burrito and a little surprise."

"Breakfast? Yep, that'll do it. You can go inside if you want while I unload this and get it going. You haven't seen my house since the updates, have you? There's a fire in the woodstove, so it's nice and warm. I even made a pot of coffee with the percolator if you'd like some. It's sitting by the stove." As if he could sense her earlier decision, he added, "I'd love to show you around."

"Okay," she agreed, abandoning her previous plan for this much better one. Because the truth was, she needed to face this, deal with her emotions, explain about the cookies.

Besides, she did want to see what he'd done to the house—the place where they'd spent hours together talking, laughing, playing cards, watching TV, making pizzas and quesadillas, and just being. The place where she'd never felt more herself—or ever been so happy.

Maybe the changes he'd made would be a good thing for her emotional state. The lack of the familiar might prevent the spark of feelings that she feared. But even if they did start to flame, she would simply snuff them out like pouring water on a fire. She'd be a feelings-snuffer. And it would be that easy, too, she assured herself, because she was so completely aware now.

Stepping inside, she quickly abandoned the introspection to appreciate the hardwood floors. Same ones, but they'd been refinished and appeared freshly waxed. The walls were different colors. He'd chosen soft ivory for the entryway and a light mushroom hue for the living room, which she liked better than the previous light blue.

Two years ago, he and Tag had totally redone the kitchen, but she'd never seen the results. And she loved it instantly. Bright blond-wood cabinets that she thought might be maple, cream-colored walls, and granite countertops in shades of brown and gray with veins of black to pull it all together. New appliances in black stainless steel. Looking around, she couldn't help but note there were no signs of Ashley making herself comfortable yet. Hmm. She wondered what that meant.

Cricket had always been a neat housekeeper, tolerating little clutter. That hadn't changed and could explain the lack of Ashley evidence. But then her gaze homed in on the cookie jar sitting on the counter—the one she'd given him all those years ago filled with homemade oatmeal cookies.

That didn't necessarily mean anything either, did it? Even if the only other items to grace the surrounding area were a knife block, a coffee maker, salt-and-pepper set and a toaster oven? Obviously, it meant *something*, but probably not what she wanted it to. The man liked cookies, she reminded herself, and it was a nice container. Airtight and dishwasher safe. *Okay, Hazel, possibly you are obsessing about the meaning of a cookie jar. Time to move on.*

The kitchen flowed into the dining area, and she placed the food on the counter before heading there. The table was the same, an antique oak pedestal he'd purchased ages ago at an estate sale. *Perfect for poker games*, he'd once informed her. She knew he often hosted poker night because all her male family members and Hannah regularly attended.

Same antique sideboard, too, upon which several framed photos were neatly arranged. Cricket and Tag posing in front of Cricket's first Cessna airplane, standing side by side, each with an arm draped over the other's shoulders, aviator shades on, looking confident, content and handsome. There was another of the wedding party at Tag and Ally's wedding. Next to that was a brilliant photo of her entire family at one of Bering and Emily's famed outdoor bashes—her mom and dad seated together in the center with everyone gathered around them. She'd never seen the photo of herself and all three of her sisters in ski gear posing in front of a newly opened Snow Sky Resort. So cute. Cricket's helicopter could be seen in the background.

An old toy airplane was parked in front of the photos, made of metal, condition well-loved. She wondered about its origin. Did it belong to Cricket? He didn't like to talk about his childhood, and it was one of the few topics they'd never thoroughly discussed. Next to the toy was an old photo she'd never seen before. Reaching out, she picked it up for closer inspection. Cricket and his brother, Lee, she realized.

For some reason, the image made her heart clench tightly with a mix of sadness and love.

The boys were standing in front of the Presbyterian church here in Rankins—the church
her family had attended all her life—which
seemed odd because the Blackburns weren't
members.

Cricket appeared stiff, arms at his sides, his
expression somber and weary. Worried, even.
Lee, however, looked completely the opposite,
cocky grin, a glint in his eye, with one arm
curled around Cricket's slim shoulders. She
estimated Cricket to be about eight years old,
so that meant Lee would have been maybe six-
teen or seventeen?

Approximately two years before she was
even born. According to what she recalled,
that would have been around the time Lee
was arrested for his first serious offense and
sentenced to a juvenile detention center. Their
father, Frank, had spent much of Cricket's
childhood in and out of jail. Where had Cricket
gone during those periods?

Neither Lee nor Frank was living in the
area by the time Cricket and Hazel had struck
up their friendship. She'd never met either of
them, had seen only a few photos of Lee. And
definitely not this one.

She'd contemplated all of this before, but
for some reason, it struck her harder now how
much that instability, drama and tension had to

have affected him. But it didn't show; it hadn't shaped him, had it? Intelligent, accomplished and successful, he was also kind and incredibly generous. He'd not only overcome his circumstances, he'd also become a true pillar in the community. She made a mental note to ask her mom more about his childhood.

The lights flickered on, startling her out of her contemplation. Replacing the photo, she registered how nice the place smelled, too. Unlike most bachelor pads she'd encountered, his house smelled of vanilla, cinnamon and fresh coffee—reminding her to retrieve the percolator from where he'd left it next to the woodstove.

In the kitchen, she found the cups were in the same location in the cupboard next to the sink. She heard the back door open, which led to the garage from the mudroom, where he'd now be removing his coat, hat, gloves and boots.

"Thank you for dropping the generator off," he told her a moment later when he entered the kitchen. "Russ called and said a transformer's out. It'll be hours before the power is back on." Russ Driscoll, she knew, was a friend of his who worked for the power company.

"Happy to help. Coffee?" She held up his mug that she'd found on the table.

"Please," he said.

Pouring coffee into his cup, she said, "Your burrito is right there in that lunch bag. You may need to put it in the microwave for a bit. I know you like extra salsa. It's in the small container."

She carried their mugs to the bar, where she set them down. "And these," she said, removing the foil from the plate to reveal the cookies. "Freshly made this morning. Hope they're still your favorite."

"Oatmeal cookies," he stated, voice dipping low while his gaze traveled up to latch onto hers. He remembered.

"Yep," she said, forcing a smile.

"Yes," he murmured, his eyes holding hers. "Still my favorite."

Had she gone too far? She felt silly. Nervously, she cleared her throat. "I figured it would be sort of like starting over, you know? To me, they kind of marked the start of our friendship. So, I was thinking they might do that again. Like a new beginning."

"I see." He slowly nodded as if thinking it over, but the whole time his eyes never left hers, and she felt something more. Her pulse accelerated, blasting heat through her bloodstream. Did he go around looking at everyone like this? If so, it was no wonder he had women fawning over him all the time. At that moment, she truly hoped Ashley had changed, because the woman she'd known was nowhere near good enough for him.

She tried to look away but only managed to shift her gaze as far as his mouth. Probably she needed to quit admiring his lips.

But then a smile slowly curved there, and he asked, "You want to see the sunroom?"

CHAPTER NINE

CRICKET KNEW HE probably shouldn't ask the question even before it came sailing out of his mouth. But Hazel had brought the cookies, and the sunroom had been her spot, their favorite place to hang out. Also the scene of the crime, so to speak, which was why it wouldn't be a good idea.

On the other hand, Hazel was right; they needed to form a different relationship, create new memories. And, he reminded himself, she had a boyfriend. So that would make it easier to keep his distance. Theoretically, he amended as he watched her walking a few paces ahead. Why did everything about her have to be so appealing?

"I *like* this," she gushed, taking a seat on the love seat and falling back against the plush velvet cushions. "So much!" She lifted her feet to rest on the matching ottoman and patted the seat next to her.

The sensible, friendly move would be to take the adjacent chair. But they'd always sat there together so they could look out the windows. And he wouldn't want her to think he was avoiding her. That would be uncomfortable, too. He placed his cup on the end table and settled next to her. She pulled the blanket from the back of the sofa and arranged it to cover them both. The movement brought her so close he could smell the sweet, tropical scent of her hair. Feel her warmth. He ached to reach out and touch her skin, still sun-kissed from her recent travels.

"It's even more comfortable than your old one. All I need is my new pillow and a…" Her voice trailed off as Mitt, his giant fluffy brown-and-white cat, lumbered into the room. Her eyes lit with pleasure.

"Cat! Cricket, you have a cat? How did I not know this?"

"I do." He smiled. "Two cats. That's Mitt."

"Wow," she whispered as Mitt padded closer, his almost comically large paws thudding on the hardwood. Cats were supposed to be graceful and stealthy and sure-footed. The ballerina of the animal world. Not Mitt. He was more like a bull in a China shop and, at eighteen pounds and with enough fur to knit a king-size blanket, he more closely resembled a small musk ox. He jumped onto the sofa next to Hazel. Standing close, tail twitching, he proceeded to give her the sniff test.

"Mitt?" she asked as the cat awarded her a passing grade by helping himself to her lap.

"Yeah, it's short for Mittens. That was his name at the shelter when he was about the size of my fist. But look at him now—you can see he's a tough guy." Mitt was purring loudly, circling, pausing here and there to make biscuits. "Needed a name to match."

"Mmm-hmm," Hazel droned sarcastically. "So tough. I hope he doesn't go for my throat. Hi, Mitt," she cooed, scratching the sweet spot behind his ears. Smart cat was already in love. He flopped onto his side, sprawling and stretching his neck so she could better reach his chin, his other sweet spot. He had several.

"That's a real possibility. I wouldn't recommend making any sudden moves."

She laughed. "And you have another one?"

"I do," he said and glanced toward the door. "And there she is—there's my sweet Valentine. Her friends call her Val."

In opposition to Mitt, Val was petite and lean with short velvety gray fur. Also, unlike her "brother," she was not particularly fond of strangers. She glided into the room and hopped directly onto Cricket's lap, where she daintily folded her legs beneath into a regal sphinxlike crouch, where she haughtily assessed Mitt's brazen ploy for attention.

Hazel quirked a brow and tipped her head. "That's the one to watch out for."

"True," Cricket agreed with a chuckle. "She is a bit possessive. So, you were saying you need a pillow and a what?"

"I said I need *my new pillow*. My Secret Santa struck again. And I was going to tack *cat* onto the end of that sentence because there's nothing I like better than taking a nap with an actual cat."

"Ah, yes," he said, relishing yet another Secret Santa score. "You and your catnaps. You can borrow one of mine anytime."

"I might take you up on that." She smiled down at Mitt. "With this one, anyway." Her gaze bounced around the room. "I like everything you've done, Cricket. It's perfect."

"Thank you. I'm glad you think so." Cricket couldn't remember the last time he'd felt this content and wholly in-the-moment at the same time. That wasn't true; he remembered very well because it had been here. With her, just like this. The years were melting away, and the sense of rightness settling over him was almost overwhelming.

He stretched one arm along the back of the sofa, admitting that his hand was only inches from her shoulder. "I thought about you when I picked everything out. Wondered what you'd think."

Her lips curled at the corners as her gaze latched onto his. "Did you?"

"I did. We used to talk about houses and decorating stuff, remember? And watch those home improvement shows."

"I remember. You were building your deck that summer."

While fantasizing about sharing it all with you, he silently added. A niggle of guilt crept over him. Was it fair to let her go on believing that she'd struggled with emotion that he didn't return? That she was the only one who'd suffered all these years? He needed to tell her. If it was possible to have a genuine chance at friendship, he needed to be honest about how he'd felt, too. Take responsibility for his part in it all.

It would be okay to admit now because she was over him. She'd moved on. He should also let her know how happy he was that she'd found someone. In other words, lie. Lying would be the right thing to do.

"Hazel, I need to tell you something."

"Okay, sure," she said. "You know you can tell me anything." Her voice was low and sincere, and her eyes were soft and shining with curiosity.

Gathering his thoughts, he let his gaze wander over her. She was so beautiful it almost hurt to look at her. He wanted to tell her that, too. And that she was the sweetest, bravest, most interesting person he'd ever met and the only woman he'd ever… Wait. What was that crawling on her shoulder? He leaned closer for a better look.

"What's the matter?"

"Don't move. There's a spider on your shoulder." From the table beside him, he plucked a tissue from its box and then slowly shifted toward her. Val, irritated by the disturbance, moved from his lap to perch on the sofa's arm.

"Sometime today would be fine with me," she whispered with a hint of urgency.

"I don't want to scare it."

"I don't want it on me anymore!" she shot back. Mitt let out a soft meow. "See? Mitt agrees."

That was when he realized his mistake. "Huh."

"Cricket, seriously! What are you waiting for?" Her tone was full-on impatient now.

He plucked the object from her shoulder. "Why, Hazel James," he said, meeting her gaze, "intrepid traveler, bold adventurer and all-around fearless human—I did not know you were afraid of spiders?" He was very close now, mere inches separated their faces, and he couldn't help but think about kissing her. Anyone would, right?

"I'm not," she said. "I just like them better when they're not crawling on me."

He turned his palm up for her inspection.

Squinting, she peered closely. "Yeah, that's a piece of fuzz."

"I know." She glared at him, and he couldn't contain his laughter. "I swear, I thought it was a spider. You have to admit, it was a little bit funny how your eyes got big, and your voice went all high." Then he went on to imitate her very badly, "'Cricket, seriously!'"

"That is funny," she said, smiling and nodding appreciatively. "It's funny that you think that's what I sound like." Then her hand shot out, latched onto his fingers and squeezed. Hard.

"Ouch!" He belted out a laugh and placed his other hand over hers, trying to reduce the pressure. "Jeez, you've got a grip on you." At the same moment that she loosened her fingers, he stopped struggling, which left their hands all tangled together. They were still close, staring into each other's eyes, and he became aware of her rapid breathing and his own and... And maybe she wasn't quite as over him as she claimed?

He could find out, he reasoned, if he carried through with that kiss. Just one, to remind her what a kiss should be like, in case, as he suspected, the chemistry between her and Kai was lacking. That was literally the only thing on his mind. So focused was he on that train of thought that the sound of another person entering his home didn't even derail it.

Until his best friend strode into the room. "Hey, doorbell's not working and what's with—" The questions abruptly halted as Tag took in the scene, zeroing in on their hands, still entwined. "Oh."

Cricket glanced at Hazel. She grinned, and with them both chuckling softly, they untangled their fingers. Not guiltily, just deliberately. But still, Tag's gaze landed briefly on Hazel before his features morphed into a puzzled scowl that he directed at Cricket.

Cricket could see the question in his eyes, along with curiosity and maybe a hint of disapproval.

"Um, hi, guys," Tag said. "What's going on?"

"Spider on my arm," Hazel explained, now looking at Tag, seemingly unfazed by her brother's expression. "Cricket decided to let it spin a web before removing it from my shoulder, which I did not appreciate. I'm here re-turning Cricket's generator. Dad borrowed it."

"Power's out," Cricket added.

"Ah." Tag nodded slowly. " That explains why you're not answering your phone. Ashley has been calling. She even emailed."

"Yep, it's dead. Haven't even plugged it in yet. What's up?"

"Can you take a cargo flight for me today? Medical supplies—it's kind of urgent."

AT FIRST, HAZEL assumed Ashley was just doing her job by helping prepare for their flight the next day. After all, she worked for Tag here at Copper Crossing Air Transport. Because Iris had held the position of all-purpose employee before Ashley, Hazel knew the job involved a wide variety of tasks. Answering phones, scheduling flights, cleaning and preparing the planes, loading cargo, helping passengers board, and on it went. So, even when Ashley exited the office with a duffel bag hitched over one shoulder and a smaller satchel strung over the other, the alternative still did not occur to Hazel.

Hazel and Kai were standing in the pas-senger waiting zone, an area located beneath a covered patio right outside the lobby, adja-cent to the runway at Rankins's airfield. There were a couple of vending machines and several benches where travelers could enjoy a very cool view of the planes landing and taking off. Hazel imagined how well that would go over with tour clients.

Not to mention the stunning scenery. The morning air was crisp and cold, and the sun illuminated bright, clear skies with no threat of precipitation. Sparkling frost blanketed the grounds, and silver-tipped mountains glimmered in the distance. The two-day forecast, while not good for JB Heli-Ski, was perfect for the journey ahead.

Beside her, Kai was on his phone, cataloging Instagram hashtags for Our Alaska Tours' future promo possibilities. Hazel could not have been more pleased with either his creativity or his work ethic.

Nerves and excitement jostled for position inside of her. She and Cricket seemed to have conquered a major hurdle. Visiting his house had been almost therapeutic. They'd had fun. All signs suggested that they could have a friendly platonic relationship. Now, if only she could get her heart and her body in line with her brain.

There had been a moment with the fuzz-spider. When she'd grabbed his hand, the air had gone all heavy and intense. And the desire in his eyes, how he'd looked at her, had tied her in knots. But she'd been the one to touch him first, and even though she hadn't meant to be flirtatious, it had sort of turned into that.

Then Tag had shown up, and the connection had passed. Good timing, she told herself, before she did or said something stupid and things turned awkward. She couldn't expect her feelings to dissipate all at once just because she wanted them to, right? Right. So, in conclusion, *she'd* experienced certain sensations, but she refused to read more into them than that. No more projecting her reactions onto him.

Ashley stowed the bag in the plane and then sauntered over to join them. "Hi, Hazel. Nice to see you. How's it going?"

"Hello, Ashley," she answered politely. "Fine." She might not despise the woman any longer, but that didn't mean they were going to be friends.

"I hear you're home for the holidays this year?"

"Yep."

"Very nice. Tag said it's been a while."

"That is also true."

Ashley was eyeing Kai curiously, so Hazel performed a quick introduction. "Kai, this is

Ashley Frye. She works here. Ashley, this is Kai. He works with me."

They shook hands and began making small talk. Hazel studied the tentative schedule she'd come up with and tried to tune them out.

"Utah!" Ashley loudly exclaimed, startling her and redirecting her attention. "So beautiful there, right? Someday, I'd love to see all those canyons. Hazel did this post on her site a while back about this slot canyon. The walls are so high that you can barely see the sky when you look up. You're surrounded by all this red rock and phenomenal light and shadows. The colors are stunning."

Ashley followed her blog? Huh.

"We have tons of those," Kai said, and Ashley appeared enthralled as he went on to describe his favorites.

"So jealous!" she said when he'd finished. "The only other state I've ever visited is Hawaii. Went to Maui on my honeymoon."

"Well, you picked a good one. Hawaii is fabulous," Kai said. "Epic hiking there, too. And snorkeling."

"Unfortunately, my ex didn't want to leave the resort or get in the ocean. Afraid of jellyfish. Such a dud. Should have been my first clue, huh?" she said and then laughed at her own joke. Which, Hazel grudgingly but silently admitted, was kind of funny.

Peeling back her jacket sleeve, Ashley peered at the watch on her wrist and then gestured at the backpacks sitting on the bench beside them. "I should probably get your bags loaded. We'll be boarding in about seven minutes." Reaching out, she snagged Kai's pack, slung it behind her and slipped one strap over her shoulder.

"I can get that!" Kai protested.

"Don't worry," Ashley said brightly, brushing him off with a wave of one hand. "It's my job." She turned toward the airplane, and, tossing a grin at Hazel over her shoulder, she chirped, "I bet you never thought you'd have me tagging along on one of your adventures, did you, Hazel James? Even if it is just to Juneau."

Tagging along? Hazel blinked slowly. Before she could even form a question to clarify, Ashley was at the plane with Kai's bag.

Hazel thought fast. Did she have a right to be upset? How much of this reaction was due to her dislike of Ashley? And how much to the fact that she hadn't made arrangements for a fourth person? The logical assumption could be made that Cricket planned for Ashley to share his room, which pretty much answered the question that had been gnawing at her since she'd seen them at the Faraway Inn. Cricket and Ashley were a couple. Why hadn't he mentioned it?

Why did this bother her so much? Jealous, yes. She owned that. She was always jealous when she knew he was dating. The last time she'd come home for Christmas, she'd thought he was going to date her cousin Adele, and she'd ended up cutting her stay short. Thankfully, that relationship had fizzled before it ever got very far off the ground.

She tried to set her personal opinion aside. From a strictly professional standpoint, it was inconsiderate not to have filled her in on these plans.

Cricket pushed through the door behind them, picked up Hazel's pack and swept a hand toward the plane. "Everyone ready?"

"For sure," Kai said, still looking at his phone.

"Wrap it up, Montauk," he said bluntly, his tone not quite snappish. "Can't use your phone on my plane."

"Got it. I was just—"

He interrupted, "When you're finished, Ashley will walk you through our boarding and safety procedures."

And that was another thing—he didn't seem to care for Kai.

"Cricket," Hazel asked. "Can I talk to you for a second?"

CRICKET WAS IN a bad mood.

No matter how he tried to spin it in his mind, the days stretched out before him like an emotional gauntlet. Two days with Hazel and... *Date*. Hours and hours of traveling—spending time in close quarters, boat rides, car rides, meals, conversations. Between hearing them laugh and listening to their incessant "travel speak," it was like being tied down and bitten by a thousand mosquitoes. While the entire town scraped their nails on a giant chalkboard.

As wonderful as it had been at the time, he now likened her surprise visit to that stupid menu tasting. He didn't want a tiny piece of Hazel; he wanted all of her. And now here he was, forced to watch while someone else got what he wanted.

The only thing worse would be starting the trip off with a visit to Otter Falls Correctional Facility. Oh, that was right—he was!

Visiting his brother in prison was always depressing. But because he still hadn't been able to deposit money into Lee's account, that meant he'd likely be spending time in the administrative offices, as well.

But wait, there was more! Today he had the added thrill of escorting Ashley on her first visit to the facility. He'd been surprised when she'd approached him a couple of months ago and asked if he ever visited Lee. His brother's incarceration wasn't a topic he discussed. But he'd soon learned that Ashley's ex-husband, Roy, had been recently convicted of fraud and was also currently housed there. Roy had mentioned to Ashley that he'd met Lee.

For reasons that she didn't disclose, Ashley wanted to visit her ex, which had been the point of her inquiry. Cricket had helped her navigate the visitor approval process and then offered to take her with him on his next visit. Despite her determination and brave face, Cricket fully expected it to be an emotional experience.

Sure, Roy was a royal-class jerk, something Cricket knew all too well as he'd found Ashley an attorney when her ex had tried to bully her into lowering his child support payments. Tag, in a generous show of support, had paid her retainer. In the end, Roy's payments were significantly increased. Regardless, seeing someone incarcerated was shockingly difficult. Not to mention the man was also the father of her three children.

Caught up as he was in his own mental quagmire, he wasn't prepared for Hazel's reaction when he followed her inside Copper Crossing's small lobby. There was no one else inside, and when she spun around to face him, the set to her jaw, the lines of tension around her eyes suggested she was not in a good mood either.

"Why didn't you tell me Ashley was coming with us?"

"Oh, uh…" He raked a hand across his jaw. "I thought you two patched things up. Ashley said you were fine."

"'Patched things up'?" she repeated flatly. "Cricket, we didn't have some sort of *spat*. There's been a pattern of behavior on her part that… You know what? Never mind." She paused to inhale a breath. "I'm over what she did, yes, but that doesn't mean I want to be her travel buddy. And besides that, a simple heads-up would have been helpful."

"I didn't mean to…" He wasn't sure how to explain without revealing Ashley's personal business. "Is this a problem?"

"Um, no, not really. I just wish you would have asked me first."

"Well, technically, Ashley was the one I needed to ask."

"What?"

"Remember when Bering pointed out how I was flying to Juneau today anyway?"

"Yes," she said with a scowl before her features transformed to wide-eyed understanding. "*Ohh*... You and Ashley already had this planned. Kai and I are the ones commandeering *your* trip."

"Correct, but—"

"No," she said, bringing a hand up, palm out in an apologetic gesture. "You know what? I'm sorry. You can invite whoever you want wherever you want to invite them. Besides, it's your airplane."

"I'm sorry, too. And I appreciate you being so cool with it. I probably should have given you a heads-up. It's just that I've had a lot on my mind. And I did need to talk it over with Ashley first. Make sure she was okay with bringing other people along with us. If you knew the situation, you'd understand how difficult this is for her." Shaking his head, he added, "That's cryptic and annoying, isn't it? What I'm trying to say is that she's going through something very personal right now."

"Say no more. It's not my business." She nodded and added a smile. Sort of a smile, he realized, noting it was more of a lip-curling that didn't reach her eyes. "I'm glad she's, um, okay. So, that settles it, then. I guess we better get going." With that, she pushed through the doors and marched toward the plane.

CHAPTER TEN

ANOTHER BONUS, HAZEL silently acknowledged, about flying in a plane this small was that it required headphones to communicate comfortably, making it easy not to talk if you didn't want to. And, right now, that was what she preferred. Not talking. Or listening. With her headset tucked into the forward seat back, she pretended to study a book about the history of Alaska's gold rush, which she'd already read but had brought along for reference purposes.

Surprising how much Cricket and Ashley bothered her. But on a positive note, this settled it. Sealed it tight, in fact. Once again, she'd been confusing chemistry with emotion when she'd misinterpreted the moment at his house. And now she got to spend two days watching him with the woman he actually wanted. Tears pooled in her eyes, and she turned to stare out the window into the blur of clouds. How was she going to get through this? These were going to be the longest two days of her life.

Thankfully, the flight was short, albeit a bit

bumpy. Cricket nailed the landing. They disembarked, gathered their bags and headed to the parking lot, where they soon gathered together. An uncharacteristically subdued Ashley stood close to Cricket, looking pale and possibly unwell.

"Ashley, are you okay?" Hazel asked because she couldn't help but be concerned.

Ashley flinched, probably surprised by the question. Hazel couldn't blame her. It was likely the first time she'd ever gone out of her way to talk to the woman where they weren't on a crash course to a confrontation.

"Oh, um, yeah, just a queasy stomach." She flattened a hand to her abdomen.

Motion sickness, Hazel assumed, further stirring her sympathy. She suffered from that herself on occasion and always carried these certain candies she'd discovered in Switzerland for that very reason. Digging one out of her pocket, she offered it to Ashley. "Try one of these. Peppermint and ginger. Nothing settles the stomach better."

"Thank you, Hazel," Ashley said, accepting the lozenge with a weak smile. "That's very kind."

Cricket caught her gaze, and she saw approval and what looked like more than affection. He held it for a beat, and there it was—that too-familiar, disconcerting buzz. Nope, she told herself, breaking eye contact. Didn't mean anything.

She said, "I ordered a car to take us downtown. Our boat leaves for Gold Bend in an hour. Exploring there will take all morning. When we get back, we'll show Kai around Juneau, let him get the layout and a sense of the place, and then start looking at potential lodgings—"

"Uh, hold up a sec, Hazel," Cricket interrupted. "You two go ahead without us. Ashley and I have plans. I've been to Gold Bend many times, and I trust your judgment. Kerry will be there to meet your boat. He'll help you out, answer all your questions. I'll text you later this afternoon, and we'll meet up."

Then he looked at Ashley. "Ready?" he asked softly, and the expression he turned on her was filled with so much tenderness, Hazel decided she needed a candy, too.

GOLD BEND WAS nothing short of awesome. Both Hazel and Kai agreed with Cricket and Bering that it should be a part of the tour. As promised, their friend Kerry was welcoming and informative. After showing them around, he introduced them to the Inn at Gold Bend's owner, who was enthusiastic about their plans.

The excursion was a complete success, and

Hazel and Kai were back in Juneau by late afternoon. She still hadn't heard from Cricket, so they grabbed a late lunch of crispy, tender-flaky halibut fish sandwiches and piping-hot, perfectly seasoned onion rings. Feeling rather miffed after checking her phone yet again, Hazel tried not to let it show. A stirring of guilt followed when she imagined how Cricket must have felt when she was in Utah and out of touch.

She and Kai set out on a walking tour, where she focused on absorbing the magic that was Juneau. Between the lights, the creative displays and the cheerful shop windows, it was impossible not to embrace a bit of the holiday spirit.

Afterward, they wandered through shops filled with unique handcrafted items. Hazel found a perfect necklace for Shay and a stuffed orca whale for Lily that was so cute she'd probably end up giving it to her before Christmas. She bought a gorgeous keepsake box with an inlaid salmon on top for Victoria's daughter, Scarlett, a twelve-year-old sweetheart who could already fish almost as well as her mom and Seth.

Hazel was so focused on her musings that it took a while for her to realize Kai was less than his usual energetic self, too.

"What do you think of this?" he asked about a finely knit wool scarf in a lovely sea-green color that reminded her of Cricket's eyes.

"Very pretty," she said.

"You think it's too feminine?"

"Uh, that depends. For your mom? Or Emma?"

"Ugh, no. *Pretty* is not what I'm going for here."

"Hold up," she said, noting the distress on his face and realizing what was likely going on. "Is this a Secret Santa gift?"

"Yes." He let out a little groan. "This is harder than I thought it would be. Even with your mom's advice, I'm struggling."

"You want to tell me who you have, and I can help?"

Expression twisting with uncertainty, he admitted, "I do, but I don't want to get into trouble."

"You think Mom is going to find out and put us in Christmas jail?"

He chuckled. "Good point."

"My mom is all about Christmas happiness. You know her charity is literally called Operation Happy Christmas, right? I promise that if Mom knew this was causing you even a smidgen of angst, she would want me to help. This is supposed to be about spreading joy, and I can tell you whoever has my name has already made me ridiculously happy. And spoiling my person is turning out to be just as fun. This whole thing is making me feel like a kid again, which is the point, right?"

"Okay." He added a sigh. "You make an excellent case. I have Cricket, which I thought would be easier because, you know, I'm around him and stuff. But he doesn't talk that much at the office. Plus, he's so... I don't want to say *grumpy*, so I'll go with *serious*." Shifting on his feet, he looked away for a second before forging ahead. "This is kind of embarrassing, but I think it's me. I can tell he doesn't like me very much, and that adds to the pressure."

"It's not that he doesn't like you." Was it? She didn't know because she, too, had noticed his behavior where Kai was concerned. Either way, it wasn't like Cricket. He could be reserved, for sure, but he was always cordial and kind. If Kai had picked up on it, she was going to have to talk to Cricket.

In the meantime, she could do this for Kai, help him be a kick-butt Secret Santa for Cricket. And, truthfully, it would be fun to make Cricket happy, too. She knew she could make him happier than Ashley could if only he would... Okay, enough with the going off on the Ashley tangent.

Determination stirring inside of her, she

looked at Kai. "Cricket can be hard to read, but he's surprisingly easy to buy for because he has tons of cool hobbies and is interested in lots of things. But you can put the scarf down—he doesn't wear wool."

"Ugh." Kai groaned and slapped his forehead. "I got him wool socks for his first gift. No wonder he hates me."

"He didn't even know it was you! How could he hate you?" Hazel reassured him and meant it because there was no way Cricket could hate someone as nice as Kai. "Come on, I have a few suggestions."

HE'D BEEN ONLY nine years old, but Cricket distinctly remembered the first time he'd visited his father in prison. First, there'd been the long journey of traveling to the facility. Which proved to be nothing compared to the ordeal of getting through security.

He'd never even seen a metal detector before that day, didn't understand the purpose. All he knew was that he'd had to remove his favorite belt to walk through the towering arch, and then a harried-looking man had hovered over him with a strange beeping flashlight, which he now knew was a metal detector of the handheld variety. But as a child, he'd felt like he'd done something wrong himself, and he'd been terrified.

Next came "the tunnel"—that was how Lee had described the seemingly endless hallway beforehand, and how Cricket would forever think of it—with its series of doors clicking open and then snapping shut behind him. Once through the tunnel, he was inundated with the clanking sounds of metal on metal, echoing footsteps and the acrid, antiseptic odors that burned his nose and throat.

That was when it had hit him. He was trapped. The room spun, and the walls closed in around him. He barely remembered the visit. All he could think about was how badly his lungs ached and how much he needed air. Afterward, it had taken Lee months to convince Cricket the sensation wasn't real. Nightmares plagued him, and he'd awaken in the middle of the night, tightly twisted in his blankets, thrashing and choking on nothing.

Trauma, shock, claustrophobia—he didn't even know how to describe the experience. No matter what the experts called it, he and Lee had vowed that they'd never end up there.

Lee had broken his vow. Multiple times. And while Cricket had overcome his debilitating fear, the undertaking was never pleasant. But today, he discovered that there was something worse than visiting Lee in prison: arriving for a visit and finding that he wasn't there.

"My brother has been released?" Cricket asked the question even though the official behind the sheet of Plexiglas had already confirmed this information. Twice.

"Yes. Ten days ago."

That explained the problems with the commissary account. Why hadn't Cricket thought of that possibility? "I didn't even know he was being considered," he said, answering his own silent musing. "Can you tell me where he is?" he asked, knowing this was a pointless question, too.

"Sorry." The man shrugged. "No."

Not that it would do much good even if he could. Lee had no home, no permanent address, preferring instead to drift from town to town, often staying with acquaintances, sometimes temporarily renting an apartment, room, trailer or cabin. Cricket frequently received mail for him. No doubt he'd gone to a friend's place to camp on a sofa until he could save enough to get back on his feet.

As an experienced mechanic, he had little trouble finding work. Unlike their father, Lee was smart enough to never steal from his employers, and thus, even with his record, he always had excellent references.

Cricket journeyed back to the parking lot to wait for Ashley and ponder the aspect that bothered him the most. Why hadn't Lee told him he was getting released? Best-case scenario, he hadn't known himself until the last minute and didn't want to put Cricket out. Worst-case scenario, he was planning something and didn't want Cricket to know.

His phone vibrated with a text. From Hazel:

Hey, any idea what time you'll show up at the hotel? Thinking about making a dinner reservation. How about that steak you've been craving?

Nope. No way. He could not do it tonight. He had his limits. With Lee's unexplained disappearance on his mind, he couldn't sit through another dinner with those two and act like it didn't bother him, not even for the promise of a rib eye.

He tapped out a response: Not sure yet. Go without me. And then, with his reluctant fingers hovering above the keyboard, he forced himself to add Have fun.

HAZEL WAS UP early the next morning. They'd agreed to meet in the lobby of the boutique hotel where they'd spent the night. Anxious and unsettled, she headed downstairs early and was surprised to discover Cricket seated in the cozy lounge next to the lobby. Long legs stretched out before him in the dark leather club chair. He was staring into the glowing flames burning in the massive stone fireplace, looking contemplative and so handsome that it made her ache.

She fetched a coffee and a donut from the complimentary bar and joined him. "Good morning," she said brightly. Nibbling on her donut, she felt exceedingly proud of her cheerful tone.

He looked up and gave her a small smile. "Good morning to you."

"Missed you at dinner last night." She took a seat in the chair across from him.

"Sorry about that. We got tied up."

"How was your day?"

"Not great."

"I'm sorry," she returned, wondering how that could possibly be true. She waited for him to elaborate. Wasn't surprised when he didn't.

"Did you guys get some scouting done? What did you think of Gold Bend?"

"We did." Glancing around, she added, "It went well. Gold Bend is fabulous. All you guys described and more—easy boat ride, fascinating history, interesting sights. And that scenery—

wow. The lodge is also perfect. Kai and I are totally on the same page."

"Why am I not surprised?"

She peered at him, trying to decide if she'd heard a sliver of sarcasm in his tone. Unsure, she added, "Would have been nice to have your opinion, too, though. Where's Ashley?" she asked, mostly to remind him why he hadn't been there to provide one.

He absently glanced around. "I don't know. Probably upstairs. She missed her flight back to Rankins and had to stay over."

"Missed her flight?" she repeated. "I didn't know she was supposed to fly back yesterday."

"Yes. Didn't I mention that?" He sighed. "She was supposed to hop on a Copper Crossing flight yesterday afternoon. But like I said, we were delayed, and she missed it."

"Is everything okay? Did you guys…?"

"Did we what?"

Gah. She hated how she didn't know what the boundaries were here. Was it too much to ask about his dating life? Did she even want to know? But she cared about him, and she could see that something was bothering him.

"Did you guys have a fight?" she asked. What kind of a person did it make her that she wanted the answer to be yes?

"A fight?" he repeated sharply, confusion

knitting his brow. Then, after a drawn-out moment, his features softened along with his tone. "Hazel, do you think that Ashley and I are a couple?"

"You're not?"

"No. We…" His lips flirted with a smile. "Ashley and I are not dating. Never have, never will. She is not my type."

Then his gaze traveled over her, and she felt her neck go hot. The look was back. And this time, she was very close to calling him out on it. But what would she say? *You're looking at me with that certain expression that makes me feel funny in a way that I like. But I need you to stop because it makes it harder to get over you. Oh, yeah, I lied when I said I was over you.* She was beginning to think this was impossible. Not to mention, why *was* Ashley here, then, if not to be with Cricket?

"But I saw you last Sunday night at the inn, in the restaurant…" Her eyebrows drifted up, urging him to fill in the blank.

"Soo…?"

"Cricket, she kissed you."

"What are you…?" He shook his head as if trying to recall the moment. "Oh. That."

"Yeah, *that*."

Chuckling, he finished the thought. "Was a

friendly thank-you type kiss. You know how… demonstrative Ashley can be."

She did know.

With gorgeous green eyes full of sincerity, he said, "Listen, Hazel, even if I were interested in her, which I am not, I would never do that to you, or to Iris, for that matter. Or make things difficult for Seth. Your mom doesn't care for her either, by the way."

That made her smile a little. "I know. Mom always says that she can forgive, but that doesn't mean she has to forget. I think I get that from her."

"I think you do, too."

"You know what? It's a relief that you two aren't together." That was a severe understatement. She was trying to tamp down the elation, reminding herself that it wasn't like he was redirecting his affection toward her instead.

"Is it?" he asked, and she could not read his stony expression.

"Yes!" she gushed, realized how that sounded, and then quickly qualified, "Because, well, you know, like you said, it might be weird for our family."

"I see," he said, his eyes searching hers. Then he looked down at his empty cup, swirled it around. "Making things difficult for your family is the last thing I would ever want to do."

That still left the question of what in the world he and Ashley had been doing together all day. And why he seemed so broody. She was about to ask when Kai appeared in the doorway.

"Hey, team!" he called, lifting a hand and coming over to join them. "Everyone is up and around. I just saw Ashley in the dining area, finishing her breakfast. Here I thought I was early, and it looks like I'm late."

MINUTES LATER, ASHLEY joined them, and Cricket had to admit that, selfishly, he wasn't disappointed that she'd missed her flight. Now he wouldn't have to be the irritable third wheel, watching Kai interact with Hazel for the entire day.

A snafu with Ashley's paperwork had delayed her visit with Roy for several hours. There were only two commercial flights out of Juneau to Anchorage, and the last one had been full. Catching this morning's flight meant a long layover that would have only delivered her home a few hours quicker than if she waited and went back with them.

She'd been a good sport about staying over, cheerfully informing him that she always traveled with a few essential toiletries—spare underwear, socks and a tube of mascara. They'd stopped at a store so she could get the rest of what she'd needed for a comfortable night. Cricket had given her the option of hanging out on her own today, but she'd chosen to spend the time helping them scout locations, which he also appreciated.

Hazel looked up from the list she'd been studying and said, "Kai and I toured several of these lodging options yesterday afternoon and evening, so we're confident that we are looking for the same things. What does everyone think about splitting up into pairs to check out the rest? If we divide these remaining places, we can probably finish by late afternoon."

"Works for me," Kai said.

"Sure," Ashley agreed.

Cricket nodded. Worked for him, too.

"Great," she said, producing a pen and making little marks on the map she held. "We'll plan on meeting for a bite somewhere around noon or one, depending on how things go. We'll figure out the where later." She handed Kai the paper.

"Sounds like a plan," Kai said and flashed Cricket an easy smile. "We'll get it done. Even if we do have one more on our list than you."

Wait... Why was he looking at Cricket like that? Surely, Hazel didn't mean for Cricket to hang out with him all day?

Hazel answered, "Just text if you guys are

running late, which you probably will be because you insist on checking out a place that I already know will be a dud." She was obviously teasing Kai, and Cricket realized he was witnessing another of their inside jokes. The ones that made him want to lock Kai in the supply closet without the phone that he seemed to love more than Hazel. Maddening.

Hazel flashed an encouraging smile at Ashley. "And, Ashley, thank you for helping us out. Don't be afraid to speak your mind. Kai will explain what we're aiming for here. But your opinion is extremely valuable to us, so feel free to point out any little thing, good or bad."

Cricket felt his irritation melting slightly because Hazel's kindness toward Ashley was endearing.

"You got it!" Ashley responded enthusiastically. "Although, everything is going to look like a palace after spending all day at the prison yesterday, right?" she joked.

"Prison?" Kai looked completely confused.

"Where?" Hazel asked at the same time.

Ashley looked at Cricket. "You didn't tell them?"

"No way, Ashley. That's your business."

Her expression transformed with gratitude. "You are, like, the nicest person—do you know that?" She reached out and squeezed his arm. To Kai, she said, "Cricket took me to Otter Creek Correctional Facility to see my ex-husband, Roy. He's locked up there, and I had some things that I needed to say to him."

"I am so sorry, Ashley," Kai said, radiating sincerity. Cricket instantly liked him better for it. "That must have been rough."

"I'm sorry, too, Ashley," Hazel said. "I had no idea."

"Thank you, guys." Ashley nodded. "I appreciate the support. It was not fun." Blinking rapidly, she mustered a smile. "So, now I am ready to go do something constructive and take my mind off it. Let's go critique some hotels!" She raised her arms as if victorious.

They all laughed.

Then Hazel looked at him. "Cricket, you're with me. Ready?"

"Sure," he said. And just like that, his day got a whole lot better.

CHAPTER ELEVEN

WITH HAPPINESS FLUTTERING inside of her, Hazel practically skipped along the sidewalk next to Cricket as she absorbed the morning's revelations. Cricket and Ashley were not *together*. She knew her relief was excessive, but she didn't care.

Sympathy for Ashley was mixed in there, too, and she felt the need to clarify a few details. "You took Ashley to see her ex-husband in prison yesterday? That's what this whole thing was about for her. It also explains where you were all day yesterday, and why you weren't helping us, and why you didn't want to tell us."

"Uh, let's see… Yes, to all."

"I thought you—" She abruptly halted her thought in midsentence. "You genuinely are a good person—you know that?"

"That's kind of you to say, but I'm just glad I finally got to put all my prison experience to good use," he joked.

"How did you even know her ex was there? Did Lee tell you?"

"It's a long story, but it was kind of the opposite." He explained about Roy inquiring about Lee and everything that came after. "Eventually, I offered to bring her to Otter Creek with me. I was supposed to see Lee yesterday, too."

"What do you mean, you were supposed to? What happened?"

"When I got there, I found out he'd been released."

"Released? When? Why wouldn't he have told you?"

"Ten days ago, and I don't know."

Hazel was curious about this, too. That photo of Lee had her thinking. She didn't want to be intrusive, but she also wanted to be supportive. "Is that unusual for him? Not to let you know where he is?"

"Yes, it is. He moves around a lot. We'll go weeks or maybe even a month at a time without talking, but he always lets me know. Gives me a phone number. I called a few of his buddies that I had contact information for, got through to one voice mail. Left a message. Also left a message for his ex-girlfriend, Toni."

"I'm so sorry."

"Don't be sorry. I accepted a long time ago that this is how it is. I'm sure I'll hear from him eventually. Right now, I agree with Ashley—ready to get my mind off it." He halted in front of a two-story green building with white trim. A dapper-looking snowman stood next to the hotel's sign, complete with a top hat, plaid scarf and a carved walking stick. "Is this the place?"

NEARING LUNCHTIME, HAZEL and Cricket had toured all the lodging options on their list. Their top two choices were the same, although they had them in the opposite order. Hazel suggested they find out Kai's and Ashley's favorite picks at lunch, and then the four of them could tour the top three or four together.

But then Kai texted, raving about Duke's Pine Lodge. Good news, he added, they had a restaurant, too, and could Hazel and Cricket meet him and Ashley there for lunch? They agreed. Since the lodge was located a few miles outside town, Hazel ordered a ride, and they were soon on the way.

At first glance, she had to agree that the modest-size log cabin nestled among a pretty stand of trees on the edge of a small lake appeared idyllic. As they got closer, she could see the groomed surface with ice-skaters enjoying the day.

Adding to the lodge's list of pros was the beautiful picnic area with a gazebo near the water's edge. Hiking trails led into the nearby hills. The sign said that one path ended at a scenic waterfall. In the summer, they had kayaks, canoes and fishing gear on hand for the guests to enjoy. Snowshoes, skates and cross-country skis were available in the winter.

Duke's had all the amenities they were after plus more, including two hot tubs, a sauna and a small but state-of-the-art fitness center. The stylishly decorated interior reflected the latest in country chic. Several cozy sitting areas were designated where guests could read, sip a drink or enjoy the scenery. There was even a "wildlife viewing station" complete with two high-powered spotting scopes mounted on tripods.

After a good long look around, she had to agree with Kai's assessment; the place was perfect. They spoke to the owner, who was also the manager, and she seemed eager to work out an arrangement for their tour groups. Hazel promised to be in touch with details.

She took a moment to revel in their success in Juneau. Between this place and the Inn at Gold Bend, they were set with lodging for the most critical portions of what they'd tentatively dubbed the Coastal Gold Tour.

"Nice call, you," Hazel said to Kai, reaching out for a fist bump.

"Thanks," he replied humbly. "I almost took your advice and skipped it."

"Good thing you didn't." To Cricket, she explained, "I didn't think we needed to look at this place. Juneau is so charming and fun that I thought we'd want something within walking distance of downtown. But Kai insisted on adding this place to his list."

"The Peace & Quiet Hotel would have worked, too," Cricket said. His gaze meandered around like he wasn't as impressed as she knew he was.

"Not as well as this place," she felt the need to point out. Because poor Kai, she thought, trying so hard to impress the boss who seemed determined to be indifferent. She needed to find out what Cricket's problem was where Kai was concerned.

"Mmm. Maybe," he said noncommittally. "Let's eat."

They enjoyed a delicious celebratory lunch in the dining room, which was as charming as the rest of the establishment, decorated with local artwork in an attractive mix of watercolor paintings, metal sculptures and mixed-media prints. All of it with a hip Alaska vibe.

Their server, a friendly, efficient young man Hazel estimated to be in his early twenties, approached their table with a dessert menu. "So,

I highly recommend the Klondike blondie with the apple-butter sauce or the mountain moose chocolate cake. *Or*, if you folks are the adventurous types, you could try our hot spiced skate?"

"Your what?" Ashley asked.

With a dramatic sweep of one arm toward the lake, he said, "We'll give you a to-go cup of our hot spiced cider, a giant snickerdoodle cookie and a skate rental. Superfun!"

Ashley's face broke into a grin. "That's funny. Kai and I were just talking about ice-skating. He loves skating but hasn't been in forever. And I never get to skate anymore without kids."

"I messed around with it a bit when I was younger. Had a few lessons," Kai revealed. "I'm not bad."

Waggling her brows, Ashley looked from Hazel to Cricket and back again. "We finished our scouting early, right? So, we can spare an hour or so? What do you guys say, four of the hot spiced skates?"

"Works for me," Hazel agreed. Why not have a little fun while they were here?

LIKE MOST PEOPLE he knew, Cricket enjoyed ice-skating. Like most of the men, and plenty of the ladies, he'd grown up with, he preferred doing it with a hockey stick in his hand and someone to bodycheck. But after spending the day with Hazel, his spirits were high, and he certainly wasn't going to be a killjoy. Especially since Hazel was an excellent skater; she'd even taken figure-skating lessons when she was young.

And even though he knew it wasn't the most selfless motivation in the world, he relished the notion of being better at it than Kai. Hazel's blatant attempts to prop the guy up were grating on his nerves.

He'd just sat down to put on his skates when his phone began to vibrate with an incoming call. He dug into his pocket for his phone. Hazel was beside him, tying her laces. Kai and Ashley were seated on the next bench over, sipping hot cider and chatting like old friends.

Despite what he'd told Hazel, Cricket was concerned about Lee. He couldn't help it. There'd been plenty of times during Cricket's childhood when his brother had been there for him. To scrounge up money for a pair of shoes, fix a hot meal or help him with homework.

Later, when Cricket was trying to make it on his own, Lee would, miraculously, after being gone for weeks, show up with groceries or rent money. Doing the best he could with the example he'd had, which wasn't much. Lee hadn't had a friend like Tag or a family like the Jameses to support him. He'd had only Frank Blackburn to rely on, and Cricket believed he would have been better off with nothing.

That was why when he saw the unknown number, he said, "I'm going to take this in case it's Lee."

"No problem," Hazel said. "We'll meet you on the ice."

It wasn't Lee. But it was Lee's ex-girlfriend Toni, who informed him that Lee owed her two hundred dollars and had promised to fix her car. But she missed him, and so did her dog, Jellybean; she had a box full of his mail, and did Cricket know where the keys were to the camper he'd left on her property?

When Toni paused for a breath, Cricket managed to ask a few questions of his own. None of her lengthy answers proved helpful, but she seemed like a nice woman, and he assured her that he'd pass on her message. He ended the call and headed back toward the pond.

Just in time to see Hazel gliding toward Kai at lightning speed. Angled slightly away, Kai appeared unconcerned. Did he even see her?

Fear grabbed hold of him and squeezed like a vise. *"Haze, Haz-zel, Haze-el,"* he murmured, hurrying toward the pond, but his skates were bulky. Slow. She and Kai were too far away.

Too far to even hear him shout. He couldn't get there. For several eternity-mimicking seconds, he felt as though his heart had stopped. He braced himself for the inevitable collision…

But then, in a graceful, fluid motion, Kai reached toward Hazel, she flew up into the air and… And that's when Cricket realized what was happening. A figure-skating lift. A few lessons, huh? That freaking…*Date*!

Kai hoisted Hazel high above his head and spun a tight circle. Like a pro, he set her gently back onto the ice, and hand in hand, smiling like a pair of, well, *figure skaters*, they cut a wide, sweeping arc. Then they rolled out a series of fluid dance steps, ending with another spin that had them all coiled together.

Finally, Kai wrapped an arm around Hazel's shoulders, squeezed her toward him and then turned, skating backward, and slowly pulled her into a hug, floating gracefully across the ice the entire time. The crowd clapped and whistled and cheered. They took a bow.

Cricket stood, immobile yet shaken. Some sort of switch turned off inside of him, or on, or possibly it short-circuited? Whatever. It had him turning around and heading back to the bench. Bending at the knees, he sat, then leaned over and placed his forearms on his thighs. Breathing deeply, he tried to recover.

Unsuccessfully. He couldn't do this. Removing his skates, he put on his boots and returned to the lodge to wait. To think.

Stew. Fret. Agonize.

Only in retrospect did he realize that probably wasn't the wisest course of action.

WHEN A HALF hour passed since his phone call and Cricket still hadn't appeared, Hazel grew concerned. Eventually, after looking everywhere outside, she swapped her skates for her boots and finally found him inside the lodge. Seated in the Moose Lounge, one of the lodge's viewing areas, he looked pale and troubled as he frowned out the window.

He didn't move as she approached and took a seat across from him. "Hey, everything all right? You disappeared on us. Did you get some bad news about Lee?"

Setting his face to blank, he looked up at her and answered with a soft, "Yeah. No, I'm fine. No news."

"You don't look fine. I know I told you I wouldn't ask about your feelings anymore." She tried to make it sound light, but something was wrong, and she couldn't stay quiet. "But this is me asking as a friend. Are you okay?"

He stared hard at her for a few long seconds, and now Hazel could see the tension radiating from every inch of his six-foot-three-inch frame. But she couldn't figure out what any of it meant.

Finally, he spoke, his voice husky and fraught. "Hazel, please, I am really trying here."

"Trying?" she repeated. "What does that mean? Cricket, you are acting strangely. Like one minute you're…you. And the next, you're all grumpy and surly. And are you aware that you are not nice to Kai?"

After grinding out a bitter laugh, he said, "I am as nice to him as I can be."

"Did he do something that I'm not aware of?"

He shook his head and sighed. "I don't know how else to say this, so I'm just going to. I can't do this anymore. I know it's not fair. I know I asked you here and that I said you could hire whoever you wanted, but this isn't working."

"What isn't working? What are you talking about?"

"I'm talking about you and Kai. Specifically, Kai as our employee. Your coworker. You need to fire him."

"Cricket." Further speech failed her, and for several seconds they stared at each other. When he didn't elaborate, she said, "You cannot be serious? He's doing an excellent job.

We've already accomplished so much. I don't know if you understand how hard he works, how many hours we've both put into this venture already. Not to mention that he's trying very hard to impress you."

"Oh," he said, voice laden with sarcasm, "is that what the ice-skating bit was about out there? Impressing *me*? He couldn't have simply skated by himself? Was it about putting his hands all over you?"

Hazel opened her mouth, closed it again. He was *jealous*? Of Kai?

Silently, he focused on her again. His gaze narrowed like he was thinking, but she recognized the look for what it was—an attempt to gain control of his emotions. Shutting down, in other words, like he so often did. Frustration surged through her. She wanted to push him for answers, ask him, beg him to talk to her. She'd promised him she wouldn't do that anymore, but that couldn't apply now, could it?

But then something strange happened. A shift, a change, a clarity transformed his expression.

Nodding slowly, he said, "You asked me ten years ago to tell you how I felt. You asked me in Colombia, and then again in Florida. And each time, I told you I couldn't. That's because I knew if I said the words, it would change everything. But I just realized something… Do you *really* want to know how I feel, Hazel?"

What was happening here? Her chest had grown so tight with anxiety that her answer came out a whispered, "Yes."

"Okay. Fine. Here goes. I know you said that you are over me, and clearly, that is the case. Unfortunately, I'm not over you. All those hours he gets to spend with you. *He* gets to make you smile and laugh and give you all the compliments that I want to give. He gets to—" He broke off the rest of his sentence with a frustrated scoff. "The scenarios are endless, and they keep me up at night. But in all of them, every single one, I want it to be *me*.

"The rational part of my brain reassures me that he's perfect for you. Reminds me how happy I should be that you've found someone you want to date."

Found someone? He thought she was *dating* Kai? Why would he…? That was when it dawned on her. *Date.* That word illuminated in her mind like an old-time movie marquee. She'd told him that very thing in Utah, that Kai was her date. But never clarified any further. At the moment, she'd liked the idea of him thinking she was on a date. But then Kai had shown up in Rankins for the job. Without her ever mentioning the status of their relationship.

Cricket looked pained as he went on, "I can see that he's a good guy, although I'm not sure he truly knows you. Not as well as he should. But that's not my business either." He raked a hand through his already mussed hair, thinking, struggling, maybe, to stay on task.

"My point is *that* part of my brain is no longer working properly. No matter how much I want it to, it cannot override how I feel. Because I am not happy. I am *miserable*. That's why I find fault with everything he does. I despise the poor guy. I know that's not logical, but that doesn't seem to matter. I've reached the point where it's either him or me—and since the company is half mine, I can't be the one to quit, can I?"

Hazel was too shocked to respond. Wide-eyed, limbs frozen, all she could do was stare. For ten years, she'd wanted him to talk, to be honest with her about how he felt. Why was he saying all of this now?

He cleared that up next. "The ironic thing is that I feel like I can say all of this now because you *are* involved with him. Like your relationship gives me the freedom to finally be honest. And I want you to be happy, Hazel. I do. Please, believe me when I tell you that. I just don't want to *see* you being happy with him anymore."

"Cricket," she murmured. "That's..."

"Messed-up, I know," he finished for her. "Now do you see how emotionally twisted I am? Do you understand why I've never talked about this? I could never say the words because... Because I couldn't do anything about it."

He brought one hand up and formed a fist in the center of his chest. "But you own my heart, Hazel. I want you to know that. That's why I don't have relationships. How can I give my heart to someone else when it already belongs to you? Ever since that summer, long before we ever kissed, I knew. I had guilt about that, too. Wanting to be with my best friend's sister, hiding my feelings from everyone—even you."

A rush of heat flooded through her. She was right. She'd been right all along. She was elated. And yet... What to do about it? He'd admitted that he'd confessed only because he believed she was in a relationship.

She wasn't sure what to do. But she knew one thing; she'd waited ten years for this day, for him to finally admit that he cared about her in this way. This was above and beyond what she'd even hoped for. No chance would she let another ten go by before... Before what?

If she responded now, she'd tell him how *she* felt. She'd tell him the truth about her and Kai. And she'd tell him she loved him. But then he'd retreat again. So, instead, she did the only thing she could think to do that would prevent any of those scenarios from happening.

"Well, okay, then," she somehow managed, slapping her hands on the tops of her thighs and pushing to her feet. "That explains a lot. Thank you for telling me." And then she walked out the door.

CHAPTER TWELVE

THERE WAS NO doubt in Hazel's mind that Cricket would reconsider firing Kai once he learned they weren't dating. The problem was, she wasn't sure she wanted to tell him. Not yet, anyway. She needed time to think this through.

Before she'd even made it back outside, her phone chimed with a text from Cricket.

I'm sorry. I'm a selfish jerk. Don't fire him.

Relief rushed through her—relief and respect because he was so... He always did the right thing, even when it was difficult. She loved that about him, even if it was, as she was beginning to suspect, the very thing that had kept them apart all these years.

She responded immediately: Thank you. You are the least selfish person I know. Can we talk soon? After we get home.

Yes.

Now she just needed to figure out what to say. How to convince him they belonged together.

Something she pondered the entire way home. Thankfully, Ashley and Kai held up the conversation, and if they noticed she and Cricket were quiet, they didn't mention it. A short plane ride wasn't near enough time to make sense of the last ten years.

She couldn't even begin to decide how to move forward, but she had to try. Because no matter how she turned the conversation over in her mind, she could not see a way where Cricket hadn't confessed his love for her. A huge part of her was overjoyed, but another part was more confused than ever. As the hours passed, her anxiety only increased. She felt like she had an opportunity here, but no concept of how to best capitalize on it.

Mother Nature granted her a brief respite. That night, only hours after they arrived back in Rankins, the frozen skies finally opened. A massive two-day pileup of snow clogged streets, driveways, pathways and parking lots, briefly crimped work schedules and inconvenienced plans.

The weather system also dumped tons of snow in the mountains. Good news for both Snowy Sky Ski Resort and JB Heli-Ski. Bad news for baking day, which was put on hold. Hazel spent the day alternately contemplating her options, texting Iris and Seth—whose flight home had been delayed—reading the new ebook from her Secret Santa, snacking and catnapping with Mica.

The next morning, the snow was still falling but in a far less frantic, must-bury-the-world type of way. These were big fat lazy flakes that you could watch drift and dance for hours and never get bored. Curl-up-and-watch-a-Christmas-movie-by-a-crackling-fire-with-a-bottomless-mug-of-hot-chocolate weather. White-Christmas weather. Definitely not agonize-over-what-to-do-about-a-guy-because-you-have-nothing-but-time-on-your-hands weather.

Then again, if your name was Margaret "Happy Christmas" James, you would declare a snowstorm "optimal candy-making conditions."

"This is perfect," she announced, bustling around the kitchen gathering ingredients. "We'll get a jump on the treat making. Candy takes up so much counter space and a huge chunk of time. We'll be done before the roads clear enough for everyone else to get here to do the cookies." Baking day would recommence in a few hours, and Hazel looked forward to the house filling with family.

Now she stirred the syrupy mixture on the stovetop and marveled over the brilliance of her mom's plan. The smell alone was a comfort. And it felt good to be moving. To be doing something constructive, instead of wallowing in nervous indecision. Plus, it gave her time to ask her mom one of the many questions on her mind.

"Mom, do you remember when Cricket was a little kid and his brother, Lee, got sent to the detention center?"

"Yes, I certainly do."

"His dad was in prison, right? When Lee was sent away? Where did Cricket go?"

Margaret, who was busy spreading butter on the sheet pans, looked confused for a second as if considering the question. "He didn't go anywhere. He stayed here."

"Here?" Hazel repeated. "You mean he lived with us?"

"Well, technically, you weren't born yet, but yes, he did. I'll never forget that day, going to the church to pick him up, and all he had was one tiny backpack. Barely anything in it. Just some clothes and that little toy airplane."

"Airplane?" Hazel repeated, her heart aching all over again for the little boy she'd seen in that photo.

"Yep. Your dad had taken Cricket and Tag

to the flight museum in Anchorage and bought them both toy airplanes. To Cricket, that airplane was a treasure. He rarely went anywhere without it."

Hazel smiled. "I saw it on the sideboard in his dining room next to the photo of him and Tag when he first got his Cessna. There's also a picture taken when he was a kid, of Cricket and Lee in front of the church."

"Yes. I took that photo." She poured almonds from a large bag into the food processor. "I found it not long ago and gave it to him. That was the day Lee left for the youth facility. The social worker arranged for him to say goodbye to Cricket. Lee was so brave and sweet to Cricket. Told him to be good and mind his manners and help me with the dishes…" Her words faded to a frown.

"He was with us for six months that first time. Then Frank was released. It ripped my heart out to let him go back with that man. I felt like I was losing my own child. I have so much respect for foster parents. Your dad talked to Frank about letting us keep him. We both did." She pressed the power button, and the sound of grinding nuts temporarily halted her story.

"What happened?" Hazel asked when her mom had finished that task. The mixture began to boil like molten lava, reminding her of the Witch's Pot. She wished she could show Cricket Montauk Caves. There were so many places she'd been to over the years that she'd enjoy sharing with him. "This is starting to thicken."

Margaret peeked into the pot. "Looking good. Keep stirring. You know how it is—even bad parents love their children." She tipped her head thoughtfully. "Most of them, anyway. Same with siblings. Lee loved Cricket the best he knew how. He had potential, too. Charming and funny and a gifted mechanic—even at that age, he was already fixing cars.

"Poor kid. Never had much of a chance with Frank as his role model. Unless they are exposed to something different, it's difficult for kids to see their parents for who they are, and often by the time they do, it's too late to alter their influence."

Hazel felt another twist of sympathy.

"When the social worker came to get Cricket, he hugged me so tight. He was just clinging and trembling, trying not to cry. It was all I could do not to cry. I held him for a long time and told him that just because he wasn't living under our roof didn't mean that we didn't want him. I knew his mom was gone, but I could be here for him. I promised that no matter where he was or what happened, I would always be his 'other' mom. When he and Tag were in school and Mother's Day craft time came around, he always made his gift for me. Still gives me a Mother's Day present every year."

No wonder Cricket had so much love for her parents. She had an awful lot herself at that moment. The truth slammed into her like a freight train carrying a ton of bricks; Cricket might be worried about how Tag would handle him and Hazel as a couple, or what Hannah would think, or even how Shay, Seth and Iris would take the news. But he wasn't nearly as concerned about them as he was about upsetting Margaret, and likely Ben, too.

"You said the first time?" she asked, now wanting to understand the entire picture.

"Yes. He stayed here several times over the years when Frank was in jail, and Lee was gone or vice versa—or both. Cricket was pretty much on his own by the time he was a teenager, and when he was seventeen, Frank got that five-year sentence." She paused, thinking. "He never came back to Rankins after that, not to stay. Lee was gone by then, working on the North Slope.

"Cricket was firmly on a different path, thank goodness. He had his pilot certification not long after he graduated high school. I think it helped that he had that talent, that gift to focus on. It gave him the motivation and the confidence he needed."

"Wow. I knew some of this, I guess, but I never really got it, you know? I didn't understand the consequences."

"You are ten years younger. As often happens with the baby of the family, everyone just assumes you know the history, too. But even if you do remember, it's from a kid's perspective, which can be rather skewed."

"That's so true," Hazel said and then grinned. Tag, Shay and even Hannah often remembered things differently than she, Iris and Seth did.

"Although, I am a little surprised that the topic never came up for the two of you. You were so close there for a while." Her mom surprised her with *that* look, the one she and Seth and Iris had long ago termed the "Mom knows" stare.

Her stomach tightened with a bout of teenage-style nerves. What the heck? "Mom," she said slowly, "what are you talking about?"

"Oh, Hazel," she said with a playful eye roll. "Did you honestly believe I didn't know where you were going after track practice, after school and all that summer, before your shift at work, or when you left to hang out with unspecified friends?"

"Um, yes," she answered primly. "That's exactly what I thought. Why didn't you say anything?"

"I did. I said something to Cricket."

"Mom! You did not!" Hazel felt her face go hot with mortification. "It's been ten years, and I still can't handle the humiliation."

"Which is why I talked to him instead of you."

"What did you say? Do I even want to know?"

Margaret laughed and began sprinkling the nuts onto the pans. "I told him that I could see you had a crush on him, a serious one, and he needed to be careful."

Hazel groaned and then stated with mock seriousness, "I had no idea you hated me that much."

"Oh, hush," Margaret said, still smiling. "There is no one on this earth aside from your father that I trust more than Cricket. I think Frank's dishonesty made him go in the opposite direction. He promised me I could trust him, and that man's word is like gold. That was all I needed to hear."

Everything made so much more sense now. In addition to all the excuses about why they couldn't be together, he'd also mentioned a promise, a *broken promise*. She'd always believed he was talking about Tag, about some sort of silly best-friends-don't-date-sisters vow. That wasn't what he'd meant, though. "Betraying" Tag would be bad enough, but letting down her mom would be so much worse in his mind.

"I thought the two of you would end up together someday. But you were so young, and I didn't want it to be too soon. I hoped you'd go away to college, live a little and figure out what you wanted. And you did. All of that, in spades. I'm so proud of you, honey. You exceeded our expectations. But I always thought Cricket might end up in your final equation, too."

Hazel nodded, gratitude and love welling inside of her. "Thank you, Mom. That's so nice to hear. But to be honest, I'm still working on that last part—the figuring-things-out stuff."

"Really? How so?" Across the kitchen, Margaret opened a drawer and retrieved a candy thermometer. "About time to check that."

A part of her didn't want to admit the truth because what if she and Cricket didn't work out? But then again, what did she have to lose?

"I do want Cricket, Mom. You were right.

I've always wanted him. And I'm pretty sure he wants me, too."

"Oh, honey! That's wonderful!" Then she paused, puzzled, processing the look on Hazel's face. "Or it should be. What are you waiting for?"

"Um, I'm not sure. I guess I'm waiting for him to realize that he won't lose his family, our family, by giving us a chance."

"Ah." Margaret joined her by the stove and dipped the thermometer into the liquid. "I can see where he might need a little help with that."

AFTER A JAM-PACKED two-day schedule of flying skiers into the backcountry, interacting with clients, answering questions, taking reservations, scheduling flights for maximum efficiency and trying to locate his brother, Cricket still wasn't looking forward to the downtime stretching before him.

That meant he now had hours to think about how he'd essentially told Hazel he loved her. Having no idea what he'd hoped to accomplish with his confession, the words had just come pouring out. He replayed the conversation endlessly. At least he'd had the presence of mind to take back Kai's firing.

Just get through the holidays. Only two more weeks until Christmas and another week until the New Year, and then they'd both be gone. Seeing her with another man hadn't helped him get over her as he'd hoped. Not by a long shot. But maybe now that he'd said the words aloud, he'd be able to let her go? A task that might be a whole lot easier considering her reaction.

All the times she'd wanted to know how he felt and when he'd finally told her, she'd walked away. That had hurt. But how could he blame her? How often had he done that very thing? And much worse was the realization that he'd ever caused her that same kind of pain.

Just as he feared, without work as a distraction, these thoughts and questions were taking up all the space in his head. Until he turned into his driveway, where he immediately and gratefully noticed that Ben had plowed the snow, a favor they often exchanged seeing as how their homes were only miles apart.

Continuing around to the back of his house, he discovered a beat-up SUV parked in front of his garage. It wasn't blocking his bay, so he pulled his pickup inside and then went back out to inspect the vehicle. The amount of snow piled on top suggested it had been there awhile, several hours at least, and the advanced age and unfortunate condition gave him a clue as to who the driver might be, although no one was behind the wheel. A set of snow-smudged footprints led to the house and back again. With a gloved hand, he dusted the fresh powder from the rear passenger window.

"Hey!" he shouted, knocking this time, because there appeared to be a sleeping-bag-clad body lying across the back seat.

Sure enough, a figure popped upright, jack-in-the-box style. A startled Lee appeared, face framed by a bright red-and-blue ski cap, the flaps tied snugly beneath his chin, tassels flopping as his gaze darted wildly around before settling on Cricket with a huge grin on his face.

Cricket couldn't help but chuckle. The window came down, and amusement mingled with relief at the sight of his brother whole and presumably healthy. It was always difficult to stay annoyed with Lee.

"Hey, little brother," Lee said. "'Bout time you rolled in. Where you been?"

"Are you kidding me?" He shot back. "Where have *you* been?"

"It's kind of a longish story."

"You're not wanted, are you?" Cricket glanced around as if the cops might show up at any second.

"No!" Lee laughed. "I got out early. Good behavior and all. I am *always* a model inmate."

"You realize the dubious distinction that is, right?"

"Says someone who has never been behind bars."

"I've been in front of them plenty, though. I went to visit you last Thursday, and you weren't there. I've been concerned and trying to track you down ever since."

"Oh." Lee's face fell. "Ah, man… Cricket, I'm so sorry. I was thinking your next visit was this Thursday. Thought I'd get here before then, which I did. I wanted to surprise you—in a good way. I have stuff to tell you. Wow, it's so great to see your ugly face. I've missed you."

This was the thing about Lee. He was so *likable*. Yes, he was a thief, but he would never hurt anyone. The opposite, in fact. To someone he cared about, he'd give the shirt off his back. Granted, the shirt might be of questionable provenance, but the point was he'd do just about anything for a friend or someone less fortunate. Or his little brother. And here he was, shivering in a cold junker car while wrapped in a cheap sleeping bag and wearing a goofy stocking cap. But still smiling. Ugh. He loved his brother, and if that made him a sucker, so be it. He just hoped he didn't live to regret it.

Cricket waved a hand. "Come in and tell me. I've got food. Homemade cookies, even, and I'll make coffee. You must be freezing."

"SETH!" HAZEL HOLLERED at the sight of her triplet brother and launched herself into his arms. She couldn't help it. She needed him right now. "It took you forever to get here."

"Missed you, too, Trippa," he said, calling her by the nickname he used for both her and Iris and squeezing her extra tight because, somehow, he always—okay, almost always— knew when she needed his support. Occasionally, he missed the cue and went straight to joke mode, but the multitude of texts she'd sent over the last two days probably helped him get the hint.

Iris took her turn at hugging Seth, who then fussed over Lily and asked Iris all the right pregnancy questions. More hugs and greetings were exchanged with Victoria and Scarlett. Then Margaret whisked Scarlett and Lily away to begin the cookie decorating.

Hazel, Iris, Seth and Victoria settled in the family room. "I didn't intend to lead with this," Hazel said. "But everyone else will be here soon, and I need to figure out what I'm going to do."

She'd already told Iris what happened in Juneau, and now she relayed the whole story for Seth and Victoria.

"I knew it," Victoria said. "I told Seth when I saw you two bickering in Florida that it was a love spat."

"To be fair, the term *love spat* was never used," Seth countered with mock sincerity.

Victoria rolled her eyes but couldn't quite contain her grin. "Sparks were flying that could only come from having a history. When I mentioned that, your brother looked at me like he thought I'd lost my mind—assured me that you and Cricket were like brother and sister. Ha!"

Seth exhaled a comically dramatic huff. "As much as I hate to admit it, that's all true."

Victoria smiled triumphantly.

He said, "But, Hazel, seriously? You and Cricket. I missed this. Totally and completely."

"Don't feel bad," Iris said. "Everyone did."

"Everyone except Mom," Hazel amended.

"What?" her siblings cried simultaneously.

She explained about that, too.

"Of course, she knew." Seth chuckled and shook his head. "I doubt we ever actually got away with anything where that woman is concerned."

"Hazel," Iris said with a little shake of her head. "Cricket is *in love* with you. *Our* Cricket."

She nodded. "That is precisely the problem. He's *ours*. And he thinks I'm someone else's."

"Let's back up a bit," Seth said. "It's completely wild when you think about it. Cricket has so much to lose. He's Hannah's business partner, probably her best friend. Bering is now his other business partner and very close friend. He works for both Tag and Bering in the off-season. Tag is *his best friend since first grade*. Pretty much everything he does involves someone from this family.

"And Mom and Dad are like the parents he never had. He spends most every holiday with us. Birthdays, parties, celebrations, Sunday brunch—the only thing that isn't James about Cricket is his last name. Having a relationship with you would cement those relationships further. But if it didn't work out, it could…"

"Possibly ruin them forever," Hazel finished for him as a fresh wave of anxiety rushed over her. "Thanks for the recap, Captain Synopsis," she joked, even as the gravity of it all overwhelmed her. Then she groaned and buried her face in her hands. "Because I am not already feeling the pressure."

"Calm down," Seth urged in a teasing tone. "All I'm saying is that before you—we—proceed to make a plan, it's important that you are 100 percent positive about this. How many list violations?"

"How many what?" Victoria asked, and Seth quickly filled her in.

A gleeful Iris answered the question. "All of them, pretty much. Though Hazel claims they don't count where Cricket is concerned. He already knows her likes and dislikes. You can sure tell from his Secret Santa gifts that he knows her very, very well. Like possibly as well as we do, Seth."

Seth scowled but didn't look unhappy, just contemplative.

"Cricket is my Secret Santa?" Hazel repeated Iris's theory, although she knew the answer before she even got the question out. It seemed obvious now. The headlamp, the perfect pillow, the cat pillowcase, the catnap reference—then there was the ebook by one of her favorite authors that came Friday evening after the storm hit.

Not to mention the scones he'd brought to work and about a thousand other little things he'd said and done in the last couple of weeks. It all made sense. Iris was right; under the circumstances, and adjusting the list accordingly, they could all be interpreted as further proof of his...*like* for her.

Nodding, she looked at her brother and addressed his concern. "Seth, I have been in love with him my entire life, even before I understood what that emotion meant. I spent a decade trying to get over him, which is how the list came to be." She briefly explained that logic.

"Okay, then," Seth said. "I'm convinced. You may proceed," he teased.

Iris, always the problem solver, said, "Now we need to figure out how you're going to approach him, what you're going to say."

"Yes," Hazel said, grateful to be talking solutions. "What have you got? I'll take even the wildest scheme under advisement."

"We know he's jealous of Kai. Maybe you and Kai could go to the Festival of Trees together? Really act like a couple. He would help you out like that, right? Maybe seeing you and Kai would—"

"No!" Victoria interrupted sharply. All eyes landed on her. "Sorry," she said and added a little wince. "I didn't mean to sound quite so…forceful. But she's already done that accidentally—and by her account, very successfully. I think the poor guy has suffered enough, don't you?"

Leaning forward, she went on, "Hazel, listen—when Seth and I were trying to figure out how to be *us*, there were so many obstacles and distractions and people trying to keep us apart. But the one thing that kept me going, that made me want to work it out, were those moments when we were alone. Just the two of us. When I had any doubt, that's what I kept going back to, that's what I focused on, and that made dealing with all the rest worthwhile.

"My advice is for the two of you to have some good old-fashioned alone time. And honesty. Tell Cricket how you feel without putting any pressure on him. Someplace where he won't be reminded of what he has to lose. And where he can see what he has to gain."

Seth was gazing at Victoria all hazy-eyed and love-glazed. "I love you," he said to her. Then to Hazel, "I agree with my fiancée. You two need a date, a real one." The sweet look he then exchanged with Victoria suggested the strategy had worked for them.

"I love the idea, too. But I still have the problem of how to get him to agree? I'm not sure he'd say yes if I asked him."

"That's easy," Iris said. "You trick him."

"Uh," Seth interjected. "From a male's perspective, I don't think *tricking* him is—"

"I don't mean in a devious way. I'm talking about a simple bait and switch. You know that Christmas benefit concert Cricket is going to with Hannah and Tate?"

"Yes, the one in Anchorage tomorrow night where Rushing Tide is performing." The band's two founding members, Clark and Ezra Mayfield, were friends with Cricket and Hannah. They'd accommodated a last-minute heli-ski adventure for the band, and they'd reciprocated with complimentary tickets to their highly anticipated and sold-out Notes of Christmas Concert.

"Well…" Iris said brightly. "What if Hannah and Tate couldn't make it, but you showed up instead?"

CHAPTER THIRTEEN

CRICKET WATCHED VALENTINE make a fool of herself for Lee, stretching and purring and turning circles on his lap while they lounged together on the sofa. Lee scratched her chin and snacked on cookies while Cricket built a fire in the woodstove. He couldn't help but think that it said something good about Lee that his notoriously standoffish cat liked him, right?

With a fire now crackling in the woodstove, Cricket fetched them both coffee and then settled in an adjacent chair.

"I've gone straight," Lee announced after he took his first sip. Val curled up for a nap. As if he'd heard Cricket take his seat, too, Mitt padded in from the other room and hopped up next to him.

"For real this time. That's why I didn't tell you I was getting released. I wanted to prove to you that I meant it. I know it's only been a couple of weeks, but I have a job and an apartment."

"Where?"

"Glacier City. I want to be close to you, but not too close—yet. My plan is to open my own shop here in Rankins eventually. But I'm aware that my, uh, reputation precedes me, and that it rubs off on you. For your sake, until I can show people that I'm reformed, I need to maintain some distance."

Cricket wasn't sure how to respond to that. Lee's goal was lofty. He'd once heard Ally's grandfather Abe say the smaller the town, the larger its collective memory. There was no escaping your past in Rankins.

Lee seemed to read his mind. "Look, Cricket, I know it's going to take a while for you to trust me. And even longer for most of the people in this town to believe I've changed. I don't blame you. Or them. I can wait. But I want you to know that I'm serious this time. I'm in therapy."

"Therapy?" Cricket repeated with all the skepticism he felt.

Lee busted out a laugh. "I know how it sounds. But I met this psychiatrist woman at Otter Creek, Dr. Easton, who specializes in rehabbing criminals. At first, I only started going to the group sessions for something to do. You know how it is?"

"No, thankfully, I don't."

Lee chuckled again. "I'm grateful for that. Every single day, I'm glad that my choices, and Dad's choices, didn't lead you astray. I'm grateful you had Tag and his family to keep you on the straight and narrow. I'm working hard to understand my stuff, like why I steal. Because you know it's never been about the money."

Cricket did believe that. He also wanted to believe his brother had changed. Or was trying to, at least. The problem was he always wanted to believe, but he'd been disappointed too many times.

"Dr. Easton started seeing me one-on-one, and then when I got released, she set me up with a new doctor in Glacier City, Dr. Monroe."

Cricket suspected that this fulfilled specific terms of his release but didn't ask for confirmation. Because regardless, how could a little therapy hurt? See, there was that wanting-to-believe thing again.

Lee said, "Since we're on the topic of lawbreaking, have you heard from Frank?"

"No. Frank knows I'm not interested in having any kind of relationship with him. I made that clear years ago. Why? Are you guys in touch?"

Lee shook his head. "No, but I heard through

the grapevine that he got transferred to a new facility and is on work release."

"Ha. Frank working? That's funny."

Lee grinned. "Never been his greatest strength, has it? Let's not talk about him anymore. Any chance you'd let me camp out here on your sofa for a while?"

"I thought you said you got an apartment?"

"I do. It was supposed to be ready yesterday, but the landlord decided to paint and replace the carpets, which is nice. But now it won't be done for at least a couple more weeks."

"Yes, you can stay as long as you need. You can sleep in the guest room. Just promise me, Lee, that there's nothing you're not telling me here. No surprises, okay?"

"I promise, little brother. No surprises."

HAZEL'S ENTIRE BODY hummed with nervous energy. Watching the main entrance, she stood by the tall Christmas tree inside the lobby of the Hotel Ophelia in downtown Anchorage, waiting for Cricket and their surprise date to the concert. With Ashley's assistance, Iris had gotten Hazel on a Copper Crossing flight by simply telling Tag she was meeting a friend in the city. That way, Hazel could avoid any questions from Tag that would result in her having to skirt around the truth—that she was attempting a romantic ambush of his best friend.

The beat of her heart was erratic and uncertain, just like she felt. Her hands were cold and clammy. Skydiving, cliff jumping, white-water kayaking—she ticked through the most fear-provoking activities she'd ever done, trying to find anything that could measure up to this level of sheer nervousness. She couldn't come up with a single comparison. A healthy dose of adrenaline-charged anticipation was completely different than this emotional...torment.

Her phone chimed with a text. Sweet words of encouragement from Hannah: I would tell you to break a leg but after trying that myself I just don't feel right about recommending. Don't worry. You've got this. Your plan is sound.

She answered with a simple Thank you. Waiting in the lobby now.

Hannah had taken the news about her and Cricket much better than she'd expected.

"Hmm," she'd said after Hazel explained everything. "I've always suspected that he was interested in someone. I just didn't know who." Brow scrunched, she'd gone quiet, thinking.

Hazel had waited. She'd understood. It would be a lot for her sister to process.

A long moment of silence had passed before Hannah slowly smiled and said, "I'm surprised

I didn't see it sooner. The way he asks about you and talks about you. I just thought he was interested because your life is so unique. And because, you know." She'd pulled one shoulder up into a shrug. "You're like a little sister." Eyes going wide, she'd amended, "But *not*, obviously."

"It's okay," Hazel had chuckled. "I know it must be a bit shocking. He talks about me?" she'd asked, not caring if it made her sound needy and vulnerable. Because she sort of was, wasn't she? She was about to put her heart on the line. Again. Sure, this time, she wasn't a naive nineteen-year-old, but still, she was unsure about how he'd react. Any proof of his affection that Hannah could provide would be a boost to her confidence.

"Yep. He's always commenting on where you are, what you're doing, where you're going next. Or asking, 'Have you read Hazel's latest blog? Did you see Hazel's post about her jet boat ride on *Whatever-a-among-a* River in New Zealand? Did you know she was trekking alone in Nepal?'"

Hazel had to laugh at Hannah's attempt to recall the name of the New Zealand river.

"I'm glad it's you, tiny triplet." The use of Hannah's childhood nickname for her, along with the support, had brought tears to her eyes.

"Now that I'm thinking about it, considering all the angles, you guys are, like, a perfect match. So much in common, adventurous, independent and the same sweet spirit."

"Thank you, Hannah. I'm glad it's me, too." She'd grinned. "Now I just need to convince Cricket. It's going to help to have your blessing."

"About that." Hannah's gaze had zeroed in on her then, this time with the candor, firmness and no-nonsense response she'd expected from her sister. "I don't think I need to point out to you what's on the line for Cricket here?"

"No, you don't."

"Good, because it's massive." She'd held her arms wide. "Like, glacier size."

"I know," Hazel had said, respecting her sister's protectiveness of him.

"I love you both. But if it doesn't work out, you have to know that I will not choose. No matter what. Cricket is the best friend I've ever had. He's one of the best men on the planet. Period. And I will not get caught in the middle of any drama, nor will I set my friendship with him aside."

"I know," she'd said again, her words low and raspy due to the emotion crowding her chest. She nodded and cleared her throat. "I wouldn't expect you to."

"And Mom and Dad mean the world to him. I honestly believe he is Mom's favorite. Shay *thinks* that she is, but she's wrong. It's totally Cricket. And he deserves it. He treats Mom like a queen. Well, he reveres Dad, too, for that matter."

"I get that, Hannah. I swear, I do." She might not have before, but she believed she did now.

"Speaking of friends, does Tag know?"

"No. I don't see the point in telling him until I'm sure that Cricket is willing to give this a go."

"Makes sense. Our big brother is going to freak. You know that, right?"

"I do."

From that point on, it had been a whirlwind, planning the date and making arrangements. Hannah had enthusiastically gifted her the concert tickets, called the Hotel Ophelia and put the room she'd reserved in Hazel's name. Iris had insisted on handling dinner reservations, and then Ashley had pulled off the flight without rousing Tag's suspicion.

And now here she stood, uncertain and terrified. What would he do when he saw her? She couldn't shake the notion that his initial reaction would tell her a lot. Would he be upset? And how was she going to go about explaining everything? She hadn't thought past the logistics. Maybe she should go up to her room and text him first? Yes, she needed to think this through, lay the groundwork, tell him she was here and ask if he'd—

"Hazel?"

She felt his hand on her shoulder at the same instant that she heard his voice. A shock went through her, both from his touch and because he'd approached from behind.

"You need to quit sneaking up on me in far-away places," she said, turning to face him and trying to smile. She inhaled a deep, steadying breath but all that did was overwhelm her with the scent of him. As if the sight of him weren't enough to leave her reeling. A long moment passed, her frozen with indecision, him peering at her curiously, waiting for her to say something.

"Hazel," he finally urged. "What are you doing here?"

She puffed out a nervous chuckle. "For some reason, I thought you'd come through the front entrance, so I was watching the door. It didn't occur to me that you'd already be here."

His sweetly curious expression transformed into one of confusion. "You've been waiting for me?"

"Yes. Sort of, um…"

"What's going on?" he asked, glancing around. "Are you here with Hannah and Tate?"

With no clever or witty explanation occurring to her, she went with blunt. "No. So, here's the deal—Hannah and Tate aren't coming."

At his frown, Hazel felt a fresh wave of doubt. He pulled his phone from his pocket and took a quick glance. "I've been checking my phone, and she hasn't texted. Is everything okay?"

"Oh! Yes, it's fine. She's fine. They're fine. I'm— Okay. That's… Wow. I'm astonishingly good with pronouns, huh?" she tried to joke, but the frantic pounding inside of her head made it difficult to think. Well, that, and the second-guessing of herself.

Concern flickered across his face as his gaze narrowed in on her. "Are you okay?"

"Yes." He didn't look convinced, and she realized she'd better start talking. Where to start? "Remember when I texted, asking you if we could talk?"

He flinched. It was slight, but she saw it, nonetheless. And combined with the flicker of regret in his green eyes, she suddenly felt like crying. This was a stupid plan. Why had she thought this sort of grand gesture would be effective? Cricket was not a grand-gesture type of person. And neither was she. She'd been horrified when Ashley had attempted one on Seth. Seth knew that. Why hadn't Seth talked her out of this?

"Uh, yeah," he answered carefully. "Are you saying you flew all the way here to Anchorage tonight so we could talk?"

"No. Well, yes. Sort of." *Get it together, Hazel.* She counted to five and then said, "I flew all the way here to ask you out on a date."

"You... What?"

"Cricket, I'm so sorry. Kai and I aren't seeing each other. We never were. Nothing romantic there at all. I can see how you thought so, though, since I told you we were on a date in Utah. That wasn't even a real date, I mean, not a *romantic* one. And then, in Juneau, I let you believe it because I thought if I told you the truth, you might..."

He hadn't moved a muscle. Even his face looked like it was carved from stone.

Desperate, she tried to give him an out. "You know what? This seemed like a good idea when Iris proposed it. You know how enthusiastic she can get with her schemes." Sure, blame Iris for her own bad decision. "I got caught up, and now I feel...silly. And then when Seth didn't talk me out of it..." Yeah, throw Seth under the bus, too. She was *such* a good sister. "No, never mind, that's not fair. I take full responsibility, and I'm—"

"Wait," he interrupted gently. "You're not seeing Kai? He wasn't your date and is not your boyfriend?"

"No, no and no. And at the risk of repeating myself—never. Not interested."

Looking thoughtful, he tipped his head, no doubt still trying to catch up with her ramblings. He asked, "What are you sorry about?"

"About taking Hannah's and Tate's concert tickets and showing up here in their place. About letting Iris make us a dinner reservation, and then flying this far without asking if you wanted a date first." Her cheeks were hot and flaming, and prickles of embarrassment paraded all along her back and across her scalp. The nervous sweat was a nice touch, too, and added to her despair. She might not be nineteen anymore, but she certainly felt that way.

"I see. So, why didn't you ask me?"

"Because I was afraid that if I asked, you would say no."

"Hazel." His eyes closed for a few seconds as he inhaled a breath. When he opened them again, his green eyes were flashing with intensity and heat. A whole lot of heat.

He held her gaze, and his voice went low and soft. "After all these years, after all the looks, the touches, the tension, the...*moments* that have passed between us? Me, flying to South America and then Utah to find you, to see you. Just to know that you were safe. The meddling and the advice and the argument in Florida." His eyes dipped to her mouth and lingered there for a couple of sexy seconds before adding, "The kiss."

Hazel's blood went hot, firing through her veins. Her entire body felt heavy and tingly.

But he wasn't finished. Gaze lifting to catch hers again, he continued, "Then there was the raging jealousy over Kai, resulting in my confession in Juneau. After all of that, plus an eternity spent trying to get you out of my head, do you really believe that I would be capable of telling you no?"

Joy blossomed inside of her, filling all the space, pushing out all the last bits of doubt. Was this actually happening?

"In that case..." Lifting both hands, she slipped them beneath his open jacket and flattened her palms on his chest. The sharp intake of his breath had her confidence soaring, her hands sliding up and her lips curving into a smile as she asked, "Can I kiss you?"

CRICKET DIDN'T CARE. He just didn't care anymore. What he'd told Hazel was true. He'd reached his limit and didn't have the strength to fight this anymore. Even if it meant complicating every important relationship in his life, so be it. He'd risk it all just to kiss her again, to hold her.

"Yes." He wound his arms around her, one low on her hip and the other curled around her neck. Dipping his head, he met her mouth for a kiss that was hot and sweet and just completely... honest.

For once, he let go and showed her all the emotion he'd kept bottled up for so long. He wouldn't have believed the reality of this moment could ever live up to either a ten-year-old memory or the fantasy he'd harbored ever since. But it did.

It was even better. Because this time, he was all in. There was no stopping too soon, no excuse-making, no walking away. No regrets. Except... He suddenly realized they were kissing in the lobby of a busy hotel.

Keeping his arms around her, he broke away just enough to nuzzle her neck and catch his breath. Then he shifted to look at her face. Eyes soft and hazy, mouth curling up at the corners, she appeared every bit as dazed as he felt.

"Hey," he said gently in opposition to his still-wildly-beating heart.

"Well," she quipped, because, of course, Hazel would make a joke when they were like this, "this evening is going *exactly* as I planned."

CHAPTER FOURTEEN

"So, if Hannah gave you her concert tickets, that means she knows…?" Cricket drew out the question. Snuggled together on the sofa of his hotel room, where they'd headed from the lobby, Hazel drank in the gorgeous cityscape splayed outside the window below them, made even more extraordinary by the glimmer and sparkle of holiday lights. "About *all* of this?"

"Yes." Hazel nodded. "And she took it better than I expected, although she basically told me that if things ever got ugly between us, she would choose you."

He tipped his head back and laughed. "We both know that's not true."

"I don't know that at all. Seth, Iris and I—Mom, too, I think—we credit you with bringing Hannah back into the family fold, so to speak. But yes, Hannah and Tate, Iris, obviously, Seth and Victoria all know. And Mom and Dad."

"Wait, your mom and dad know?"

"That's a big reason why I'm here. Mom

sort of helped me see things differently." Hazel recapped the conversation she and Margaret had had over candy making. "She told me about going to you that summer and talking about…me. Which is super embarrassing." She paused to cringe. "She said you promised her that you could be trusted with me. That day, after I kissed you, I remember you saying that you broke a promise. I assumed you meant like some sort of bro-pact you'd made with Tag. But you were talking about Mom, weren't you?"

"Yes," he admitted and then let out a groan. "Breaking that promise was difficult to live with. So many times, I thought about confessing or…"

"Confessing to what, though?" She reached over and took his hand, and he entwined his fingers with hers, and she didn't think she'd ever get over the novelty of touching him. "I kissed you."

"I knew how you felt about me, Hazel. That's why your mom came and talked to me, to make sure I understood what I was dealing with. The whole point was for me to avoid that sort of behavior."

"What you were dealing with? You mean like a lovestruck teenager?" She added a bark of laughter. "Trust me—I knew what I was doing, Cricket. I shouldn't have kissed you that day. I took advantage of your kindness. I should never have put you in that situation. If Mom and Dad knew what happened, how you reacted, they'd only be more impressed with your behavior. I was—" she searched for a word "—shameless. And you did the right thing by sending me away."

He appeared to be thinking this over, so she leaned in to kiss him again because, seriously, they had years to make up for, and she didn't want to waste another minute musing about the past. Cricket seemed to have the same thought because he didn't hesitate to gather her close, and there was an urgency this time, mixed with the sweetness.

Finally, she pushed away enough to see his eyes. "Still shameless, apparently," she whispered.

"Fine by me," he shot back. His expression was brimming with affection and his self-satisfied smirk was so adorable that she almost kissed him again.

"When we were in Utah, and you told me about how you interpreted what I said to mean that I didn't care about you the same way, I felt—*I feel*—terrible about that. Because nothing could be further from the truth. But I've always known that if I ever admitted the truth, there'd be no going back."

No going back. That was the part she loved the most.

"I understand all of that now," she said and thought, *I love you.* The words lay heavy and restless on her heart. Like they'd been tethered there for too long, and she needed to free them. Probably too soon to spring a declaration of love on him. Which was funny because how could something this old feel new? "I wish I would have figured all of this out sooner."

"It wouldn't have mattered," he said. "It was only seeing you with Kai that made me realize that my feelings were never going to go away." She cuddled against him, laying her head on his chest.

He paused, thinking. "I told myself I could handle it. If I could just enjoy your company until you went to college, you would forget about me and move on."

Hazel said, "Mom told me she thought— hoped—we would end up together someday. But she wanted us both to be sure. And she wondered if I could even *be* sure of how I felt at nineteen. Does that change things for you?"

"YES, IT DOES," Cricket said. And it was true; those words changed everything. At this point, he'd been willing to take a risk without knowing for sure Margaret and Ben would be supportive, but the thought that he wouldn't have to was the headiest sort of relief.

"I thought it might," she answered softly, and Cricket loved her even more for understanding. For not telling him that her parents' approval didn't matter when they both knew that it did. He couldn't let himself think about what might happen if this didn't work out. Because now that he had her, he couldn't let her go.

Although… "Couldn't help but notice that your list of family members currently in the know did not include Tag."

"Yeah, I didn't see the point in going there until I knew for sure that you'd… That we would, you know, proceed."

"Have you given that any thought? How to tell him?"

"I was thinking we'd tell him together. He'll be fine once he hears the whole story," Hazel declared confidently.

Cricket wasn't so sure. She didn't know her brother quite as well as he did. Tag had always counted on Cricket to have his back. He was not going to be pleased that he'd gone behind it to pursue his sister. How was he going to explain to his best friend that he was in love with his sister? His much younger sister. And, not only that, but he'd also loved her for years and never said a single word. A quiet minute passed, and he decided to let the matter go for now. No point in speculating about a conversation he had no trouble putting off for the evening. Or for as long as possible.

"So, tell me about this date you came here to treat me to."

"Better yet," she said, sitting upright. "Let me show you."

THE FIRST STOP on their date that Hazel had planned included dinner at Lulu's, a mutual favorite restaurant that served filet mignon in portions much larger than a taste. Only moments after they entered the place and gave their name, a young woman appeared and showed them to a secluded table in a corner near the Christmas tree.

They sat, and the hostess said, "I understand you two are celebrating tonight?"

Eyebrows nudging upward, Hazel grinned at Cricket. "I'm guessing Iris assumed that if we made it here for our reservation, we'd be celebrating." To the hostess, she answered, "Yes, we are."

"Fabulous! We're thrilled that you chose Lulu's for your special occasion. My name is

Janna, and I'll be taking care of you tonight. I understand that Iris is your sister?"

"Yes," Hazel answered with a touch of hesitancy, no doubt wondering, as was he, what Iris was up to.

"You are lucky to have such a wonderful sister. She arranged something very special for you two tonight. An appetizer, which will be out momentarily, and…"

Another server appeared with a bottle of wine, which he proceeded to open and pour into two glasses and then place before them.

Janna said, "We'll leave you to choose your entrées, and I'll be back in a few minutes to take your order."

Cricket couldn't remember ever feeling this way, which cemented how firmly entrenched Hazel had been in his heart all these years. They talked about everything and nothing, and it was remarkable how relaxed and comfortable and content he felt—and yet electrified at the same time.

When dinner was over, they hired a car to take them to the concert venue. They got out a block away to avoid the traffic and crowd of the sold-out performance.

On the sidewalk, he took her hand, and they headed for the auditorium. That's when he recognized that as much as he'd been looking forward to seeing Rushing Tide, he was reluctant to go inside. Knowing the chaos awaiting them at home, he'd rather spend the remaining hours alone with her. No way would he spoil their first date by admitting as much, though, especially when she'd so carefully arranged it all.

They were nearing the queue at the entrance when she slid a glance at him. Slowing her stride, she said, "Cricket?"

"Yep?"

She steered him to one side, away from the crush of people. "Would you think it was awful if I wanted to skip the concert?"

Dipping his head as if to answer, he kissed her first and then whispered against her lips, "Awful would be spending our first real date together in an auditorium surrounded by other people."

Her smile was radiant. "Let's go," she said.

Back on the sidewalk, Cricket watched a young couple emerge from a popular coffee shop. Strolling hand in hand, they had that dreamy in-love look about them, which he appreciated because he knew he had it, too.

"Hey," Cricket said, "you two on a date?"

"Uh, yeah," the guy said, glancing around a bit nervously.

The woman also looked wary but curious if slightly amused.

"Have you ever heard of Rushing Tide?"

"Um, yes!" she cried. "They are one of my favorite bands. And they are playing right there." She pointed at the auditorium. "There's the line. Are you guys going?"

"We have tickets," Cricket replied. "Front row."

"Jealous!" she returned. "Have fun. We couldn't afford the tickets. We have a two-year-old and a new baby at home. This is our first night out in…" She confirmed with her partner, "Months?"

He nodded. "Three months."

"You want to go?" Cricket held up the tickets.

With skepticism all over his face, the guy asked, "How much?"

Cricket glanced at Hazel, who was smiling beside him because undoubtedly, she knew exactly what he was up to. "What do you think?" he asked.

Hazel handed the woman the two tickets and said, "Merry Christmas."

"Are you…? Is this a joke?" The woman beamed.

"Nope. Go have fun."

After convincing the couple that the tickets were a gift and refusing any payment, the couple thanked them profusely and headed toward the concert.

Hazel pulled her phone from her pocket and tapped the app to get them a car.

"Well done," she gushed. "That was fun."

"It was," he agreed. "I thought it might take a few tries."

Hazel sighed. "It's so awesome to make someone's Christmas a little brighter, isn't it?"

Cricket had to agree.

"Like how you've made mine. Cricket, seriously, you are the best Secret Santa in the history of the world. Thank you."

"You figured it out, huh?"

"Iris did."

"And she told you?" Surprising, the pang of disappointment he felt at that news. "Why would she—"

"So she could use your superior gift-giving as evidence of your interest in me."

"Not have told you sooner?" he joked, stepping close to pull her into his arms. Their car arrived, and they climbed into the back seat for the short ride to the hotel.

Only hours ago, Cricket reflected when they'd settled inside, the last thing he would have expected was to be here with Hazel tonight. Earlier, when he'd spotted her in the lobby, he'd been overcome with joy—his usual reaction where she was concerned. On the heels of that had been curiosity and the burning hope that she wasn't there with Kai.

When she'd revealed they weren't a couple, his relief had been so intense he could barely think straight. And then he'd realized that her revelation made his previous confession impossible to avoid. Just that fast, the decision was out of his hands. As if he had to be with her now no matter what. End of story.

But that wasn't the end, was it? This wasn't a fairy tale. Aside from the difficult conversation he needed to have with Tag, there was the practical issue of their careers, which would give the term *long-distance relationship* a whole new meaning. His life was in Rankins and Our Alaska Tours was just getting off the ground. They had a lot to discuss.

But not tonight, he thought as Hazel leaned in, cupping his jaw and urging him to look at her. When he happily obliged, she kissed him, and for a split second, he was...whole. At peace. With all of his being, he wished that this moment, this sensation, was all that mattered.

"NOTHING LIKE DIVING right into a James family dinner to get the new-boyfriend awkwardness out of the way," Hazel joked the next afternoon as they pulled into the driveway of her parents' house. They'd just returned from Anchorage, having spent a leisurely morning in the city. After a late, delicious breakfast at the hotel, they'd wandered around and done some Christmas shopping, neither of them eager to leave the bubble they'd created.

"Looks like everyone is here…"

"Except Tag," Cricket amended, noting the absence of his pickup and Ally's SUV. As the time grew closer to break the news to Tag, Cricket didn't share Hazel's confidence. And what if Margaret and Ben weren't as supportive of them as a couple as Hazel believed? Any family member could disapprove and make this difficult.

"Maybe that's a good thing," she said. "It might be better if we tell him privately."

Cricket parked and flashed her a curious smile. "Oh, so you *are* worried about how he's going to take the news?"

"No! I'm not *worried.* It just seems like more of a respect thing between the two of you. I could never begin to understand your relationship. I've never had a friendship like yours. I'm lazy when it comes to friends because I've always had these built-in besties named Seth and Iris. My partners in crime and chaos. My adult life has always been too unsettled to establish and maintain a solid friendship like you guys have. I have tons of acquaintance-type friends, and that's enough for me.

"But that's you and Tag, right? And probably Hannah, too. The people you'd call to help you cover up the crime you accidentally committed. In your case, that would be Hannah because we both know Mr. Do-Gooder would never stand for any lawbreaking going down on his watch, accidental or otherwise." She laughed.

Cricket realized she was watching him, a small smile playing on her lips.

"What?" he asked.

"I was just thinking that the closest thing I've ever had to a non-related best friend is you. You were the one I called from Colombia."

"I've never had the kind of closeness we shared with anyone else either. Which explains why I couldn't get you out of my head all these years. All I've ever wanted is you."

"Well," she said, lips slowly curling upward, "You have me now."

"I certainly do," he whispered, leaning over to slip one hand around the back of her neck. This would be a perfect time, he decided, to tell her that he loved her. That way, no matter what happened, she'd know that he'd said it without caring about the consequences. But first, he needed to kiss her.

Her eyes closed as his mouth found hers.

"Hey!" The thumping of a gloved fist on his window accompanied the shout.

Tag. He groaned. Hazel flinched. They parted.

"What is going on?" Tag asked in that too calm voice that suggested he was anything but.

"Oh, boy," Hazel murmured as Cricket powered down his window. "Hey, Tag," she leaned over and called cheerfully.

"Tag," Cricket said, "we were just discussing when and how to tell you."

"Tell me what exactly?"

"Hazel and I are together."

"Together," he repeated with a nod. He looked off into the distance and for a long moment it seemed as if he wouldn't respond. Then he faced them again. "Do you have any concept of how complicated this could get? If it doesn't work out—"

"It will," Hazel said confidently. They both climbed out of the pickup.

"But what if it doesn't? This is a disaster." Tag glanced toward the house where Iris and Seth were now descending the porch. "You know what?" he added smoothly. "Let's see how everyone else takes this news." He swept both hands toward them like some sort of melodramatic showman. "Hey, you two, guess what? Cricket and Hazel are together."

"Yes, we know," Seth said slowly, taking a cue from Tag's tense tone and body language. "And we support them."

"We're very happy for them," Iris chimed in. "They've been—"

Tag interrupted with a scoff. "What was I thinking? *Of course you two are!* Hazel could rob a bank, and neither of you would bat an eye. How was I the only one who didn't know about this?"

"First of all," Iris said in an overly serene tone that did little to hide her obvious irritation. "If Hazel robbed a bank, there would undoubtedly be an excellent reason for her doing that. So, yes, I would drive the getaway car. But secondly, what I was trying to say is that Cricket and Hazel have cared about each other for a *very* long time. They were both concerned about how the family would take the news. Cricket was extra concerned about your reaction."

Tag was shaking his head. "Well, Cricket was right to be worried. Because he understands how many relationships and connections are on the line here."

"As do I," Hazel replied smoothly, "but this *relationship* is no one else's business but ours."

"Wouldn't that be nice?" Tag asked. "If relationships actually worked that way? But that's just it, Hazel—you don't get it. You're never here. Your visits home last about as long as your relationships. Our family dynamics don't affect you on a daily basis. But Cricket is *here*. He lives here in Rankins and you don't. His work, his life, is tied to all of us."

Looking at Cricket again, he added, "You are invested in this family, and when this relationship, or whatever it is that you're doing with my sister, goes south, it will affect all of us. And you more than anyone." Then, without waiting for a response, he glared at them, marched back to his pickup and climbed inside.

"Should I go after him?" Seth asked.

"No," Iris and Cricket said at the same time.

Iris added, "He needs to calm down. I haven't seen him this upset since he was dating Ally and she got called before the hospital board."

Cricket agreed. He knew better than to try to talk to Tag when his friend was this worked up. Truthfully, he couldn't blame him.

Tag drove away. Hazel looped her arm

around his elbow, and the four of them went inside.

"Cricket!" Margaret said. "I have the best news!"

"Let's hear it," he replied, managing to feign enthusiasm.

"Missy from Bellis Tech just called. At some point, you emailed her on behalf of Operation Happy Christmas?"

"I did. Way back in September, but I never heard anything."

"Missy apologized for that. The email was forwarded and overlooked—an assistant got fired, and etcetera, before she finally saw the message. Long story short—they've donated two hundred tablets."

"Two hundred?" he repeated, now understanding Margaret's excitement. "I requested fifty, hoping for half of that." They were for a rural school district where Ally had been raised. "That's enough for every student K through 12."

"I know! Can you believe it? Someone from Bellis is delivering them to the church tomorrow. I called Rebekah, and she said she'd meet them there, so we can pick them up anytime."

"Margaret, that is outstanding. And I'm going to add my own bit of good news. I have three dozen Squixits getting dropped off today."

"Oh, my! This is so great!" She gave him a quick hug. "Do you know what this means? We have nearly every item on our wish list. And what we don't have, we have enough in cash contributions to purchase."

Not even the confrontation with Tag could squelch his satisfaction. They'd done it. Or at least the most challenging aspects, anyway. They only needed to pick up this final load of donations, then organize, wrap and deliver. Cricket was confident these last steps would be a breeze with the network they'd put into place.

Reading his mind, Margaret said, "Cricket, I believe we're going to pull this off. Operation Happy Christmas indeed!"

CHAPTER FIFTEEN

OPERATION HAPPY CHRISTMAS INDEED. Hazel silently repeated her mom's declaration with a particular glow in her heart. This was shaping up to be the best Christmas ever aside from the temporary setback called Tag. But even that episode couldn't crush her joy. Her brother would come around. What choice did he have? Once he calmed down and heard the whole story, he'd see reason.

Hazel tucked the Secret Santa gift Kai had bought for Cricket into her bag and drove to Cricket's house early the next morning before work. He was booked solid with heli-ski flights, so this was the perfect opportunity to help Kai elevate his Secret Santa status. Even though she was pretty sure Cricket would ease up now where Kai was concerned.

She knew he still kept a spare key under the edge of the brick planter because the day she'd visited, she'd jokingly asked him. Unlocking the door, she slipped quietly inside. On her way to the kitchen, light from the living room caught her eye. And then stopped her cold. A partially lit Christmas tree stood in the corner. It seemed odd that Cricket would leave the lights on and—

"Good morning," a voice said from behind her.

With a little yelp of surprise, she turned, instantly recognizing Cricket's brother. Even though years had passed since the photo was taken, he had the same mischievous grin and laughing green eyes. "Lee?"

"Sorry," he said, fighting a chuckle. "You must be Hazel."

"Yes. Jeez. Hi. You scared me."

"I caught that," he said. "Imagine how I felt when I heard a prowler in the house."

"I'm sorry, too! I didn't think anyone would be here, so I let myself in."

"In my experience," he joked, "that's an excuse that does not hold up in court."

Hazel felt her jaw drop open. And then she couldn't help herself—she laughed. "Cricket said you were funny."

"He said some pretty nice things about you, too."

"We should definitely sit down and talk about them. How much time should I schedule—two hours, three?"

His grin was a mix of amusement and approval.

She hitched a thumb toward the living room. "The tree must be your doing? It's gorgeous."

"Thank you," he said with a bright smile. "I'm, uh, trying." He waved toward the living room, where she could see the tangle of strands and bulbs littering the floor. "I'm in the mood for a real Christmas this year."

"You and me both, Lee."

Reaching up, he scratched his cheek. "Only problem is—I'm not sure exactly what that entails."

CRICKET ENTERED HIS house from the garage into the mudroom. He paused, needing a moment to process the unexpected but extremely pleasant sensations greeting him. He was used to coming home to darkness and silence typically broken only by the patter of Mitt's paws or an impatient meow from Val.

Not this morning. Laughter mingled with the cheerful strands of Bing Crosby's "White Christmas." Gingerbread and cinnamon wafted pleasantly on the air. Following the smell, he discovered a platter of pumpkin pancakes still warm on the counter. From there, he could see straight into the living room, where Hazel and Lee were busy decorating a Christmas tree.

Strands of multicolored lights already danced along the branches.

His heart did this happy skippy thing as he took in the sights. His big brother perched on a stepstool with a glittering ornament in one hand. Hazel, a string of Christmas garland wrapped around her neck, was beside him, gesturing at the tree. On the floor, Mitt wrestled with an oversize knit stocking while Val critiqued them all from the comfort of the sofa back.

"A little higher," Hazel told Lee. "See how that branch next to *that* one is completely bare? Yes! Right there. Perfect."

"Good morning," Cricket said, strolling farther into the room.

Hazel whirled around, lighting up like the star on top when she saw him. And wasn't that the nicest feeling to come home to? "Cricket, hi! What are you doing here?"

"Uh…" he drawled, glancing around as if he wasn't quite sure himself. "Last I checked, this was my house, although it's changed a bit in the last few hours." He stepped over and bent to kiss her neck. "Nice necklace," he whispered. A little shiver ran through her, making him wonder if causing that reaction would ever stop being a thrill.

"Thank you. Lee gets all the credit for the tree. This was all him."

"No way!" Lee protested. "Hazel's been here for two hours. I hope you don't mind," Lee said. "I wanted to surprise you and have it all done when you got back."

"Which is why you invited my girlfriend over to help?"

"Oh," Hazel said and laughed. "No, I brought you a Secret Santa gift."

"You are *not* my Secret Santa."

Glaring playfully, she said, "How could you possibly know that?"

"Because my first gift was a pair of wool socks."

Lee brought one foot forward and pointed his toe like a ballerina. "I appreciate them, though. He re-gifted them right here on these sorry dogs."

Hazel chuckled. "Mom would approve that you're spreading the Christmas cheer around." Wool made Cricket itch, and she was extra glad she'd prevented Kai from missing the mark again. "You're right. I'm merely the delivery person. Like Lee with the tree, your Santa wanted to surprise you."

She retrieved the large gift bag from beneath the tree and handed it over. Inside was a six-pack of his favorite Grizzly Quake microbrew, a party-size bag of white-cheddar jalapeño popcorn, and a book about famous pilots and their planes.

"Hmm. Delivery person and personal shopper, perhaps?"

She shrugged her shoulders in an adorable but futile attempt at conveying innocence. Must be Kai, he deduced and then felt even worse about how he'd treated the guy. He needed to try to fix that.

Lee stepped down from the stool. "What happened to your busy schedule?"

"We had two groups of skiers cancel. One rescheduled for later this afternoon, which means I won't be able to take you to Glacier City today." Lee's SUV had broken down, and it was currently at the auto shop where he was working. Since Cricket had a final load of donations to retrieve, he'd offered Lee a lift.

"No problem. Toni offered to come and get me if I needed a ride."

Hazel asked, "What about the donations, though? Aren't you supposed to get those today?"

"I'll figure something out tomorrow. I have another packed morning, but I can go in the afternoon."

"Tomorrow, you can't," Hazel reminded him. "We have a meeting with the bus guy about the Denali tour. And don't forget the Festival of Trees is at seven."

Operation Happy Christmas's organizing, wrapping and distribution started the day after. That meant he was going to have to see if Tag could fetch the donations. Ashley had gone for them once already, but if he asked her, then Tag would know he hadn't asked him. It would be obvious he was avoiding Tag, even though they both knew they were avoiding each other. Not to mention someone would have to cover for Ashley at work, and with the holiday season upon them, Copper Crossing was swamped.

"I can do it," Hazel volunteered. "I can drop Lee off and bring back the donations."

"I don't know… I can probably find someone else, or—" He was about to mention Tag.

Hazel waved him off. "No, I'll do it. I don't want you to have to ask Tag. This way, there won't be any delay. I know what a carefully coordinated operation this is, and we're getting close to game time."

"Honestly, Hazel, that would be amazing," Cricket said.

"I don't want to put you out," Lee said to her.

"It's no trouble, I promise. Someone has to get the donations and I still need a few Christmas gifts, so I'll stop for a little shopping.

And it will be fun to be my mom's hero for a change."

She winked at Cricket and handed him a box of ornaments. "You take over here for me. I'll head into the office now, get a few hours of work done and get Kai set up for the rest of the day. Lee, I'll pick you up after, and we'll head out. I'll be back before dinner. Easy-peasy."

THEIR PLAN WORKED PERFECTLY. Until someone else's worked even better.

Hazel dropped Lee off at Dubby's Auto Repair just before two o'clock. Shopping went smoothly, and she scored every single item on her list, including a final gift for Shay. Ahead of schedule, and with high spirits, she drove to the church to pick up the donations. By the time she, Rebekah and another volunteer got everything loaded, the sky had darkened to a steely gray, and a light, steady snow was falling.

Precipitation had not been in the forecast, but the van had new snow tires and all-wheel drive, the roads were freshly groomed and the radio was tuned to an all-Christmas station. Nothing to worry about. A cup of strong, hot coffee and she'd be good to go.

A quick search on her phone located an espresso shop just down the block, where she drove through and ordered their largest dark roast along with some bite-size vanilla peppermint scones. Waiting for her bounty, she texted Cricket:

Dropped off Lee. The drive was super fun, and everything went great! Your brother is hilarious! Shopping done. Van loaded. Counted all the tablets and toys. Grabbing a coffee and then hitting the road. Can't wait to see you tonight.

She added a heart emoji and thought about how he'd told her that she owned his heart. And yet, he hadn't said "the words." But then again, neither had she. Ten years of believing she might never hear them suddenly had her impatient. Tomorrow night, she'd tell him, after the Festival of Trees. Their first public outing as a couple, and she could not wait!

Cricket responded with his usual wordy reply:

Great! Drive safe. Me too. xo

But she couldn't complain because he'd become quite the texter where she was concerned.

The road between Rankins and Glacier City cut through a massive wilderness area, and, at about the halfway mark, the countryside was at its most desolate. Traffic was light.

The snowfall tapered to intermittent wispy flakes as she reached a long straight stretch across vast, brushy, willow-strewn fields known as Parchment Flats. Prime moose country. So, when she spotted the large lump in the middle of the road, a heaviness immediately settled over her. Judging from the size, she guessed it to be a moose calf.

A quick glance in the mirrors confirmed no vehicles were behind her. Slowing the van, she tapped her emergency flashers and pulled over onto a wide spot in the road, maybe ten yards shy of the obstruction. She could see now that the lump was brown, moose-colored for sure.

Slipping on her parka, she then climbed out of the vehicle and went to investigate. Something odd about it, though. Puzzled, she stepped closer. Beneath the fresh layer of snow, it looked like fur, but there were no legs visible or a head, for that matter. What the heck?

That was when she heard the sound of another car approaching. Good, maybe someone could help her decide what to do. Because regardless, the object was a traffic hazard. Turning around, she discovered there was no other car. It was the van! Rapidly backing away.

"Hey!" she shouted and then watched helplessly as the driver executed a sudden U-turn and sped off.

The reality hit her fast and hard—she'd been set up. She squinted at the "moose" and moved closer. Kicking at the mass with one foot, she discovered a large chunk of brown fleece draped over two cardboard boxes.

Anger boiled inside of her as she reached for her phone to dial 911. Stomach plummeting, she realized she'd left it inside the van. Along with her hat, scarf and gloves—and…everything else. Including the tablets! And oh, no, all those toys.

Quickly, she disassembled the fake moose and tossed it to the side of the road. She tried to recall if she was closer to Glacier City or Rankins. There was that gas station/mini-mart several miles outside Rankins where Highland Road hit the highway. But that was still miles away. Looking around, she realized there wasn't a house or even a side road that might lead to a home anywhere in sight.

Analyzing the event objectively, she had to concede it was the perfect location for a car theft. Dang it. She zipped her jacket to the top, flipped up her hood, fastened it tight and started walking back toward Glacier City.

"IRIS, HEY, IT'S CRICKET. Have you heard from Hazel?" Cricket paced the floor at the Faraway Inn. Across the room, Margaret was on the phone with Ben. Lee hadn't responded to his texts and wasn't answering his phone either.

"No," Iris said. "She's not back from Glacier City yet?"

"She's more than an hour late and not answering her phone."

"She said she had shopping to do. Maybe she stopped somewhere to—"

"She texted me," Cricket gently interrupted and relayed the details. "There haven't been any accident reports. I don't know why she would be late at all and not let me know."

"You're right. She wouldn't. Especially after how bad she felt about Utah. Unless something is wrong with her phone."

"That doesn't seem likely. And even if there was, she should still be back by now."

"It doesn't. I'm going to hang up and have Flynn call the hospital in Glacier City."

"Okay. Your mom is on the phone with your dad. If he hasn't heard anything, I'm going to look for her." Another call came in. "Iris, I have to go. It's Lee calling."

He switched over and heard his brother's voice. "Cricket, what's going on? My phone was in my backpack. I'm just now seeing your messages."

"When did Hazel drop you off?"

"One fifty-two. I know the exact time because my shift started at two. Why? What's going on?"

"She hasn't made it back yet." He quickly explained. "Did she mention she was planning on stopping anywhere else?"

"Just the Christmas shopping, and the church, but if she texted you…" He trailed off, thinking. "I don't like this."

"Me either." A fresh surge of worry bolted through him. Cricket tried not to let his imagination run wild even as all of Iris's tragic Utah scenarios ran through his mind.

"Is there anything I can do? Do you want me to go look for her?"

"Um, not yet. But can you keep your phone with you?"

"Absolutely. Let me know as soon as you hear something."

He hung up and looked at Margaret, who was already watching him. She shook her head. "Nothing. No one has heard from her."

Cricket picked up his coat. "Flynn is calling the hospital in Glacier City. I've got to try to find her."

"Okay." A pale Margaret nodded. "Ben is

calling Hannah and Shay. He and Seth and Victoria will be right behind you."

HAZEL LINGERED AT an intersection, torn between trying to flag down help or taking a chance and venturing down a side road to find a house. The darkness was a problem, though, and the snow had picked up again. Vehicles were few and far between, and initially, she'd been spooked about the robbery and unsettled about who she might accidentally flag down. Head bent, she'd stayed as far off the side of road as she could, convinced she'd come upon a house. Possibly, she'd had a bit too much fun with Lee on the way up and misjudged how uninhabited the area was.

All the traveling she'd done, the situations she'd found herself in, meant she wasn't terrified. Bears were hibernating. She wasn't even excessively cold. Yet. The temperature was falling fast, though, and despite tightly cinching her hood, her face was feeling the bite. Her legs were a bit chilled, too, encased as they were only in jeans. Her feet were doing fine in hiking boots with thick socks. The insulated jacket she wore was perfect for the conditions, although she wouldn't have minded another layer beneath it. She longed for her scarf and missed her gloves and hat. As long as she kept moving, she'd likely be fine until Cricket or her parents or someone found her. Or she stumbled upon a house. There had to be someone living nearby. She yearned for the welcoming glow of Christmas lights.

The next car, she decided, she'd signal for help. Long minutes ticked by without a single car, irrationally causing her to speculate that road was closed. She sighed.

How soon before Cricket and her family became concerned that she was late? How much time had passed? More than an hour, she guessed. She was glad she'd texted to let him know her ETA. They'd lightheartedly joked around about his "rescue mission" to Utah, and she'd promised him that she would never intentionally ignore a text from him ever again. Even if she was upset. Surely, that meant he'd err on the side of caution, right?

A question that prompted her to speculate about how she'd ended up in this situation at all. What kind of person would plot to steal a van full of Christmas gifts for Alaska's less fortunate? Despicable. Because the more she walked and thought this through, the more convinced she was that the culprit had to have targeted the charity. The tablets were valuable and last she'd heard Squixits were selling online for quadruple their retail price.

She was so disappointed in herself. She knew better than to leave a vehicle like that. Why hadn't she at least removed the keys? Stupid! She cautioned about that type of carelessness on her blog with an entire page dedicated to Travel 101. One of the first rules was never to leave your belongings unattended! Always keep your valuables on your person. Rules you didn't think about so much when you were on your home turf.

Ugh. How was she going to break it to Mom that she'd lost everything? Worse was the aching disappointment thinking about all those little kids who needed those tablets for school, who'd asked Santa for a special toy, seniors who wouldn't be getting books and blankets. Folks who needed winter coats and socks.

Headlights appeared in the distance. Hazel waved both arms. The vehicle slowed and then veered off. She picked up her pace. If they had a phone and she could just call Cricket, then… But the car turned onto a side road and disappeared into the darkness. There were no lights that suggested homes, though, as far as she could see.

Another car appeared, driving way too fast. She waved, but it didn't even slow. *Jerk!* she thought. But then again, maybe not. Maybe they hadn't seen her or possibly they were dealing with an emergency of their own. She shouldn't have waited so long to flag down help.

Frustration welled inside of her. Worry began to mingle with the cold and crept up her spine.

As if to underscore her unease, a discordant, hair-raising howl pierced the darkness. Another joined in, and then another, until there were too many too count, the sounds mingling together, unsettling and eerie and uncomfortably close. She immediately knew the source. Because she'd always believed that if you were ever lucky enough to hear that sound, even once in your life, the chorus of a wolf pack was something you would never forget.

Moose country, she reminded herself. Why hadn't she thought about wolves?

SIX YEARS AGO, Hazel had called Cricket in the middle of the night. He'd never forget the rasp of terror in her whispered voice. *I think they're going to hold us for ransom,* she'd said after first rattling off her location as precisely as she could. *Cricket, I don't know what to do. I'm scared.*

She'd been traveling through Colombia with a small, diverse group of friends and acquaintances hailing from several countries. Near the border with Venezuela, their van was halted at a roadblock by a band of gun-wielding thugs. All six travelers were detained.

Hazel spoke some Spanish, enough to piece together their conversations, and at first, she wasn't overly alarmed. The men seemed mostly concerned with whether they were carrying weapons or drugs. She assumed they'd search their bags and let them continue traveling. Until she heard the phrase *dinero de rescate* and began to fear the worst.

One member of their group had a second cell phone the would-be kidnappers hadn't found. They'd taken turns making calls.

Tell them anything that will stall what's happening, Cricket had instructed. *And that—* The call had dropped just before he could assure her that he'd do everything in his power to help.

Cricket immediately called their friend Senator Jack Marsh, who'd proceeded to contact everyone from the State Department to the highest officials in the Colombian government, while Cricket had raced to the airport. Hours later, when he'd arrived in Colombia, where someone from the consulate had met him, he'd learned the entire group had been freed, although their vehicle had been confiscated. He'd climbed into an SUV along with two government officials and headed to the remote location.

Those hours had been the worst of his life. And even then, when he'd finally taken her in his arms, he still hadn't told her how he felt. He'd known that admitting how much he cared about her would be pointless. When he found her this time, he wouldn't make that mistake again. Everything was different now, so why hadn't he already said the words?

On the left shoulder of the road, he saw a figure barely illuminated in the edge of his headlight beam. Was it a person? He let off the gas. Definitely a person, he realized as he crept closer and they waved. He stopped across the road and bailed out of the pickup.

"Hey!" he called. "Do you need—"

"Cricket!" Hazel shouted and ran toward him.

He ran, too, and when they met, he lifted her in his arms. "Hazel." He breathed her name, his heart pulsing with joy, tears pooling in his eyes.

"I'm okay," she said as he lowered her to the ground, answering about a million questions with those two simple words. "I knew you would come looking for me."

Biting back his fear, he said, "Don't I always?"

She snuffled out a laugh and kissed him.

Taking her hand, they headed to his pickup. "You're shivering. Let's get you warmed up." He opened the passenger door, she climbed in, he shut it, jogged around to the driver's side, got in and cranked up the heat. He moved the pickup farther off the road and called Margaret. She assured him that she'd spread the word. He sent a text to Lee:

She's safe. I'll call you later.

"Take off your jacket," Cricket said and removed his, too. Then he reached into the back seat for a blanket. "Come here." She climbed onto his lap, where he wrapped her up and held her close. He adjusted the vents and scrubbed his hands over her arms and legs and back until she was ready to talk.

After a moment, she inhaled a deep breath and said, "Someone stole the van."

CHAPTER SIXTEEN

TURNED OUT THAT they were closer to Glacier City, and since the town had a larger police department, Hazel opted to go straight there and file a report.

The station wasn't nearly as busy as she'd feared, and soon after arriving, they sat down with a detective, a tall woman named Gail Carthy. Fortysomething and attractive, she had a square chin, sharp blue eyes and an easy, sympathetic smile. Hazel liked her instantly.

Hazel told her story, providing all the details she could recall, answered questions and then asked a few of her own. Margaret had all the relevant information about the van, which she emailed to the detective.

"I'm guessing we'll find the vehicle soon," Detective Carthy told them as they wrapped things up. "Empty, of course, and probably clean of prints, and stripped, depending on how big of a hurry they were in and how smart they are. Getting away with car theft is tricky here. There just aren't that many roads and places to go where you won't be spotted. Unfortunately, I don't hold out much hope for recovering the merchandise."

"Thank you, Detective," Hazel said and shook her hand. Cricket did the same.

"We'll keep you posted. And please, call or text me anytime, if you think of any further details. Nothing is too insignificant. Often, after the shock wears off, victims will remember things."

VICTIM. AS CRICKET drove them back to Rankins, he couldn't get that word out of his head. Hazel was fine. He knew that. If he didn't already revere her courage and fortitude, he would now. Seated beside him and humming softly to the Christmas station on the radio, she appeared to be handling the whole ordeal better than he was. But still, the fact remained that she *was* a victim. And he couldn't stop thinking that if he'd made the drive to Glacier City as planned, she would never have been driving the van.

A million other what-ifs followed. What if she hadn't put on her parka before she'd gotten out of the van? What if she hadn't been wearing hiking boots? What if she'd noticed the robbery sooner, ran toward the van and they were armed? Or they'd taken her? Or run her over?

His brain kept circling back to an obvious connection that he didn't want to make. No matter how he turned the situation over in his mind, he couldn't find a way to explain the theft that didn't make him wonder about Lee's past.

It was so obviously planned.

"Hey." Hazel reached over and squeezed his shoulder. "Are you okay?"

"Yes, I'm fine. But I've been wondering about something."

"What's that?"

"Why didn't you tell Detective Carthy about Lee?"

"Tell her what?" Hazel asked before immediately answering her own question. "Oh… Cricket, no. Lee did not do this. He wouldn't! How dumb would he have to be? You've said yourself that he has a code, that he never steals from people who, in his mind, can't afford it. Besides, he's put that life behind him."

This was all true. His brother was anything but dumb and always chose his marks carefully. That was why Cricket was reasonably certain that Lee hadn't done it. But was he involved somehow? Who had he told about the van full of tablets and hard-to-find toys? And what did he truly know about his brother's criminal leanings, aside from what Lee claimed? Lee had learned from Frank, who was a liar and a con man. Maybe Lee was more like Frank than Cricket knew.

The "going straight," therapy, moving back to Rankins, Dr. Easton, the Christmas tree—what if it was all a big act?

"AND THAT, KIDS, is why you never leave your car unlocked on the side of the road," Hazel announced after they'd finally made it back to Margaret and Ben's, where she relayed the story of the theft once again.

"Oh, honey." Ben wrapped an arm around her shoulders for a sideways hug. "My brave one."

"Mom, I'm so sorry about the tablets and the toys and everything else."

Margaret shook her head. "All that matters is that you're safe."

"Don't forget about that piece of fuzzy brown fabric," Seth quipped. "She saved the heck out of that, too."

"Seth!" Victoria elbowed him. "Your sister just suffered a terrible trauma. This is nothing to joke about. She could have frozen to death or—"

But Hazel was already laughing. "Vic, thank you. You are sweet, but I'm fine. Seriously, the wolves were freaking me out more than the cold or the robbery. Thankfully, I was smart enough to slip on my parka before I got out of the car."

"Wolves!" Scarlett cried. "You saw wolves?" Wolves were a particular fascination for the girl, who was enthralled with all things Alaska. Bering had promised to take her out to one of his remote cabins, where they had a good chance of spotting some.

"Couldn't see them. Just heard them. I wasn't overly concerned they were going to get me. But they do sound kind of spooky and…"

"Smug," Iris finished knowingly. "Wolves are so smug." Iris was terrified of both wolves and bears and pretty much every other predator in the animal kingdom.

"Smug?" Seth repeated with a chuckle.

"Yes, smug. I can guarantee they were rubbing it in like schoolyard bullies and telling all their friends about how Hazel was stranded. Or possibly how to make Hazel gravy." She breezily waved one hand. "It's difficult for me to translate with complete accuracy since I wasn't there to interpret, but that's the gist."

They all laughed. Scarlett looked downright envious. Hazel loved her family, especially her "trips" for helping her find some much-needed humor in this situation.

But that didn't make the larger problem any

better. Hazel looked between her mom and Cricket. "I am sorry, you guys, because Seth is right. You've worked so hard on Operation Happy Christmas, and now those kids won't get their tablets, and people won't have gifts because I stupidly got out of the van to save a piece of brown fabric."

"That's not what I meant," Seth said, turning serious. He reached out and squeezed her forearm. "I was just trying to make you laugh. Hazel, whoever did this would have found a way to steal the van, anyway. If you were too heartless to stop for a fake moose, they would have pulled out in front of you, or nudged your bumper, or worse. And I don't even want to think about what that worse might have been."

"He's right," her dad said confidently. "It's pretty clear that the thieves knew exactly what was in that van."

THE NIGHT BEFORE, Cricket had known he was almost out of both gas and coffee, but by the time he'd left the Jameses' house, he'd been too tired to do anything about either one, so here he was at the Super-Stop Quick-Mart with double intentions of fueling up. The place was surprisingly busy so early in the morning.

"Hey, Cricket!" Park Lowell shouted, bailing out of his luxury SUV.

"Good morning, Park."

Cricket lifted a hand to wave. Park pulled on a stocking cap and scurried his direction.

"Heard about those tablets getting stolen," he said when he'd crossed the small parking lot. Park was a member of the board of Snowy Sky Resort, an Operation Happy Christmas volunteer and a huge town gossip. "Is it true Hazel James was carjacked while driving the charity's van?"

"No," Cricket calmly returned even though he was already getting irritable. "She wasn't carjacked. The van was stolen, yes. Hazel was not inside the vehicle at the time."

"But still, that's awful. All those gifts—and the tablets! Wow. What a shame."

"It is," he agreed. The pump clicked off, and Cricket busied himself with replacing the hose and attaching the cap on the fuel tank, hoping Park would end the conversation and move along.

He didn't budge. "So, uh, I heard your brother, Lee, was back in town?"

"You did, huh?" Cricket responded cagily even as that old, familiar rush of apprehension and shame blossomed inside of him. Park didn't have to say what he was thinking. It wasn't helping that he still hadn't heard from

Lee. Several calls and texts since the night before without a response.

"How's ol' Lee doing, anyway? He, uh, living here in Rankins?"

Cricket reined in his temper because really, how could he blame Park, or anyone else, for wondering what he'd been agonizing about himself?

"He's good. I'll tell him you were asking about him. I gotta run, Park. I'll see you later." Skipping the coffee he'd planned to get for the journey, he hopped into his pickup and headed up to Snowy Sky.

The resort was an easy drive into the mountains outside Rankins. Once he arrived, he was able to put the encounter with Park behind him. Park was a busybody. No reason to think anyone else would make a connection between the robbery and Lee. He headed for the lodge to grab that coffee and have a quick word with Hannah.

He'd traveled approximately six steps inside the door when a voice called out, "Cricket!" Regina Worley, Snowy Sky's office manager, hurried over to him. Midfifties, plump, she had pretty red hair that she always wore swept up into a bun, where she often had a pencil nestled among her twisted locks. It was cute. Regina was also supersmart and an encouraging, positive presence around the resort. "I am so sorry to hear about the robbery. Is it true that all of the Operation Happy Christmas gifts were stolen?"

"No, Regina," he answered patiently because there was no way he could be anything but with Regina. "That's not true." He quickly explained.

"Oh, well, that's good. I'm glad Hazel is okay."

"Me too."

"What's going to happen about the gifts?"

"I don't know," Cricket replied.

"Hal and I already made another donation."

"Thank you, Regina. That's extremely generous."

"Piper posted about this travesty on the paper's Facebook page, so I imagine the community will step up. And I heard Laurel is putting an article together, too." Laurel owned the *Rankins Press*, the town's newspaper, where her younger sister, Piper, worked as a reporter.

That kind of attention would help recoup some of the loss for sure. Unfortunately, that also meant speculation about Lee would spread. Soon, everyone in town would be gossiping about Lee's return and his potential involvement in the robbery. If they weren't already. Cricket tried to quash his own doubt.

"You let me know if there's anything else I can do to help."

"Will do. Thank you, Regina."

Cricket was already walking away when Regina added, "Hey, I heard your brother, Lee, got out of jail…"

ALL HIS YEARS of piloting experience meant Cricket was a master at putting everything out of his mind except the current flight. A feat he managed as he transported several groups of heli-skiers and deposited them onto the snow-covered slopes.

Later in the afternoon, he made it back to town with enough time to swing by the hardware store for cat food, the bank to deposit a check and then the Cozy Caribou for a take-out sandwich before he was due at Our Alaska Tours for a meeting. Including an additional three inquiries at Snowy Sky, he was asked about the robbery, or Lee, or Lee and the robbery nine more times. Two people asked point-blank if Lee was responsible. Three people speculated that Frank was involved.

Still no word from Lee. Frustrated and disheartened, he couldn't bring himself to stop at the grocery store to buy coffee. There would be no avoiding people there, and he was tired. His plan was to pilfer enough coffee from the office to make his morning pot and then shop very early in the morning when the store would be empty. Maybe. If he heard from Lee.

As he walked into the Our Alaska Tours office, his spirits were low and his patience threadbare. Hazel, Kai and the bus company rep, Brian, were already seated at the conference table. Hazel and Kai were extremely prepared for the meeting, which was a massive relief because, admittedly, Cricket's mind wandered to all the old familiar bad places.

When the meeting concluded, and Brian departed, Cricket hoped neither Hazel nor Kai would ask his opinion on anything they'd discussed. Hazel and Kai chatted about the details while Kai began to gather his belongings to leave for the day.

Cricket wandered over to his desk, where he found another Secret Santa gift. The bundle was wrapped in a fuzzy lap blanket that the cats would adore. Inside there was a mug with an awesome Our Alaska Tours logo emblazoned on the side. It was creative, original, professional-looking, and he was sure Kai had designed it. He'd heard him whispering with Hazel about it. But for Cricket, the true prize was the two-pound bag of dark roast Holiday Blend coffee.

Instantly, the weight on his shoulders lightened. Now he could go days before he had to brave the grocery store. Unbelievable, the happiness a bag of coffee could bring.

He looked at their employee. "Kai?"

"Yeah, boss?"

"Thank you."

Kai did his best to look confused and nearly pulled it off. "For what?"

Cricket smiled. "For all of your hard work. You're doing an exceptional job here. We're incredibly lucky to have you. I don't know if Bering has said anything yet, but we're hoping you'll stay on after the season if you're interested in working for us long-term."

Kai stared, slowly blinking as if he couldn't quite believe what he was hearing. "What are you...? Seriously? Stay here in Rankins and work for you?"

"Yes, we can talk about the details later. I know you have to get going so you can get set up at the festival. But I hope you'll at least consider an offer. We'll sit down and write something up."

"Uh, wow. Okay, yes. Thank you, Cricket. I will."

He left wearing a huge smile, and Cricket was completely aware of Hazel eyeing him speculatively. Approvingly. Finally, a bright spot in this dark day.

"Well," she said in a crisp tone, and he could feel his own grin brewing because he knew her comment was going to make him laugh. "That went well. I see that you two are, um, patching things up?"

And it did. "Yes, with any luck, we'll soon be BFFs like you and Ashley."

"Funny," she said flatly but couldn't entirely suppress her chuckle. "Seriously, Cricket, thank you."

"Hey, he earned it. I freely admit that you were right about him all along. He's great. But have you noticed how much less annoying he is now that he's not dating you?"

"I have, actually. I experienced a similar phenomenon with my BFF. Her *demonstrativeness*—is that a word?—toward you has now become sort of sweet."

Stepping close for a quick hug, he kissed her. She was so precious to him, which reminded him of how easily he could have lost her. When he pulled away, he asked, "Any word from Detective Carthy?"

"No. Not since this morning." As predicted, the police had found the van. The crime scene techs were processing for clues and fingerprints, but the police weren't optimistic. "Don't expect to hear from her again anytime soon."

Unacceptable, he thought, how someone was

going to get away with this crime. Instead of coming to terms with what had happened, the fear was growing in his mind.

Hazel slipped on her coat. "I need to get going, too. I'll see you at the inn around seven? I still have to pick up my dress from Janie. She altered one of Iris's for me. Iris and I are going early to help Shay with a few last-minute details."

"Okay."

"Hey," Hazel said, reaching out and taking his hand. She peered at him intently. "Are you all right? You seemed a little distracted during the meeting."

"I will be," he declared. Because, hopefully, he would be, just as soon as he talked to Lee.

THE FESTIVAL OF TREES was always held at the Faraway Inn. Hazel felt a unique stir of delight and anticipation as she took it all in. Strategically placed around the dining room, the trees stood tall and proud in all their sparkling and glittering glory. Patrons, decked out in their finest, were mingling, exchanging greetings, chatting and admiring the cleverly themed trimmings. Whimsical, cheerful holiday centerpieces decorated the tables. It was probably corny, but it was like she could feel the Christmas spirit swirling around the room.

For the last few years, Shay had served as the festival's organizing committee's chairperson. Part of the event's appeal was how they kept the program fresh and fun by adding new twists and taking away other elements when they became stale.

This year, they'd added a social hour with a silent auction and raffle. Individuals and businesses could donate goods or a service in addition to or in lieu of a tree. Our Alaska Tours was raffling an all-expenses-paid signature tour for two. Hazel was thrilled to see that people were lingering around the poster and brochure they'd made, and with the handsome and charming Kai on hand to answer questions, tickets were selling fast. Kai seemed especially engaging, and she couldn't help but think Cricket's accolades and job offer had a little something to do with that.

According to Shay, who was also beaming, the evening was shaping up to be the most successful benefit ever. Tickets had sold out, and bidding for the silent auction items was exceeding her expectations.

"Nice necklace." Hazel complimented the glittering letters on the silver chain.

"Isn't it gorgeous?" Shay gushed, lifting the charms to show Hazel, who knew each one contained the intricate engraving of the names along the swooping curve of each letter—an *S, J, M* and *C*.

"Shay, Jonah, Maggie, Caleb," Hazel said. "That is so cool."

"I know. From my Secret Santa. Who would be thoughtful enough to include Caleb on here? I'm not even joking, I had tears when I opened it. Don't tell anyone, but when I find out who mine is, I'm going to ask them to give Jonah some gifting tips."

"My lips are sealed," Hazel promised.

Looking around, she realized that except for the kids, her entire family was in attendance. Everyone except...

"Hey, where's Cricket?" Iris asked, joining her by the silent-auction table, where she'd bid on a blown-glass lamp donated by local artist Kella Jakobs.

"Not here yet."

"Everything okay?"

"I hope so." Hazel sighed. "I don't know... He was acting funny earlier. Kind of distant. This whole robbery thing has shaken him."

As the minutes ticked by and he didn't arrive, she struggled to hold on to that holiday glow.

"LEE, CAN YOU hear me? Where are you?" Cricket was almost shouting into the phone.

"Yeah, bare...ly." A staticky Lee's voice came through the horrible connection. "I got... tied...something."

Cricket strode through the lobby of the Faraway Inn, moving toward a window, where he hoped for clearer reception. He stopped in time to hear Lee, in a voice now clear and crisp, ask, "How's Hazel?"

"She's fine."

Lee's sigh of relief came through, too. But it didn't last. "That's great. She's...awes... Crick..." He moved again.

"She is. Are you coming back tonight? I'm at the Festival of Trees, but I'll be home later, and I need to talk to you."

That made it worse. "Sorry...van. Some... need...tomorrow."

"Lee?"

The line went dead.

Cricket groaned in frustration and tapped his phone off. *Sorry van?* What did that even mean? He hated how much he was doubting his brother.

He stepped inside the dining room just as the mayor approached the podium. His deep voice boomed across the room. "Good evening, ladies and gentlemen. Welcome to the Festival of Trees. Thank you all so much for being here tonight. Wow. Do we have some extra-special trees up for grabs this year, or what?" Applause broke out. He went on to outline the evening's schedule while Cricket homed in on Hazel's location across the room.

She stood with a group that included Iris, Ashley and Kai. He began to weave his way through the crowd, but soon halted again when the mayor changed direction. "As many of you know, Operation Happy Christmas, a charity started by our own Margaret James, had their van stolen yesterday. The vehicle was full of gifts and valuable electronics. If anyone has information on who may have committed this terrible act, please call either the Rankins or Glacier City police departments."

Cricket braced himself for an evening of inquiries and suspicion. He focused on Hazel. If he could just reach her side, and remain there, maybe he could get through this evening. Maybe then the walls would stop closing in on him. Taking a step forward, he restarted his journey when a familiar voice had him halting again.

"Cricket."

"Hey, Tag," he said, turning toward the sound, relief rushing through him. He could use his friend's support right now, too. "I've been meaning to call you. I—"

But Tag's tone was pure ice when he interrupted, "What were you thinking?" The tension emanating from him was matched only by the force of his stare. Apparently, he wasn't quite finished being angry.

"About what, specifically?"

"How could you have put my sister in danger like that? She told me that she drove Lee to Glacier City yesterday."

"What are you implying, Tag?" But he knew, and it pressed directly on the already-exposed raw nerve that was the robbery.

Tag huffed. "That didn't come out right. I know you wouldn't purposely put Hazel in danger."

"No, I wouldn't," he said, irrationally defensive because he was getting angry now, too. But not at Tag. At himself.

Tag looked away for a few seconds before seeming to reach a decision. Looking squarely at Cricket, he said, "I'm not the only one wondering what Lee was doing yesterday after Hazel dropped him off. Everyone is talking about it. Crab Johnson is convinced that Lee and Frank pulled it off together. If you can look me in the eye and tell me that the possibility of Lee being involved hasn't occurred to you, I'll drop this right now."

And that was the moment that Cricket realized how pointless his efforts truly had been.

All of them. Almost forty years of doing the right thing, being the best person, student, pilot, citizen, rotary club member, volunteer— the best *friend*—he could possibly be, and none of it mattered. Because he had put Hazel in danger, however inadvertent it may have been.

And he'd never be forgiven. Not completely. Because he could never forgive himself. Without another word, he turned around and walked away. From everything.

Hazel caught up with him in the lobby. "Cricket!"

For a second, he considered that maybe he should just keep on walking. What was the point in dragging this out? But he'd promised that he wouldn't hide his feelings anymore. The least he could do was keep that promise.

"Where are you going?"

"I'm going home." But not for long, he silently added.

"What? Why? I saw you and Tag talking. Then I saw you leave. What did he say to you?"

"He didn't say anything that everyone in that room isn't thinking—or talking about. He just took it up a notch because he loves you. And I…" *I love you, too.* No, he wouldn't say it and complicate this further. Suddenly, he was glad he hadn't yet spoken those words aloud. It would be easier to let her go.

"You what?"

"Hazel, I can't stand the thought of what could have happened. You could have been killed."

"But I wasn't! Cricket, I am fine. It barely fazed me."

"But it should have. It fazed me." He clapped a hand to his chest before gesturing toward the dining room. "And Tag. And the rest of your family, even though they are all too kind to say what Tag did. You heard your dad and Seth talking about how much worse it could have been. And now the whole town is wondering if Lee had something to do with it. This is my fault."

"Not the whole town! And not my entire family. This robbery was in no way your fault. You don't even know if Lee was involved, and *I* don't think he was!"

"That doesn't matter. You don't get it, Hazel. The speculation alone is enough. My brother, my dad, their choices—the consequences of being a Blackburn have always affected me, and they always will. I can't change that, but I won't let it harm you."

"So, that's your answer? To *leave*? To give everyone a reason to believe that their unsubstantiated gossip bothers you?"

It did bother him. It bothered him because the gossip was usually true, or at least mostly accurate. She didn't understand, and he couldn't expect her to, could he? She was a James. Her family name was beyond reproach. She'd never been the victim of a scandal or gossip the way that he had.

"It's about so much more than that, Hazel. All these years, it made it easier in a way to keep my distance, knowing I wasn't good enough for you. But then this—us—happened, and I thought... For a little while, I let myself believe that maybe I'd finally escaped the Blackburn reputation. Your mom and dad seemed fine about us being together, and I'd worked so hard to overcome my family name, so maybe I deserved to have what I wanted. But then Lee came back, and the robbery just reminded everyone—including me—of who I am and where I come from.

"I should have known better to think we could... Tag is right. I put you in danger. I should never have let this go so far. And I don't know what to do."

"What do you mean you should have known better? Are you talking about us?"

He didn't answer.

"Cricket?"

He couldn't bring himself to say the words.

"Please," she whispered, her voice thick with

emotion. Tears shimmered in her eyes, and he could see how much he was hurting her. And his own pain was so intense he could barely hold on to her gaze. "Can we please talk about this? I don't see this the same way that you do."

"You don't have to. Because I know that I put you in danger simply by being me—and I don't just mean physical danger. If it hadn't been the van, it would be something else eventually. I'm, uh… I need to go right now, Hazel. I need some time. I have to talk to Lee and figure things out. I'll be in touch."

CHAPTER SEVENTEEN

SHOCK AND CONFUSION churned inside of Hazel as she watched Cricket push through the door of the Faraway Inn. *I'll be in touch?* she scoffed. What was that? Like they were business associates. And what did he need to figure out? Because it sure sounded like he meant their relationship.

The truth stabbed into her heart. Slowly, the pain spread from there, making it difficult to move, or to breathe, or even to think clearly. She was losing him. And after they'd overcome so much to get here.

What to do?

She wanted to leave, too, even took a few steps to follow. Not smart, she immediately realized. With Cricket gone and the rumor mill already grinding about Lee, she wouldn't give people something else to talk about. Which was also why she decided not to confront Tag in front of the entire town. But, wow, she was angry with him. And now she was a little angry with Cricket, too. Why didn't he fight back?

Maybe, after he talked to Lee and was confident that he wasn't involved in the robbery, they could work this out? They had to because she'd already begun to plan for a life with him. She refused to give up.

But what if he was pulling away for good this time? That was when she realized that regardless, she couldn't go through this again—this hope and dejection, hot and cold, Cricket and no Cricket. She needed him to be all in. Or out. But what if he chose out? Fear and despair joined with her anger, and the crack in her heart began to widen.

No, no, no, she told herself, blinking back tears. She would not cry. Not yet. She inhaled a deep breath, forced a smile and went in search of her lifeline, her people. Where were Seth and Iris?

She knew she and Cricket were worth fighting for! How could he not see that? And Tag and his opinions? Right now, she didn't care that it was all wrapped in a veil of caring. Her brother was just... Ugh! Yes, stay focused on the anger, and she would get through this evening and *then*...

Then *both* of these men would hear from her. Tag first. She was preparing her speech when she reentered the dining room.

"What's wrong?" Seth demanded, appearing at her side.

"Are you okay?" Iris asked from the other side.

Okay, so maybe there'd be no hiding of emotions where these two were concerned. There was a surprising amount of comfort in that.

"Everything and no," she answered them both.

Iris said, "What happened?"

"Tag attacked Cricket, and then Cricket may have broken up with me."

"Attacked him?" Seth repeated anxiously. "With what? Is he okay? Where are they?"

"I think she means a verbal assault," Iris said. "Not with, like, a baseball bat or whatever it is that you're thinking—that is what you're thinking, right?"

"Maybe," Seth confessed. "My money would be on Cricket. Don't tell Tag I said that."

Iris gave her head a little shake and said, "You are such a guy sometimes."

"Thank you?" Seth said and shrugged an agreeable shoulder.

To Hazel, she attempted to clarify, "Tag and Cricket had an argument? What do you mean, he broke up with you? Tell us everything that happened."

DETECTIVE CARTHY HAD phoned him early this morning while he was already on the way to Glacier City. Stopping by the station seemed simpler than talking over the phone, especially since he had questions of his own.

"So, you're saying you haven't heard from your brother?" Detective Carthy stared Cricket down as he wondered how many different ways she could ask the same question?

The Glacier City police station was significantly busier this morning than it had been when he and Hazel were last here. Presumably, the holidays were as busy for criminals as they were for everyone else.

"Like I said, not since last night." He reached across the desk and handed her his phone, the string of texts between him and Lee displayed on the screen. "Go ahead and pull up the call log, too. You can see the call at 6:53 p.m., which, as I already explained, was cut short. I texted him an hour later. He responded, saying he'd call when he had better reception. That's it."

Cricket was very aware that trying to find Lee could be a waste of time, but that didn't matter at this point. It was something he had to do. He'd cleared his schedule, arranged for another pilot to take his flights for the next several days. His friend Laurel had agreed to care for the cats if he didn't make it back to Rankins for a day or two.

"Is Lee a suspect? Is that why you want to speak to him?"

"No. There is no evidence that your brother was involved," she answered. "He has a solid alibi. He was at work. Several people have verified." Cricket didn't let his relief show. Better that the detective thought he had no doubts.

"That's good," he answered confidently, hoping to learn more.

She went on, "The evening of the robbery, he voluntarily came in for questioning because he assumed we'd want to speak with him. Cooperated fully. He also seemed extremely anxious about Hazel and adamant that we solve the case."

Cricket nodded. All good.

"What I wanted to speak with you about is your visit to Otter Creek Correctional Facility the other week."

"Oh. Uh, not much to tell there. I went to visit Lee, but he'd already been released."

"Right. That's what the visitor log shows. What I can tell you is that we have information that the crime may be connected to Otter Creek."

"What does that mean?"

"We have an informant who has given us details about the robbery, which leads us to believe someone, or multiple persons, may have planned it from the inside."

"Is that informant Lee?" he asked even though he couldn't see how that was possible.

"No. But since Lee was recently released from there, I'd like to see what he knows."

"I think if he knew anything, he would have told you." Cricket didn't know that, though he wanted to believe it. But he also knew that informing was a huge violation of the thief code.

"What I'm thinking is that he might not know that he knows. I'd like to speak with him again."

"Ah. I see. When I hear from Lee, I'll let him know."

"I appreciate that, thank you."

Detective Carthy smiled, finally. "How's Hazel?"

"Completely fine," he said. "It's like it didn't even bother her."

"I got that vibe from her. In my experience, there are people in this world who are just good at that, at extracting the positive parts out of life and discarding the rest. She seems to be one of them."

"I agree. She is like that." He loved that about her.

"But sometimes the effects of trauma can

take a while to hit a person. My advice is to be aware of that, too."

"I will. Thank you, Detective."

Two thoughts ran through Cricket's mind as he left the station. Was it wrong not to say where he thought Lee might possibly be? It seemed so far-fetched, though, that it felt safer just to go see for himself. The second was, would the police follow him? No, that was ridiculous. This wasn't a television drama. No one had been murdered or injured, and the detective stated outright that Lee wasn't a suspect.

Toni Mullens's home address hadn't been difficult to obtain, and neither had the location of the vacant property she'd mentioned. A simple records search on the borough assessor's office website had revealed two properties in her name. Now Cricket typed the address of the first property into his phone's navigation. As he set off, he wondered if this was what it felt like for a police officer to have a hunch.

He would have just called Toni and asked but didn't want to put her in a position of covering for Lee if his worst fears were in play and Lee was hiding from law enforcement.

He'd know soon enough, and roughly a half hour later, after driving out of town, his phone alerted him that he'd arrived. The driveway appeared almost like a tunnel through the thick brush. The path was unplowed, but there were relatively fresh tire tracks.

He proceeded forward. A dilapidated shack soon came into view. It appeared unlivable. No windows with the roof caved in on one side. But he was far more interested in how the tracks led around behind the cabin. He proceeded that direction, where he discovered an old tarp-covered camp trailer with Lee's SUV parked beside it.

Like he'd been expecting him, Lee emerged from the camper before he could even turn off the engine. Waving, he tromped over to the passenger side and opened the door. "Hey, little brother!" he called cheerfully, tossing his backpack over the seat and climbing in. "Good timing. Car won't start again. Thought I could make it until my next paycheck to put in a new alternator. You saved my bacon. I was just getting ready to hike into town."

"Lee, what is going on? Why haven't you called me back?"

"Uh," he said, gesturing around as if the answer was obvious, "even if I had decent service here, I couldn't. Phone's dead. No electricity. Car's dead. Couldn't charge it. Nightmare."

That was all perfectly valid.

Lee reached out to adjust the vent and then

turned up the fan. "No joke, I almost froze to death last night. It reminded me of that winter when Dad took off for like two months and didn't pay the power bill. Remember that?"

"Yeah." How could he forget going to bed at night in his winter coat and snow pants and still piling on every blanket in the house? After about a week, Cricket had offhandedly mentioned to Tag that he was tired of eating frozen food.

The next day, the power was back on. Only later did he learn that Tag had told Ben and Margaret, who'd then paid their overdue bill and continued paying until Frank had returned.

"How did you know where to find me? You call Toni?"

"No. Well, I called her a while back, after I went to the prison and you weren't there. She hadn't heard from you yet, but she mentioned an old camper you'd left on her property, and I took a chance you might be here."

"Huh. Good thinking."

"Why didn't you drive back to Rankins last night? When I called your work, they said you took a couple of days off."

"I had some things to do, people to see, questions to ask, which I did, but then I came here to pick up stuff that I left in the camper, and the car died again. Speaking of being stranded in the cold, how is Hazel? I could barely hear you last night, but I thought you said fine. She's all right, then?"

"I did say fine. No lasting effects, as far the cold goes, anyway."

"What do you mean?" Concern transformed his expression. "Did someone hurt her?"

Me, he thought. *I hurt her, and that's the last thing I wanted to do.* "No. But she's… Lee, I don't know how to tell you this, but you're the talk of the town in Rankins. People think you had something to do with the robbery."

He scoffed. "Does Hazel believe that?"

"No, she doesn't," he scoffed. "It didn't even occurred to her. The police asked all their questions, where she'd been and who she was with before it happened. She gave them your name and told them where she dropped you off, but never mentioned that you have a record."

Lee's smile was electric. "You need to figure out how to keep her."

Cricket couldn't bring himself to say that he didn't think he had a right to.

"Did you tell them?" Lee asked.

"No."

"But it occurred to you?"

"It did." He sighed. "I'm sorry, Lee. I'm not going to lie. And I've been a little freaked out that I couldn't get ahold of you."

"Good. You start lying to me, and our brother-ship is over."

"Brother-ship?"

"Yeah, you know—a friendship but with brothers."

Cricket couldn't help but smile. "It's been a while since we had one of those, huh?" Surprising how much he longed for that again.

Lee turned serious and said, "Listen, Cricket, I know that's my fault. I never wanted my wayward life to affect yours, even though I know it did just by association. I know that because Dad's antics ruined everything for me. Instead of fighting back, I gave up. You didn't, and I'm so proud of you for that. But the one thing I've never done is lie to you. And I swear to you, right now, that I didn't have anything to do with that robbery."

"I believe you." And he realized how much he'd wanted to hear Lee say those words. A wave of relief washed over him because he did believe him. Maybe they could do this. If Lee went straight—for real this time—maybe they could put their past away for good. Be a real family, a respectable one. At the very least, they could have a true brother-ship.

But then Lee slammed him right back into reality. "But I might know who did."

"I'M NOT GOING to apologize for trying to protect you, Hazel," Tag announced after Hazel marched inside his office at Copper Crossing Air Transport and shut the door. She had Ashley to thank for alerting her to this brief window of opportunity to confront her brother uninterrupted. Ashley had also posted herself at the reception desk to guard the door and field calls.

Hazel moved to the chair directly opposite his desk and sat. "How is accusing Cricket of putting me in danger trying to protect me?"

"Let's be clear—he *did* put you in danger. Lee is a known criminal with criminal associates and connections."

"Not a violent one!"

"He's a thief."

"A former thief. He's changed. He's a good person, Tag."

"And your proof of this change and new-found goodness," he articulated in a tone rife with sarcasm, "is the brief conversation you had with him on the way to Glacier City right before the van you were driving was stolen out from under you?"

"Not entirely." They'd spent the morning decorating a tree, she wanted to add, but didn't, because he had a point. A small one, but regardless. "He's making true efforts at reform."

Lee had told her about going to therapy, but that information was not hers to share. "Trust me. I'd tell you to ask Cricket, but that would undoubtedly be a disaster. Ask Mom and Dad."

"*You* go ask Mom and Dad. While you're at it, ask them all about Cricket's childhood."

"I did," she shot back.

"Then you didn't get the whole story." Tag heaved a frustrated sigh. "You weren't there, Hazel, when we were growing up. Cricket needed someone—someone consistent—in his life, and that was not Lee. He breezed in and out of Cricket's life and could not be counted on. He had no one he could trust."

"That's not true. He had you—and Mom and Dad."

"Yeah, he did."

"Exactly! Who was there for Lee? According to Mom, no one. Except for Frank, a hard-core convict. How can you expect a child who has had very little moral guidance himself to know what to do for another child? Lee did the best he could with what he had," she added, unashamedly stealing a quote from their mom.

"He grew up! What's his excuse been for the last twenty-some years?"

"I'm not making excuses for his breaking the law in the past, for the life he chose for himself. But he did his best to keep Cricket out of it—unlike Frank, who dragged Lee into his life of crime. And he's changed, Tag. He's legitimately trying, and he deserves this chance. He didn't have anything to do with this."

"You cannot possibly know that."

"Innocent until proven guilty," she countered. "I know that."

When he didn't respond, she tackled another aspect. "Aside from your issues with Lee, what about Cricket and how you treated him? Your best friend, who has *always* been there for you. And for Hannah, Bering, Dad—for everyone in our family. Including me. In whatever way we need."

"*Pfft.* Beside the point."

"No, it is the point! Six years ago, when I was nearly kidnapped for ransom by thugs in Colombia, Cricket was the person I called in the middle of the night."

"You—you were..." he sputtered. "What?"

She gave him the brief version and then said, "Cricket called Senator Marsh and then flew all the way to South America to get me. He begged me to tell you guys, but I swore him to secrecy for just this reason—your overprotectiveness." That wasn't entirely true; Iris's unreasonable fears and her parents' ongoing concern about her safety in traveling alone were also factors. "I knew that if I called you, you'd never stop questioning my career choice."

He didn't argue. They both knew it was true. He often opined anyway when he had concerns about a country or a region being unsafe. He and Iris both did that.

"Humph." He paused, and for a moment, she thought he might relent. Nope. Folding his arms across his chest, he shook his head. "Cricket should have told me about that, too," he said, implying the omission was another betrayal.

"He dropped everything so he and Iris could fly to Utah because he was worried. Cricket cares about me, too."

"Yeah," Tag scoffed. "I'm aware. I *saw* all the *caring* going on, remember? I can't unsee it. My retinas are scarred. Even though it's apparent that I was the last to know."

"Oh, my…" She rolled her eyes. "How old are you? It was just a kiss. Cricket is right—it's a good thing you didn't know about what happened ten years ago."

"What happened ten years ago?" he demanded.

"We kissed. Let me clarify. I kissed him. My point in telling you all of this is that Cricket and I have a history, too. One that goes back all the way to high school for me."

"You had a *relationship* with my best friend, who is ten years older than you, while you were in *high school*? That's it…" Reaching up, he slid both hands around the back of his neck, linked his fingers and squeezed—his signature gesture of frustration. "This is even worse than I realized. I am going to kill him."

"No, you're not even listening! I have been in love with him since then. The kiss didn't happen until I was a freshman in college."

"Oh, that's so much better," he drawled, "that he waited until you were *nineteen* to take advantage of you."

"He *never* took advantage of me, Tag. If anything, it was the opposite. I seized an opportunity to act on how I felt."

"Okay," he said calmly, placatingly. Placing his hands, palms down on the desk before him, he went on in a condescending tone, "What I'm getting out of this is that my best friend has had a secret life that I know nothing about. And that secret life has involved cavorting around with my little sister and either putting her in danger or covering up the fact that she was in danger. Multiple times. Clearly, he is even more like his dad and his brother than I realized."

"That's enough." She popped to her feet. "This is pointless. You are irrational."

Trying not to stomp, she left the office, very firmly closing the door on her way out.

"I'm guessing from the anger-march and the door-slam that didn't go well?" a cringing Ashley remarked.

"He's impossible. Just…" Hands fisting with frustration, she struggled to find the right word.

Ashley helped her out. "Stubborn? Inflexible?"

"Yes! And a complete…"

"Stickler? Perfectionist?"

"Yes!"

"I know!" she agreed. "You Jameses can all be like that."

"Hey! I thought you were supposed to be helping."

"I am." Ashley belted out a laugh. "That's not an insult. Your brother is the best boss in the entire world. Not to mention he's become a very good friend. All I'm saying is that he has very high standards. For himself and those around him. You all do. And the loyalty is… above and beyond. Must be nice to be a part of such a…clan."

"Sometimes," she conceded. Then immediately felt guilty and amended, "Most of the time."

"He'll come around," she predicted. "How

could he not? The only person as good as he is just happens to be the man you're fighting about." Ashley grinned. "I love Cricket. You've got yourself a good one there, Hazel James."

"Thank you, Ashley," she said and meant it. Possibly, the biggest holiday miracle was this friendship that she seemed to be forging with her archenemy.

Glancing furtively toward Tag's office before focusing on Hazel again, Ashley lowered her voice and asked, "Did the detective call you today?"

"No. Why?"

"Well, she just called me."

"Why would she call you?"

"To ask about my visit to see Roy in prison."

"Why would she want to know about that?"

"Because I think I might know who stole the van."

CHAPTER EIGHTEEN

"LET ME GET this straight," Seth said to Hazel, carefully folding the end of the wrapping paper into a neat triangle. "You and Ashley are going all Cagney and Lacey to solve the robbery?"

"Not *solve* it necessarily, just see if there's anything to Ashley's theory." Hazel ripped off a length of tape and handed it to him.

She'd found him here early this morning in their dad's study, scissors in hand, surrounded by a pile of boxes and rolls of wrapping paper. Because he'd been traveling for his job the last few months, he'd cleverly had all the gifts he'd purchased for Victoria and Scarlett sent here to their parents' house.

"And her theory is that her ex-husband masterminded the theft from the comfort of his cell?"

"You make it sound very far-fetched." Hazel took the wrapped box, plopped a bow on top and set it aside.

Eyebrows up, chin down, the expression on his face was confirmation that he thought precisely that.

Ignoring the look, she handed him another gift from his cache, a package of shiny metallic fishing lures for Scarlett. "This is very cool. You're going to be an awesome stepdad—and dad, too, if you and Victoria decide to have more kiddos."

"Thank you," he said. "I love hearing that. But that doesn't distract me from the point of you going vigilante crime solver here."

"Okay, listen, when you hear it from Ashley's point of view, it makes a lot more sense. You know how Ashley is still close with her former sister-in-law, Stefanie?"

"Yeah. Stefanie is married to Roy's brother, Darrell."

"Right. Their kids are around the same age, and they've managed to stay friends through the divorce. Anyway…"

With Seth wielding the paper and scissors, Hazel assisted with tape and bows while she relayed the story Ashley had told her yesterday at Copper Crossing.

After they'd returned home from Juneau, Ashley had been chatting with Stefanie, who'd revealed that Darrell had visited Roy in prison the day after Ashley. Upon his return home, Darrell had asked Stefanie a bunch of questions about Operation Happy Christmas. Like, how involved was Ashley in the charity. And what part did her boss, Tag James, play in it all. When Stefanie had asked why he was so interested, he'd mumbled around, suggested they donate and then quickly changed the subject.

Huge red flag for Stefanie because Darrell thought everything about Christmas was a pain in the neck, and he was about as generous as Roy, who found the collection basket at church personally offensive. Ashley and Stefanie often joked about how cheap the brothers were. Ashley had found Stefanie's story a bit strange, too, but didn't give the matter any further thought.

"Hazel, listen," Ashley had revealed to her, "I told Roy about Operation Happy Christmas. He was angry because he had a call scheduled with the kids and no one answered. He demanded to know why. So I explained how I'd driven to Glacier City that day to pick up the donations because Tag and Cricket both had flights.

"The detective didn't call about the robbery when she spoke to me. She just asked random questions about Roy. But after I hung up, I started thinking. I remembered that conversation with Roy and what Stefanie had said to me, and I swear, the hair stood up all over my entire body. I was just struck with this thought that, I don't know, he did something."

"Ashley—"

"Wait. Do you know that Roy despises Tag

and Cricket? He blames Tag and Cricket specifically for my 'attitude' where he's concerned."

"What?" Hazel had asked. "How?"

"Cricket is the one who suggested the attorney who restructured our parenting agreement and Tag paid my retainer. Every month, he takes a little bit out of my paycheck to pay him back, but only after I threatened to quit if he didn't. Anyway, Cricket took me to meet the attorney. Later, things got ugly with Roy and his attorney, but both Tag and Cricket encouraged me not to give up. I probably would have if they hadn't been so supportive. Point is, Roy blames them for nosing into our business. He's still enraged about the increase in child support."

"Wow," Hazel had said. "That's a completely twisted but believable motive."

"I know. When I think about it, though, this is right up his alley. Roy is clever, and he would know how much it would bother Tag and Cricket to have stuff stolen from a charity. Stealing from them personally wouldn't have the same impact. He would not care that he was hurting little kids and less fortunate people in the process. All the better because it would bring negative attention to them, which it has.

"Revenge, humiliating people, destroying reputations—that's Roy. Have you noticed how much people have been gossiping about Cricket and Lee? This is the biggest news to hit this town in ages."

"True." Hazel knew that was a huge part of Cricket's problem.

"It seems over-the-top, though, right? Rehashing all of their dad's crimes? And Lee's. The way people are saying that you should never have been driving that day? Or how the donations should have been better transported. I mean, that's stupid. I went and picked up a load of donations, and so did your mom. Not for one second did I think I needed an escort."

When Ashley had gone on to explain about the storage unit, Hazel had decided it was worth a shot. They'd quickly come up with a tentative plan, and Ashley had stopped by the office after work to firm up the details.

"Okaay..." Seth drawled when she'd finished the tale. They both sat back and admired the mound of colorful packages.

"Great!" she cried, purposely misunderstanding his response. "I'm glad you approve. So, you can cover for me while I'm gone? And can you wrap all of my gifts, too?"

"Cover for you?" he repeated flatly. "What are we, back in high school?"

"You won't have to lie. I told Mom and Dad that I'm going to Glacier City to get a new phone and finish my Christmas shopping, both of which I will also be doing. While we're there, we'll drive to the storage place and take a quick peek inside their unit. That's it." With a chopping motion, she emphasized her words: "In, out, done." She added a casual shrug. "Then we're shopping and doing lunch.

"I just thought it was wise to let someone know all the details. You know, on the way, *way* off chance that something was to go wrong."

Seth frowned. "I don't like this plan. Why don't you just tell Cricket? Or the police?"

"Tell them what, though? We know it's a long shot. We don't want to say anything until we know for sure." She didn't mention that she hadn't heard from Cricket since he'd left the Festival of Trees. So far, he hadn't been "in touch" as he'd promised. She kept telling herself it was because she didn't have a phone.

And now she couldn't shake the thought that solving the robbery would solve their issues, too. If she and Ashley could prove that Roy was behind this, Cricket would see how his concerns regarding Lee were unfounded. It would explain the renewed and, if Ashley's theory was correct, exaggerated Blackburn buzz going around town. And then maybe Cricket would let this go and realize they were meant to be together.

Even though, deep inside, the fear lingered in her that he might never reach that point. Because he was right. What would be the next thing to fill his mind with doubts?

For now, though, she had to do this. "If there's anything in the storage unit that doesn't belong, we'll call the police immediately."

"What if the robbers are, like, hanging out in there?"

Hazel went stone-faced and said, "Like the secret bad-guy lair is *inside* the storage unit, and they're all sitting around in there playing Russian roulette and smoking cigars?"

"Sort of," Seth confessed with a self-conscious grin. "Maybe."

Laughing, she admitted, "I asked Ashley the exact same question." They took a moment to laugh together before Hazel added, "She says the place is one of those high-fenced kinds with a ton of security cameras, and there's no way people could come and go without looking suspicious."

"What if you get arrested for trespassing or something?"

"That's the beauty of it. Ashley's name is on the unit. She has a key. Technically, it's still theirs together. She even has some stuff there. Including Christmas decorations, which gives her the perfect excuse."

"Huh. It seems like Roy would have to be pretty stupid to hide stolen goods there."

"But he's not going to think that anyone suspects him. Why would they?"

"You know the part that no one is going to believe, right?"

"What?"

"That you and Ashley are going shopping together. You need a better reason to be running around with her."

"I know. That's why we're taking Iris, too."

"You're taking our pregnant sister along on your covert operation?"

"Yeah."

"Oh, this is just great," he said, his tone plainly stating the opposite. Then he groaned and scrubbed a hand across his jaw. "From Cagney and Lacey to Charlie's Angels. What could possibly go wrong?"

"GOOD THINKING WITH the thermos of coffee," Lee commented from the passenger seat of Cricket's pickup. "Every respectable stakeout needs coffee. And..." he announced, reaching behind him and retrieving a box from the back seat, "donuts."

Hefty Haul Storage was one of those vast and secure gated compounds with multiple drab gray buildings planted in neat rows, all with uniform, orange-painted sliding doors. A code was required to open the gate to the complex. Individual units were then accessed with keys.

He and Lee had been parked on a side street overlooking the parking lot for hours, and Cricket was beginning to question their plan. Which basically consisted of watching the storage business where Lee's contact, "a former associate," revealed that the stolen goods had possibly been taken.

What if this was the wrong place? What if the thieves had already been here? Or if they'd discovered that Lee's contact had ratted them out and they weren't going to show up at all? Maybe this was a wild-goose chase. And precisely the reason why he hadn't shared the information with Detective Carthy. They needed some evidence. Not the legal kind necessarily, just the reassurance that they were on the right track. Once they felt strongly about this possibility, then they'd tell the police.

"You going to marry her?" Lee asked, working on his second buttermilk old-fashioned.

The question was like a spike to his heart. "No," he said. "We're not... We aren't right for each other."

"What are you talking about? You're a perfect couple. She's nuts about you. And you're in love with her, right?"

"Yes, but sometimes relationships need to be about more than that." Just saying those words aloud had his chest going tight all over again. He knew he needed to talk to Hazel, but what would he say? Ironically, her current lack of a phone was proving temporarily convenient. He'd texted Iris, saying that he'd be out of touch for a couple of days, and could she pass the information on to Hazel.

"Huh." Lee took another bite of donut and stared thoughtfully out the window while he chewed. Finally, he asked, "Like what?"

Her safety, her reputation, the fact that our brief relationship is already causing problems within her family. Tag would never let this go. Hannah had texted this morning to say that if Cricket didn't show up for Christmas Eve, then she wasn't going either. No way could he go with things so tense between him and Tag. Hannah would make no secret about why she wasn't there, setting off a chain reaction and further irritating Tag. While Cricket appreciated her loyalty, this was more ammunition for Tag to use against him. And what if other family members followed his lead?

Shay would undoubtedly agree with Tag. Seth and Iris, of course, would stand "publicly" with Hazel no matter what they might secretly believe. And on that score, he couldn't be sure. Iris was a good friend, but she and Tag were close, too. Iris would weigh the pros and cons and analyze every angle, whereas Seth would focus on Hazel's happiness. According to Hazel, Margaret and Ben were okay with their pursuing a relationship. But that was before the robbery.

The robbery had changed everything, and Cricket could not allow Hazel to side with him against her family. He would not be responsible for tearing the family apart.

"Now we're talking…" Lee picked up the binoculars and held them to his eyes. He whistled. "Stakeouts would be way more fun if the scenery was always this nice."

It was apparent Lee was referring to the three women who'd just exited the silver SUV that had pulled into the lot and parked. A vehicle, he noted, that looked a lot like Iris's. As the trio walked toward the entrance, something about the woman on the side closest to them reminded him of Hazel. He reached for his binoculars.

"You know what, that one kind of looks like—"

"Hazel," Cricket finished, confirming his suspicion at the same time. "With Iris and Ashley. What are they doing here?"

"Ashley," Lee muttered appreciatively. "I've always liked that name. Is she single?"

"Lee."

"Sorry," he said, chuckling and clearly not sorry. He lowered his binoculars because the women had disappeared inside the gates of the compound. When he glanced at Cricket, it was obvious from his expression that he was concerned, too. "I know, I'm also thinking that… Can't be a coincidence."

Cricket started the pickup and backed up.

"Where are you going?"

"We're going over there. Something goofy is happening." He maneuvered the pickup onto the road and crossed into the parking lot of the storage facility.

"You realize we'll be on camera now, right?"

"Yes," Cricket said, angling the pickup into a parking spot. "We have to find out what's going on. Somehow Hazel got the same information as you." He grabbed his phone. "I'm going to call Iris."

"Wait a sec." Lee held up a hand. "A car just pulled in behind us."

A full-size SUV drove by them and parked on the other side of the lot. Lee noted to Cricket that the plates had been removed from the vehicle, likely so they wouldn't be captured by security cameras, which suggested illegal intentions.

"I'm guessing they're going to move the stuff."

Two men sat in the car talking and gesticulating before getting out. One was wearing a stocking hat, and the other had a baseball cap pulled low over his forehead. Stocking Hat slipped on a pair of sunglasses while Baseball Cap paused a few seconds to take in the surroundings.

Lee said, "That's Mason."

"You know him?" Cricket said to Lee, his blood turning ice-cold as he pulled up Iris's contact.

"Yep," Lee said, putting on his coat. "He's our guy. Get ready, make the call. We need to get those gals out of there. Mason was at Otter Creek, released a few months before me. Petty thief, pothead—steals to support his habit, or tries to, anyway. He's about as bright as a burned-out bulb. Accidentally stole a firearm and got sent to prison. If she doesn't answer, I'm going to hop out and stall them."

"How do you accidentally steal a firearm?" Cricket asked, willing Iris to answer.

"That's easier than you might think. He broke into a garage, grabbed a toolbox full of high-quality tools. Popular items. Valuable, easy to steal, easy to pawn. Except underneath the tool tray was a handgun. Mason was in a hurry, didn't look through it. Also, didn't realize he tripped a security alarm. Cops picked him up. Done and gone."

That actually did sound easy, from a thief's perspective.

"That's why it's important to do your research."

"IDIOTS," ASHLEY DECLARED with a bitter chuckle. "They didn't even bother hiding it."

Hazel, Ashley and Iris stood in the storage unit, carefully considering the stolen tablets, toys and other merchandise. They couldn't quite believe their eyes. They'd all worn gloves in case they needed to move boxes and bins around to search the place, but everything was neatly stacked near the door right out in the open.

"Iris, can you take some photos?" Hazel asked. "I don't have my phone."

"Brilliant!" Ashley said. "I'll take some, too." Both women photographed the items from several angles.

Hazel said, "Let's get out of here and call Detective Carthy." *And Cricket*, she thought. *Need to call him, too.*

"Wait a sec…" Iris muttered, peering at her phone. "Cricket is calling me." Iris answered,

"Cricket, hi." A few seconds later, her eyes went wide. "You're where?" Scowling intently, she listened for a few seconds. "Yep, got it. Understood."

Hazel was looking at Ashley, whose tense expression seemed to match her own.

"Mmm-hmm, we're going." Iris tapped on the screen.

"Iris, what—"

"We need to get out of here!" she cried. Waving them toward the door, talking while they moved, she explained, "Cricket and Lee are in the parking lot, and he said two guys pulled in, and they're pretty sure they're headed here, to this unit."

Hazel felt a surge of adrenaline-charged fear. They rushed outside, and she quickly pulled the door closed. Ashley secured the lock.

Swiftly glancing left and then right, Ashley suggested, "You know what?" She pointed in the opposite direction from which they'd arrived and started walking. "Let's go this way, so we don't pass them. Because if it's Darrell or one of Roy's buddies, he'll recognize me, and maybe you, too, Iris. Better to avoid them if we can."

Hazel and Iris followed, and they picked up the pace, jogging around the corner and then traversing the side of the structure until they came to the gap between that building and the next. Slowing to a power walk, they followed the path and exited into the parking lot where Cricket and Lee were waiting.

"We need to call the police," Hazel said. "Everything is there in the unit. We think Roy set this up to get back at you and Tag."

Ashley quickly provided a few key details.

"That makes stupid sense," Cricket said.

"Confirms what I heard, too," Lee added.

"The police might take too long!" Ashley blurted. "If they're moving the stuff, they could be long gone before the cops get here, and we won't be able to prove anything. We need to stall them somehow." She turned back toward the entrance.

"Hold up, there, cowgirl!" Lee said. "What's your plan?"

"Classic damsel in distress," Ashley rattled off. "I'll ask them for help moving my grandmother's piano and then pretend like my key isn't working. You know, 'Oh, no! This is the wrong key. I need to go to my car. Can you come with me?' If it's my former brother-in-law, I'll say I'm here for Christmas decorations."

"Wow." Lee nodded approvingly. "That would work. But I might have a slightly safer idea than you alone facing off with two criminals. They walked into the unit, so they will have to get their SUV to load everything. They are probably boxing everything up to camouflage it. We probably have a little bit of time."

"Hazel," Lee instructed, "call the detective and explain as much as you can. Cricket, come with me."

"What about us?" Ashley asked, handing Hazel her phone. "Her number is in there under Detective. Text the photos, too!"

"Good idea," Lee said and then pointed at Iris. "Baby-On-Board, you need to stay here."

They all agreed with that.

Cricket looked at Ashley. "How do we get to your unit?"

"Come on," Ashley urged, already re-punching the gate code.

Hazel quickly found the number for Detective Carthy and hit the call button.

Cricket said to Hazel, "If they get by us, do not engage, okay? We already know who one of them is, and the storage unit has security cameras, so we'll have their photos, too. It'll be enough."

Hazel nodded, and she and Iris headed toward Iris's SUV.

"Detective Carthy!" Hazel exclaimed when the call was answered, relief surging through her. "This is Hazel James. I have information for you regarding the robbery."

CHAPTER NINETEEN

ASHLEY WALKED THROUGH the entrance with Cricket and Lee, the gate clicking shut behind them.

"You're coming with us, aren't you?"

"Of course, I am," she said stubbornly. "It'll be faster. We can argue about it later."

With an appreciative grin, Lee swept an arm forward, inviting her to lead them. She took off at a jog, and he and Lee followed.

When they reached the third set of buildings, she veered right, saying, "This way." They continued until they reached the path between buildings three and four. Ashley stopped, then pointed and whispered, "Unit 338. Two from the end. You can see the open door from here."

"Perfect," Lee said. "Cricket, I'm going to turn my phone on Record and walk out where they can see me. Ashley, be sure you stay close to the building, out of sight, in case they recognize you."

They agreed and hurried toward the unit.

As they neared the spot, Lee paused and held a hand to his ear to indicate he wanted to listen.

The men weren't exactly whispering, and they all heard. "Did he know about all these tablets?... Make sure they're all the same model... Are you gonna tell Frye how many there were?... Are we going to sell them all in Anchorage?"

Lee checked that the phone was still recording and then walked into position about ten feet in front of the open door. He stood for a minute, listening and watching them go through the loot, before calling out, "Hey, Mason! Whatcha doing in there?"

"Blackburn?" a hesitant, surprised voice answered. "What are you doing here?"

"Looking for you," Lee answered, tossing a quick glance at Cricket. "We want those tablets."

Mason lunged toward the door and tugged it down. They could hear agitated talking and cursing coming from inside.

A smiling Ashley moved a little closer to better hear the commotion. Movement from the edge of the building caught Cricket's attention. Hazel, he realized, as she jogged in their direction.

Lee stepped close and slapped the metal

door with the flat of his gloved hand. "Hey, Mason, can you hear me?"

"What are you doing, Blackburn? If this is a joke, it's not funny."

"Unfortunately for you, no, it's not a joke. We want what you've got in there."

"What do you mean, we? Who's with you?"

"You remember Lenox?" Turning to Cricket, he whispered that Lenox was a very big friend of his from Glacier City.

Another voice, much deeper than Mason's, yelled, "Dude, you are dead meat. You hear me? You don't know who you're talking to. You are done for. I'm going to—"

"Shut up!" Mason yelled. "Lenny will—"

"Stop!" Lee shouted and, shockingly, they both went quiet. "You realize the futility of your threats, right? One of us is holding all of the cards here, and it's not you."

"Oh, yeah?" Deep Voice shouted again. "We've got the stuff, and I—"

"I told you to shut up, Diggy!" Mason shouted again at his cohort. Muted, angry mutterings followed.

Hazel reached Ashley and extended her hand for a fist bump.

Lee looked over his shoulder at them, then made a face and rolled his eyes. *Amateurs*, he mouthed before addressing the thieves again,

"So, here's the deal. I know everything you've got in there, and it's time to negotiate."

"Are you kidding me?" Diggy shouted. "We ain't—"

"Hey!" Lee interrupted again. "Mason, you need to get your buddy under control. You know what? We're not going to discuss this by shouting through the door. Someone might hear us—or, more specifically, that tough guy you've got in there with you. Do you have a cell phone? You did get a burner phone for this job, right?"

"Uh, yeah."

"What's your number?"

A pause, then more excited chattering. Mason recited the number, and Lee typed it into his phone.

"Got it. Sit tight. I need to think a minute," Lee told them.

His brother turned and held up a finger. *Stalling*, he mouthed, and Cricket knew they were all hoping the police wouldn't be delayed.

WITHIN MINUTES, IRIS texted that the police had arrived and were on their way to the unit. Cricket and Lee met Detective Carthy and two uniformed officers at the corner of the building and quickly recapped the events that had occurred since entering the storage compound.

"Let me get this straight," Detective Carthy said, her gaze bouncing between Cricket and Lee. "You locked two men inside this storage unit?"

"No, ma'am," Lee answered and then clarified. "Two robbers are inside there, but they shut us out. I may have implied that someone they know to be a, uh, scary guy was with us. As far as I could see there are two men inside the unit, Mason McGee and some dude named Diggy. I have it all on video. They walked in to check the stolen property and planned to load it all in that SUV back in the parking lot when we inconveniently interrupted."

"I see. We know Diggy well." Detective Carthy paused to nod at the additional police officers who'd just arrived. "And, Ms. Frye, it's your storage unit?" she clarified with Ashley.

"That's correct," Ashley said. "It's rented in my and my ex-husband's names." She held up the key. "Here's the key."

She turned to the officers and said, "We need to get them out of there and take them in. We'll need a forensics team, too. Let's—"

"Excuse me, Detective?" Lee interjected politely. "Before you proceed, I have an idea."

"What sort of idea?" Detective Carthy asked with a knitted brow and a healthy infusion of skepticism as she motioned some of the officers toward the unit.

"I managed to get Mason's cell phone number." He quickly explained and then asked, "Would it be possible to borrow your phone to contact him and ask a few questions?"

Carthy narrowed her eyes in thoughtful consideration before handing it over. "Fine, but I'll need to see the texts."

"Sure thing," Lee said. He entered the number and tapped out a text with Cricket peering over one shoulder and the detective over the other.

Hey, Mason. It's Lee.

The phone buzzed almost immediately with a response: Not cool going silent like that man. Where u at?

Lee explained, "I want him to know that I know what he has."

Lee: Thinking. 200 tablets is quite a score. Let's split it all.

Mason: ur crazy dude.

Lee: Maybe. But we aren't leaving.

Mason: How much?

Lee: Half.

Mason: Half!! NO WAY! I don't know how u found out but if Roy set us up he's a dead man!!! He promised if we do this for him we keep what we got. Everything in the van no matter how much.

Lee shrugged and gave Detective Carthy a look. "I got the sense that he'd talk. Like I said, his day job is not working for NASA."

With her head shaking and eyebrows arching high, Carthy muttered, "After all these years, you would think these things would fail to surprise me."

Finger up in a "just a sec" gesture, Lee went on to type another message:

Is it just you and Diggy or is someone else in on what you stole?

Mason: Just us. Fendy was sposed to do job w us but he bailed.

Lee: Ok good. Leaves more for us. Who you guys selling to? I know a guy pays top $

Mason: Jimmie K we already promised 100 tablets but maybe we can work out deal w rest.

Lee clarified for the detective, "Jimmie K is a guy in—"

"Yep. We know him. Keep him talking," the detective told Lee, her tone now hinting at respect for Lee's strategy.

Lee: What about the toys?

One of the policemen walked over and showed Carthy a page in his notebook. "This guy Mason has a record, mostly petty stuff until this last one." He tapped a pen to the page. "Theft of a firearm."

Mason: Let's deal.

"Any idea if Mason is dangerous?" she asked Lee.

Lee: 50/50 Let's split the stuff here.

"Mason, no," Lee said. "He's low-level and harmless. Aspiring professional gamer who steals to support his challenging but rewarding lifestyle of getting high and shooting virtual bad guys from the comfort of his grandmother's basement. Ironically, that last stint Officer Bowen is referring to was the result of an accidental theft of a handgun." Lee filled her in.

Mason: 70/30 We sell it and split the cash.

Detective Carthy nodded, a smile playing at her lips. "We'll take it from here, Mr. Blackburn. Officer Greene will escort you folks to the parking lot for now. But we'll need you all to stop by the station and make statements."

HAZEL WAITED IN the lot, watching while Lee and Cricket visited with a laughing Officer Greene. Ashley had gone to Iris's SUV to fill her in on what she'd missed.

Hazel took a moment to ponder the events of the morning, allowing her fear to dissipate and the adrenaline to settle. Lee had been completely brilliant. Ashley was awesome and brave. It was all wreaking a bit of havoc with her emotions. She got a little choked up thinking about the lengths Cricket had gone to for his brother, for her, and what the five of them had just accomplished together.

She tried not to think about what would have happened if Cricket and Lee hadn't been here, and these men had found her, Ashley and Iris inside the storage unit. Would they have believed their story, or would they now be locked inside? These guys might appear harmless, but, as Lee had suggested, desperate people did desperate things.

But just like with the robbery, none of those bad things had happened. Forcing herself to shift back to the present, she focused on the man who was walking over to stand beside her.

"You okay?" he asked gently, and she could see the concern in his gaze.

"Fine. But, Cricket, we owe you and Lee the hugest thank-you."

"I'm grateful we were here, but I owe you just as big of a thank-you. This wouldn't have worked out nearly as well if you ladies hadn't come here to confirm that the stuff was in there."

"That was all thanks to Ashley. She figured it out and she was very convincing, so it seemed worth a look. Plus, I knew she'd come here and check no matter what, and there was absolutely no way I would let her do that alone."

"Of course you wouldn't. It's nice that you two…uh…"

Hazel let out a soft chuckle knowing he'd been about to repeat the statement he'd made before they'd gone to Juneau. "It's fine, you can say it. We've definitely patched things up.

Iris is right about her. She has changed. She's actually very cool."

"That makes me happy," he said, his body more relaxed now, his eyes filled with affection.

"Your brother is a rock star," she said as the detective moved away to confer with her colleagues.

"Yeah," Cricket said. "I have to agree. He should have been a cop instead of a criminal." She couldn't help but note the pride in his tone.

"I was thinking the same thing."

"Who better to catch a thief than a thief?"

"Reformed thief," Hazel corrected.

"True. And this pretty much seals the reformed part. Once word gets out that he ratted out one of his own, no one from his former life will ever trust him again."

"Oh, wow…" she breathed, a fresh dose of admiration and fondness welling inside of her. "I didn't even think about honor among thieves and all of that. Why would he…?"

"He was furious about what happened to you and angry about the rumors. That second part not so much because of himself, but because of what people were saying about me."

"That's so sweet and brave. Do you think he's in any danger?"

"He says no, as long as he steers clear of

certain people. The good part is that Roy isn't a true thief. Meaning, he's not a part of that world, so it's not like we double-crossed some Mafia crime lord or intercepted a drug shipment from the cartel. This was motivated by revenge against me and Tag."

"Ironic how you and Tag's collective niceness was the true source of this fiasco, don't you think?"

"I do."

"Are you going to tell him, or am I?"

"Let's figure that out later."

Ashley had returned and was now sidled up next to Lee. Leaning in, she reached out, touched his shoulder. He glanced up and replied. They couldn't hear the conversation, but their laughter mingled and carried.

Hazel observed, "I know Ashley can be a little—what did you call it—demonstrative? But I'm pretty sure she has a crush on your brother. That's some high-level flirting going on right there."

"Lee is clearly sweet on Ashley, too, so..."

"What do you think?"

He shrugged. "As long as Ashley knows what she's getting into, I'm okay with it. You know Lee, he's honest about his past. But he says he won't get romantically involved with anyone until Dr. Monroe thinks he's ready. He's serious about therapy."

"I'm so happy for him, for both of you," she said, and then, because she couldn't stand it a moment longer, she took his hand. Relief filled her from top to bottom when he didn't pull away. Even better, he linked his fingers with hers.

"Feels like I have a brother again. But, you know, I don't want to get my hopes up too high."

"That's understandable. Maybe keep them about here." With her free hand, she indicated a spot just above her head. "Like midrange."

Reaching out, he nudged her hand a bit higher. "Or possibly here."

Lifting her eyebrows, she nodded agreeably. "Optimism. I like that."

"Me too." He chuckled. "Lee said that Dr. Monroe recommended I come in for a few sessions of therapy, too, and maybe Lee and I together for some family counseling."

That would be amazing, she thought, but asked instead, "What do you think about that?"

"I'm okay with it. I don't see a downside."

"I don't either. It could be good for both of you."

Hazel wanted to ask whether this was all enough. Did the proof that Lee didn't have anything to do with the robbery change anything? And did agreeing to therapy mean he was ready to let go of the hold his family's past had on him? And what about his concerns regarding her family?

She needed to know where they stood.

Turning quickly toward him, she said, "Cricket—"

"Hazel—" he said, shifting to face her at the same time.

Their gazes collided and held. No, more like fused. And at that moment, Hazel saw so much in his expression—sweetness, affection, regret, vulnerability...and desire? Yes, she was pretty sure there was plenty of that, too.

Just like it had on their first date, her heart took flight. But this time, it soared, shaking something loose inside of her. The love she felt for him was overwhelming, impossible to contain. Inhaling a breath, she geared up to say the words aloud.

But then he started moving. "Come here," he said, keeping a firm hold on her hand and urging her away from the others.

Pulse pounding, stomach fluttering, she followed. This was it. She would just tell him, and if he didn't return the words, she didn't care. Well, she did care, but that wasn't why she was going to say them. She needed to let him know, wanted him to hear how deeply she cared about him.

There was a bench off to one side of the entrance, and that was where he stopped.

Facing her, he took her other hand and said, "Hazel, we've been through so much, and I...I always thought that I'd know if the time was ever right for us to be together. The problem with that belief is that I realize now that there will never be a time when I feel that way."

And just like that, the air whooshed from her lungs, accompanied by a crackling sound in her ears, as if she could hear her heart crashing back down.

"But that's my issue. I've learned a lot about myself the last couple weeks."

Wait. What?

"I can see now that the time has always been right for us, just not for me because I was scared that I wasn't enough for you. I hope you can forgive me for not seeing that, for not accepting what was right in front of me. And that is you. It's always been you.

"I love you so much. I thought you deserved better, that you should be with someone perfect, or at a least a man who doesn't come from a family of con men and thieves and criminals. Your family means a lot to me. They are what

I've always thought a family should be, and for you to have less than that—"

"Stop," she said. Her legs had turned to jelly, so she brought a hand up and pressed it to his chest to steady herself. "You love me?"

He untangled their fingers so he could hold her shoulders. "Yes. Of course I love you. So much that I want everything to be right for you, including who you spend your life with. That's why I wanted to like Kai. As excruciating as it was for me, the best thing that ever happened to *us* was me seeing you with him.

"On the surface, he seemed perfect for you. But I could see that he wasn't as perfect as me." He paused, his expression earnest and sweet, and she was pretty sure it was the cutest thing she'd ever seen. "I don't mean that I'm perfect—I mean that no one will ever love you like I do, Hazel. It's not possible."

Now tears were gathering for a different, better reason. The best of all reasons, but she refused to cry and blur this moment. Blinking them away, she said, "I think I'm perfect for you, too."

"You absolutely are. The only person who is. And I'm sorry I wasted so much time."

"Well," she said, bringing her hands up to twine around his neck while he adjusted his hold to her waist. "I wouldn't say it was wasted. Supposedly, the best things in life are worth waiting for. There's actually this little-known principle called the waiting correlation. The longer you're made to wait, the better the thing is that you waited for. So…" She offered a half shrug. "By my calculation, that means you should be nothing short of spectacular."

"The waiting correlation? Huh." Lips twitching with laughter, he drew her even closer. "Any chance you made that up?"

"Maybe," she admitted teasingly. "But it's a sound theory. I'm going to make a new list detailing all the amazing things about you that were worth waiting for. I'll call it my 'Romance Is Worth the Wait List.'"

He chuckled and then tipped his head down so that his mouth hovered just above hers. "Have I mentioned how much I love you?"

"Yes, but a spectacular guy would repeat it multiple times a day. That's something I can add to the list."

"I love you, Hazel James," he said, just before his lips met hers for a kiss. No, not *a* kiss. *The* kiss. Hazel would never have believed that kissing him could get any better. How wrong she'd been. Because *this* and knowing that he loved her was unlike any sort of happiness she'd ever experienced. Ever. And that was saying a lot because Hazel had literally traveled the world trying to find something, any-thing, that matched this rightness, this utterly consuming mindfulness, this…this perfect sense of peace.

Cricket pulled away and hugged her tight. Nuzzling her neck, he placed his mouth close to her ear and whispered, "Despite the undue and possibly unrealistic pressure you've placed on me to be spectacular, I promise to spend the rest of our life together adding items to that list. I promise, Hazel, that *we* were worth the wait."

CHAPTER TWENTY

"THIS IS UNACCEPTABLE," Margaret told Hazel while turning a pan of fresh-baked rolls onto a cooling rack. "Cricket has spent every Christmas Eve with us since... I don't even know how many years it's been."

"I know, Mom." Hazel hated breaking this news to her. "And I'm sorry. I'm sad, too. I couldn't talk him into it. He doesn't feel right being here."

Operation Happy Christmas had been an unqualified success. Since the thieves were caught red-handed, they'd been offered a reduced charge to provide details about Roy's and Darrell's involvement. With the robbery solved, the police had released most of the tablets and other items, keeping just a few for evidence.

Distribution of all the gifts had gone smoothly, and Hazel knew her mom had been looking forward to their annual fun-filled family Christmas Eve. But even if Cricket had agreed to come, the evening would be anything but fun.

"Tag still won't talk to Cricket. Hannah is angry with Tag. Shay is upset with Hannah. Iris is extremely disappointed that everyone won't be here." Iris's disappointment went deeper than that because she was Margaret's Secret Santa and had reserved a professional photographer to take a family portrait. But Hazel couldn't give that part away even though the family photo wouldn't take place without Cricket and Hannah.

"I'm torn because I want to be with him and you all. But he's insistent that I stay here." Hazel had agreed to do so only when Cricket and Lee had made plans to go snowshoeing, and Lee reassured her that he'd be preparing his "famous" cast-iron steak for the two of them. "He feels terrible because the last thing he'd ever want is to be the cause of holiday tension in our family."

"He doesn't want to be the cause of *any* tension in this family, and that's a big part of the problem."

"What do you mean?"

Tag strode into the kitchen, derailing their conversation. "Seth just told me Cricket isn't coming tonight."

"That's what I hear," Margaret answered.

"I think it's my fault."

Margaret gave him a silent, tight-lipped,

raised-brow look that clearly conveyed *Oh, really, ya think?* She opened a drawer, removed the aluminum foil and handed it to Hazel. "Cover those up, will you?" She waved a hand toward the dinner rolls, pies and cookies already laid out on the island.

Hands on hips, she faced Tag. "It is your fault, to a large extent, anyway. You were awful and unreasonable to your best friend but—"

"Thanks, Mom. That makes me feel tons better."

"Don't interrupt."

"Sorry."

Waving him forward, she walked toward the fridge, opened the door and then removed a large bowl. "Here, hold this." He did, and she then proceeded to stack two smaller dishes on top. "Put those over there." He dutifully carried out her request and then came back for more while she continued, "*But* you did it out of love for your sister—"

"Who does not need her big brother to protect her," Hazel interjected.

With a little huff, Margaret turned and pointed at her. "Didn't I just tell your brother not to interrupt? Why would it be okay for you?"

"Sorry, Mom."

"And," she continued, telling Tag, "your protectiveness is endearing." She headed toward the large pantry closet, where she disappeared briefly and then emerged with a stack of plastic containers. "You've always been an excellent big brother to all of your siblings, Tag, and we're very proud of that." She paused. "However, I did hope that when you all grew up, you'd lay off a bit."

Tag flipped up his palms in a helpless gesture, questioning her logic. "They're still my sisters."

"True. And Cricket is still your best friend. I understand you were hurt by his not confiding in you."

"I never meant for this to happen. And I certainly didn't intend for our...disagreement to tear our family apart."

"Disagreement?" Hazel repeated sharply and immediately apologized. "Sorry, Mom, but it was way more than that."

Tag didn't argue. Surprisingly, he conceded, "Hazel is right. I overreacted. Slightly. I'm not sure how to fix it. What do I do? Should I go over to his house and talk to him? It's Christmas Eve."

"No," Margaret stated firmly.

Tag's expression looked nearly as miserable

as Hazel felt. Why wouldn't her mom want him to fix this?

Inhaling a big breath, she announced, "We're all going."

"Mom, what?" Hazel gaped at her mom and felt her spirits lift. The brilliance of this plan lit her up inside with the force of a million Christmas lights.

"We are all going to Cricket's house for Christmas Eve. That's why you're covering up those dishes. Tag, I need you to transfer everything that we removed from the fridge into these plastic containers. Then load them all into the coolers, which I will fetch for you in a minute."

To Hazel, she said, "Those we'll put into some totes. The clam chowder needs to be ladled into those two slow cookers on the counter, but we'll do that last."

She walked to the doorway and shouted, "Ben?"

"Right here, hon," her dad said, appearing in the other doorway.

"Oh, hi," she said, granting him a sweet smile. "There you are. Can you get Seth and Victoria and Scarlett? I need Victoria in here, and then you and Seth and Scarlett start loading all the gifts into the cars."

"We're going to Cricket's?"

"That's right. So, we need to text Emily, Janie, Iris, Shay and Kai to let them know to go there instead."

"You forgot Hannah," Tag pointed out, scooping salad out of a glass bowl and into a plastic container.

"No, I didn't," Margaret said.

Tag exhaled his exasperation. "Let me guess—she's already going to Cricket's?"

"Yes. She said she wouldn't be joining us unless Cricket was, too."

"Do you think we need a tree?" Ben asked. "We could take the one I bought at the festival the other night."

"He's got one," Hazel said, her heart overflowing with love for her parents and hopefulness that Tag was beginning to thaw.

"Um, Cricket?" Lee said. "Why are there so many cars in your driveway?"

"That is an excellent question, Lee," Cricket answered. The path to his garage was blocked, so he pulled up and parked beside Ben's pickup.

"You didn't tell me we were having company. I only bought two steaks."

"I didn't know we were."

"I suppose I could do a stir-fry."

Cricket laughed. For about the millionth time, he thanked fate and Dr. Easton for returning his brother to him. After an early-morning snowfall, the skies had cleared, setting the conditions for a fantastic day of snowshoeing. Thanks to Lee, he'd adjusted to the reality of a Christmas Eve without the entire James family as long as he got to keep the James that he wanted the most.

But evidently, they had other plans.

Cricket and Lee entered the house to a chorus of Christmas greetings.

"I've never been to a Christmas Eve surprise party before," Lee quipped, accepting a cup of eggnog from a laughing Iris.

"Uh, what's going on?" Cricket asked.

Margaret stepped forward.

But then Tag said, "Mom, I'd like to go first—if that's okay with you?"

"Sure, honey." She smiled her approval.

"Tag, really," Cricket interjected, "you don't need to—"

He held up a hand. "Yes, I do. But first, I need to make a point." Glancing around, he caught Iris's gaze and said, "Iris, do you remember that Christmas when you were mad at Hannah and hid all her gifts?"

"Uh, yeah," Iris answered with exaggerated defensiveness. "But to be fair, she ruined my favorite sweater, and I was only twelve at the time."

"I remember, too," Hannah chimed in. "One of the gifts wasn't found until *two years* later."

Tag pointed. "Yes, that's the one! Thank you, ladies. I appreciate those details. Who remembers the Christmas when Dad forgot to order the prime rib, and the grocery store was sold out, so we had ham instead?"

"Yikes," Seth said with a cringe that left everyone chuckling. "Are we allowed to talk about that?"

"I think we all remember that one," Shay added. "Because Mom doesn't like ham, and she was so irritated that she made Dad cook it, and then we all had to suffer."

Cricket smiled. Ben didn't cook, and the ham had been so dry it was nearly inedible.

"I reminded him three times," Margaret said, shaking her head at the memory.

"Just for the record," Ben chimed in, "I order the prime rib every year on the Fourth of July now."

Everyone laughed.

Tag turned toward Shay. "Shay, do you remember that Thanksgiving when we had a fight and weren't speaking?"

"You mean the one where you were a huge jerk because I told your annoying girlfriend, Kendall, that she wasn't invited to dinner after you told me you didn't want her here?"

"Um, yes, that's the one." He winced then joked, "In this case, I don't know that of those details were necessary, but thank you.

Then he looked at Cricket. "The point here is that we fight, we disagree. Sometimes—" here he stopped to stretch his arms wide "—we screw up. You've witnessed it all. We're family. That's what we do.

"We also get together for the holidays. Unfortunately, occasionally, these things cross over. That doesn't mean we get to opt out—out of the family part or the holiday in question.

"It was Mom's idea to come over here tonight because she can't imagine a Christmas Eve without you. We're *all* here with her because we can't imagine it either. Especially me."

Cricket nodded, his heart clenching tightly in his chest. "I get it. I can't imagine a Christmas Eve without all of you either."

"Great!" Hazel said, stepping beside Cricket and coming to his rescue. "You guys can hash out the apologies and details later. Let's eat."

The prime rib was for Christmas day. Christmas Eve dinner was a more casual, drawn-out affair of clam chowder, homemade rolls, an assortment of salads and a buffet of desserts. Plates and bowls were filled and consumed and refilled, and, afterward, Tag found Cricket

ione in the kitchen, where he'd gone after taking orders for hot cocoa.

"I'm sorry I was a jerk," Tag said, stepping
up to help, topping the steaming mugs with
marshmallows.

"I'm sorry I kissed your sister," Cricket said,
trying not to smile. "But you'll be happy to
know that—"

"Stop," Tag interrupted with a groan. "Can't
we just leave it at that?"

"Calm down. All I was going to say is that
you'll be happy to know that it caused me years
of anguish and regret."

"You're right," Tag said, beaming. "That
does make me extremely happy. In fact, that's
a Christmas gift right there."

"I thought so. Now, please, take this cup
with extra marshmallows to Hannah." He
pointed. "And tell her you apologized."

Tag dutifully picked up the mug and headed
off to make peace with Hannah. Nearing the
door, he turned back and said, "Obviously, I
misspoke about that tell of yours."

Cricket was still smiling when Margaret entered the room and said, "I know you've been
through a lot and Tag very eloquently made a
point similar to the one I'm going to make, so
I'll keep my speech short...*ish*."

Cricket nodded, his heart full of love and respect for this incredible woman, the only mom he'd ever known.

"I've given this a lot of thought. Cricket, you've always been so careful not to upset anyone in this family. You've become the peacemaker, the neutral one. I think that way down deep in your heart your eight-year-old self has been afraid that if you rocked the boat you would lose us. That we might walk away from you, too. So, you were very, very careful not to do that.

"But then you and Hazel finally got together, and Lee came back, and then the robbery. All these happenings had consequences that were out of your control. You accidentally upset the balance of this family. And that scared you. So, you decided to leave us before anyone could leave you."

With the tidal wave of emotion gathering inside of him, Cricket didn't trust himself to speak. He nodded. Margaret had a gift for seeing these huge truths and then summarizing them neatly.

"What I need to say is that even if you and Hazel don't work out for some reason, which you will because you are the two most kindhearted and reasonable of all my children." She paused to let that compliment sink in. "But let's say you don't for some unthinkable reason. We will find a way to get past it. You've been a member of this family for a long, long time. And not because you're perfect, or because you never rock the boat, but because you're you. We love you. Unconditionally. Okay?"

"Okay," he said, letting a few tears fall because they were the good kind, the right kind to shed on Christmas Eve. She hugged him, and it felt easy to agree because Margaret was right. He was a part of this family. And there was no way he and Hazel weren't going to work out. Cricket knew that now. Because he'd do whatever was necessary to make them work.

So far, Christmas Eve had been an unqualified success. Thanks to Lee, Tate, Hannah and Shay, the dishes were done, and the house had been tidied. Secret Santa identities had been revealed and the final gifts opened. The family had departed for their own homes with plans to gather at Margaret and Ben's for Christmas dinner the following afternoon. Soon after, Lee said good-night and headed to his room. Mitt and Val were curled up on Cricket's easy chair in front of the woodstove.

While Cricket got comfortable on the sofa,

Hazel fetched the gift she'd bought for him from under the tree.

"You're sure you want me to open this now?" he asked. "And not in the morning?"

"Positive," she said because they needed to talk about what it meant, and now she was nervous. Was this too much too soon?

"It's a backpack," she blurted after he'd torn away the wrapping paper but before he could finish removing it from the box.

"I see that," he said, hoisting it onto the sofa beside him. "A fancy one, too, from the look of it."

"Yep, I know it can't beat the dog Hannah got for Dad, but it's made especially for traveling." In true Hannah fashion, she'd "won" the Secret Santa event by presenting Ben with an adorable rescue dog she'd named Fisher in honor of his profession. To Hannah's credit, Ben was overjoyed by the gesture.

"So," Hazel said, twisting her hands in her lap because she couldn't believe she was going to tackle this topic now. But Cricket had made a good point at the storage facility. There might not always be a perfect time to say what you needed to say. And after years of waiting, she wanted their future settled. "I've been thinking—"

"Yes," he said, cutting her off with a kiss. "Thank you. I'd love to."

"You know what I'm thinking?"

"You want to take me on an adventure."

"Yes," she answered slowly, "I do. But…"

Patient and curious, he waited for her to continue.

"A very *long* adventure." *Several of them*, she added silently.

"Ah. What are you proposing?"

"Cricket, we've waited so long to be together that I don't want to spend time apart. There, I said it. But I'm also not ready to give up my business, my blog, my life. So, my proposal, as you termed it, is six months traveling, six months here at home. With the time to be divided however we choose. I know you need to be here for JB Heli-Ski for a few months in the winter and probably a few months in the summer for Our Alaska Tours, especially until the business gets off the ground. Obviously, there will be years when the time doesn't divide up perfectly or that we have to go our separate ways for brief periods, but I think if we make that our goal, we can get close. What do you think?"

"What about my cats?"

Hazel took one of his hands in both of hers. "I love that your first question is about your cats." For more reasons than the obvious one. He hadn't said no, and that gave her hope. "I was thinking that if Lee lived here, too, then the cats would be okay."

"Huh. That would work. It's almost annoying how much Val loves him. You've given this a lot of thought, haven't you?"

"I have. And I want to add that I think it would be good for you to sometimes get out of this town. Like I do. And see the world—with me. Victoria Falls, Machu Picchu, Aranui Cave—all the places you've said you'd like to see—with me. Time to just be yourself, to focus on yourself—and me, of course," she added with a smile.

"Cricket, I know you—and I know you have an adventurous spirit. You would enjoy traveling, especially with me, because I'm *really* good at it, and I want to do it with you."

"I see." He nodded, all stoic and somber, and she couldn't read him. "Is that all?"

Exhaling a sigh, she squeezed his hand. "Yes, but I want you to know that I'm also fine with a long-distance relationship, too, if that's what you want. We'll work it out."

Gently, he turned one of her hands palm up and then linked his fingers with hers. "Hazel, I'm going to ask you a question that I've asked you before. Likely, I'll ask you a variation of it every single time we're at an important crossroads in our life."

"Okay."

"Do you honestly believe that after everything we've been through, after all the time we've spent apart, and now that we are finally together, *and* knowing how much I love you, that I would be capable of telling you no?"

Happiness exploded inside of her, and she realized how much she'd wanted to hear that answer.

"In that case…?" she said and scooted closer.

"Yes." He breathed out the word with a playful sigh. "You can kiss me."

Laughing, she leaned in and did just that.

* * * * *

If you've missed a James family romance,
check out the Seasons of Alaska miniseries
available from Carol Ross
and Harlequin Heartwarming at
www.Harlequin.com!